Additional Evidence

By James Anderson:

ADDITIONAL EVIDENCE
ASSAULT AND MATRIMONY

Additional Evidence

JAMES ANDERSON

CRIME CLUB
Doubleday

NEW YORK LONDON TORONTO SYDNEY

All of the characters in this book
are fictitious, and any resemblance
to actual persons, living or dead,
is purely coincidental.

A Crime Club Book
Published by Doubleday, a division of
Bantam Doubleday Dell Publishing Group, Inc.
666 Fifth Avenue, New York, New York 10103

Doubleday and the portrayal of
a man with a gun are trademarks of
Doubleday, a division of Bantam
Doubleday Dell Publishing Group, Inc.

Library of Congress Cataloging-in-Publication Data

Anderson, James, 1936–
Additional evidence / James Anderson.
p.   cm.
I. Title.
PR6051.N393A66   1988   87-36533
823'.914—dc19   CIP
ISBN 0-385-24621-8

OG

Additional Evidence

PROLOGUE

Linda Matthews had had no idea the attack was coming.

But then, just a few seconds before, neither had her attacker.

However, although the murder had not been planned for this moment, it was not the result of a sudden loss of temper. The knowledge that it might be necessary had always been there—and had been gradually growing throughout the conversation.

Then, at a crucial moment Linda had abruptly turned her back. She had had no reason to do this. It had been an act of dismissal, almost of contempt. And that had been the trigger.

A silk square had been dropped casually on the back of a chair. It took just a moment to snatch it up, grip it by two corners, take three short steps towards Linda, throw the square over the blond head, let it fall to the neck and start to pull.

A slow-motion camera would have captured the expression on Linda's beautiful face a split second after she felt the pressure against her neck as one of disbelief and amazement. But this changed rapidly to terror. Her face lost its beauty, became contorted. Her long scarlet nails tore at the silk band that was digging deeper and deeper into her neck. She swayed frantically from left to right. But, although in many ways a perfect physical specimen, she was not strong. Moreover, her killer had the advantage of surprise, superior position and—now that the attack had been launched—utter determination.

Within seconds Linda's face had become a hideous, discoloured blob. Her struggles grew ever more feeble. Her hands pawed at the air for a moment before falling helplessly to her sides. Then she slumped heavily to her knees. She knelt like a puppet, supported only by the hands that were squeezing the life from her body.

That was virtually the end. The murderer remained, standing quite still, relaxing not the slightest until the last tremor had ceased—then let go of the square. Linda toppled forward onto the thick cream carpet.

The assailant stood still for a moment, staring down at the body; then, breathing heavily, knelt and groped for the girl's pulse. It gave not the slightest flicker. The short, shallow, wasted life of Linda Matthews was over.

The killer rose. It was incredible. It had all been so quick, so easy. How simple it had been to become one of those dreaded figures, a murderer. And in one sense, how little difference it had made. Linda had been standing; now she was lying down. That was the only change in the room. The second hand of the clock continued to circle the dial, and in the corner the garishly coloured manikins on the TV screen mouthed mutely at each other, just as they had before.

Nevertheless, a girl was dead. And this fact was going to mean complications. There would be problems. There would be danger. However, there was no reason why everything should not turn out all right. Provided only there was now no panic . . .

The murderer looked around the room. Was there anything that had to be done before leaving? Anything to retrieve? Any traces to remove? Anything to destroy?

This was where deliberate thought and precise, careful action were going to be essential.

The next ten minutes were spent in a quick but thorough search of the flat. Fortunately, the place was not large—just a sitting-room, bedroom, bathroom and tiny kitchen. Moreover, Linda had not lived here long—and perhaps had not planned to stay much longer. As a result, there were no drawers or cupboards stuffed with papers and other bric-a-brac needing to be rifled. In fact, in the whole flat there was only one small object which was clearly going to have to be removed.

The murderer stood motionless in the centre of the sitting-room, casting a final look round—but carefully avoiding glancing down at the inert form on the carpet. That was it. There was nothing more to be done.

Now came the real danger: leaving. Luckily this was an exclusive block. People kept themselves to themselves. They didn't hang about chatting with neighbours in the corridors. And it was a time of day when residents were least likely to be either coming home or going out. So, with just a little luck . . .

The murderer went to the front door, opened it about an inch and peered cautiously out.

CHAPTER ONE

On the same Monday evening in August that Linda Matthews met her death, Alison Grant sat reading in the sitting-room of her modern detached house, a quarter of a mile from the sea front of the busy and prosperous south coast town of Fermouth.

Alison was a quietly dressed, quietly spoken young woman of thirty-three. Her light brown hair hung loose in soft curls, which she personally thought was a style too young for her, but which her husband Stephen liked, so she had stuck to it for years. Her eyes were brown too; her brow deep, her nose nondescript, her mouth wide, her chin determined. No one had ever called Alison Grant glamorous but there was a seemingly unchanging serenity about her, which often combined with a flashing smile and a glint of mischief in the eyes to give a vivacity and warmth to her face that would long outlast simple glamour.

For some time Alison remained absorbed in her reading. But then suddenly she jerked her head up. Her heart seemed to miss a beat.

That, surely, had been a sound in the hall? She told herself that she had to have been mistaken. It must have been something in the road outside. She was alone in the house. Every door was locked. Only Stephen and she had keys. And Stephen was in Dublin.

For seconds she remained rigidly still. There was silence. She began to relax a little and cast a glance at the clock. Not quite 10 P.M. Too early for burglars.

Then she heard another sound. And this time it was unmistakable. Footsteps. Just two footsteps on the parquet floor between the mat and the sitting-room door. There was somebody out there.

Fighting back incipient terror, Alison let the book she had been reading slip from her hand and slide down between the cushion and the arm of the chair. She got slowly to her feet. Her heart was pounding. She stood quite still, holding her breath, staring at the door. Seconds passed. Then the knob started to turn.

Her hands rose to her mouth. The door was opening. She tried to scream. But nothing came out.

Then the door was pushed wide and Stephen entered the room.

Alison gave a gasp. "Stephen! What on earth—?"

She broke off as she suddenly noticed his face. It was white and his expression was one which in twelve years of marriage she had never seen before: sheer unadulterated panic.

She stared at him. The sight of steady, phlegmatic Stephen in a state of what was clearly pure funk had the effect of increasing, rather than abating, her own fear.

He came right into the room, closing the door behind him. He smiled. But the smile was such a parody of his usual cheery grin that it would have been better if he had scowled.

He said thickly, "Hello." Even his voice sounded different.

Somehow she managed to speak herself—stupidly, dazedly. "You're supposed to be in Dublin."

"I—" He stopped, then started again. "I got the business over early. Decided to surprise you."

She managed to get a grip on herself. "You certainly did that. You nearly frightened me to death."

"Sorry. I wasn't thinking." It seemed that every word he spoke was an effort to him.

"Stephen," she asked suddenly, "what's the matter?"

"Matter? What do you mean?" He spoke sharply, staring at her. His expression was suspicious, almost aggressive.

"You know what I mean. Your face. You look awful."

"Oh. Do I?" He walked across the room to the cocktail cabinet and picked up a bottle. With his back to her he went on.

"Well, as a matter of fact, I am a bit shaken up. Nearly had a smash. Lorry pulled out right in front of me. Had to stand on the brakes. Quite unnerved me."

He turned round. He had poured himself a full glass of neat whisky, which he now proceeded to down in one go.

She forced herself to say, "How nasty. Where was this?"

"Oh. Coming out of—out of Queen's Road."

"Really? Unusual to see a lorry in that part of town at this time of night."

"Well, it certainly surprised me." He attempted another smile, then turned suddenly and picked up the bottle of Scotch again.

"Did you report him?" she asked.

"Who?"

"The lorry driver."

"Oh no. Didn't seem worth it. No witnesses. Do you want a drink?"

"No thanks."

He refilled his glass, then walked to the couch and sat down. His colour was returning, but there was still that look in his eyes which she had never seen before. Something ghastly had happened—she was certain of it. Something he was afraid to tell her about.

He made what was clearly a supreme attempt at normality. "How have things been here?"

"All right."

"Anything interesting happen?"

"No, nothing. Tell me about the trip."

"Oh, quite satisfactory. Got on very well with Brannigan. I've agreed to represent him."

"Oh, I am glad. I loved his last book."

"I've got the typescript of his latest one here—" He broke off and looked round. "Oh, I must have left my case in the car." He took a drink.

"Do you think you'll be able to place it?"

He looked up. "What?"

"The book."

"Oh yes. They'll be no problem. I only read the first couple of chapters during the flight, but it's first-rate."

"That's good."

"Yes."

"Do you want something to eat?" she asked.

"Oh—no thanks. I had something on the plane. I'm not hungry."

"As you like. Coffee?"

"Yes, that would be nice."

"I'll get some."

She made her way to the kitchen, her mind in a whirl. They were talking to each other like a couple of strangers. It was awful. What *could* she do. Somehow she had to make him tell her what was wrong. The trouble was, he could be so stubborn. Once he had decided to keep a secret, there was no dragging it out of him.

She made coffee and carried a tray back to the sitting-room. Stephen was standing up again, smoking a cigarette. Further evidence of something wrong, she thought. He'd given them up two months ago.

He saw her eyes on him and looked a little embarrassed. "Just felt like one," he said. "Found half a packet in the drawer. Sorry."

She put the tray on a low table. "Don't apologise. It's up to you."

He looked round for an ashtray, found one and stubbed the cigarette out. Then he sat on the couch again and took the cup of coffee she handed to him.

She seated herself in the chair opposite and poured herself a cup. "Tell me about Dublin," she said. "What's Sean Brannigan like?"

"Oh, very Irish. Very charming. I thought we'd be talking for hours, but he told me after ten minutes I could represent him. Apparently he'd only wanted to size me up and he quickly decided I was OK. Then he went off to a party. Wanted to take me along, but I thought if I could get back tonight, I could have a whole day at the office tomorrow."

He was talking more naturally now, but there was still a jerkiness to his speech, and he was clearly finding great difficulty in concentrating.

After a few more desultory remarks they both fell silent. It was plainly a relief to him to do so, and Alison felt she just couldn't keep up the effort of trying to draw him out. After a while she turned the television on. An old movie was being screened. It was a good cover—she was able to pretend to be following it while actually busy with her thoughts; and she was sure the same applied to Stephen. She watched him covertly. He fidgeted constantly and kept glancing at his watch. It was as if he were waiting for something. But what? He did sometimes get phone calls late at night, from publishers or fellow literary agents in the States, Australia or Japan, but he would always mention it if he was expecting one.

She began to dread the end of the film. For then they would have to start talking again. Or patently avoid doing so. Of course, soon they could go to bed. But she had never felt less like sleep, and she was certain Stephen hadn't either.

The film ended. Alison would have been hard put to even give the name of the principal character. She continued to sit doggedly through the final commercial break, the run-through of the next day's programmes, the weather forecast and the announcer's determinedly cheerful good night. Only when the screen went blank was she forced to get up and switch off the set.

She glanced at Stephen. Usually he would make some comment on the movie: "Very good," or "Not bad," or "What a load of rubbish." But tonight nothing.

Alison drew a deep breath. She *had* to make him talk. She said resolutely,

"Stephen."

He gave a start. "What?"

It was clear that until that moment he hadn't realised the TV was off. Or perhaps he hadn't even noticed it had been on.

"We must talk," she said.

"Sure. What about?"

"About—"

At that moment there came a ring at the front door.

It was so unexpected that Alison gave a start. As for Stephen he jumped as though he had been shot. He got hurriedly to his feet and stood staring stupidly at the sitting-room door. Much, she thought, as she had two hours ago.

"Who's that?" His voice was a whisper.

"How should I know?" She answered impatiently.

"It's after midnight."

"I *can* tell the time, Stephen."

"Don't let anyone in," he said.

She stared at him in amazement. "You expect *me* to go?"

At this he seemed to pull himself together a little. "No—no, of course not. Sorry."

He turned abruptly and went out to the hall. Alison followed him. The doorbell rang again—a long, peremptory, insistent ring.

"All right, all right." He muttered the words irritably. From behind she saw his shoulders go up as he took a deep breath; then he stepped forward and opened the door.

Two men stood there. Alison could see enough of them only to tell that they were dressed in dark suits with white shirts and sober ties. And she knew immediately just what they were.

"Mr. Stephen Grant?" It was the shorter of the men who spoke.

"Yes."

"We're police officers." He briefly held out some form of identification. "Could we have a word with you?"

"Now?"

"If you don't mind, sir."

"It's very late. We were just going to bed."

"It *is* important, Mr. Grant."

"What's it about?"

"It would be easier to explain indoors, sir."

"Oh—very well."

With bad grace, Stephen stepped aside and the two men came into the hall. The one who had spoken was the older, looking to be in his early fifties. He was short for a policeman, no taller than Alison herself, slim and wiry, with grizzled grey hair, a small military-looking moustache and surprisingly bright blue eyes. In some remarkable way he contrived to look weary, cynical and alert all at the same time.

The second man was twenty-five or thirty years the younger. He was over six feet tall with shoulders to match. He had a round red face, with a cheerful expression. He looked like a young farmer who played second row forward for his local rugby club.

The first man said, "I'm Detective Chief Inspector Bidwell. This is Detective Sergeant"—he paused—"Primrose." The incongruity of the name seemed to strike him as he said it, and the look he cast at his colleague as he introduced him had a definite air of irritation about it. Primrose, though, seemed quite unaware of this and gazed around him amiably.

Stephen said, "I hope this isn't going to take too long." There was an air of bluster about his voice and manner that was new to Alison.

He turned now and saw her. For a moment it was as if he'd forgotten she was present. Then:

"This is my wife," he said shortly.

"So I assumed, sir." Bidwell gave Alison a stiff little bow.

"Come into the sitting-room, won't you?" she said. She turned and led the way. She knew now that she had been waiting for this all the evening. Stephen was in trouble. He had mentioned a near-accident. Had there, in fact, been a real accident? Had he failed to stop? Had he actually killed somebody?

The two policemen followed her into the room. Stephen brought up the rear. He closed the door and stood looking at them.

"Well, what do you want?"

His manner was curt, his voice hard. On top of her apprehension, Alison felt embarrassment sweep over her. And surely, at the very lowest level, if he *was* in some sort of trouble, it was bad tactics to antagonise the police.

However, his rudeness plainly slid off both Bidwell and Primrose. The former just said, "It might be better if we spoke to you in private, sir."

"Oh. Yes, well, my study perhaps? It's very tiny but—"

"No," Alison said loudly.

The three men all looked at her and she flushed. "No, Stephen. I have a right . . ." She tailed off.

He swallowed. "Yes, of course." He turned to the chief inspector. "Say what you have to say here, please."

"As you wish, sir." Bidwell paused, then said, "You're acquainted with a Miss Linda Matthews, Mr. Grant?"

"Matthews? No, I don't think so." Stephen answered very quickly. Then it was as if he realised his response had been too glib. "At least, I can't place the name offhand. Of course, I come into brief contact with so many girls in the course of my business—I'm a literary agent—and publishers' offices are naturally crowded with them. They change their jobs all the time and it's difficult to keep track of them all. So I suppose I may have—"

Bidwell interrupted. "No, sir, Miss Matthews could not be described as in any respect a literary lady. Anyway, we're talking about a local person."

"Oh, I see. Well, I'm sure we don't know any girl by that name in Fermouth." He glanced at Alison. "Do we, darling?"

Alison shook her head. Bidwell ignored her.

"Why do you keep referring to her as a girl, sir?" he asked.

Stephen started. "What's that?"

"Twice you've used the word. But from what I've told you about her she might be any age—ninety or more."

"Oh, I see. I—I don't know, really." Stephen was floundering. "I suppose—"

Alison cut in. "Don't you think 'Linda' sounds quite a modern name, Inspector? I assumed you were talking about a *young* person, too. If you'd said 'Emily' or 'Violet' I'd have imagined an old lady, I think. But 'Linda' I'd visualise as a girl."

"Means 'Snake.' "

It was Sergeant Primrose who had unexpectedly spoken. Alison looked at him sharply.

"I beg your pardon?"

"The name 'Linda' means 'Snake,' so I read once. I'm not casting any aspersions on Miss Matthews' character, you understand. But snakes were thought to be beautiful long ago, so it must be a fairly old name, wouldn't you think?"

"This may be all highly educational," Stephen said harshly, "but my wife and I would like to know what this old lady has to do with us. Why are you standing here questioning us about her in the middle of the night?"

Bidwell regarded him silently for about ten seconds before replying. "Firstly, your original use of 'girl' was correct: Linda Matthews was twenty-seven or twenty-eight years old. Secondly, we're discussing her in the middle of the night because she was killed earlier this evening. Thirdly, we're not questioning *Mrs.* Grant about Linda—only you, sir. And fourthly, we're standing here because we were invited into this room but have not been invited to sit down. Does that answer all your points, Mr. Grant?"

Stephen had gone white—whether from anger or fear Alison couldn't tell. Certainly when he spoke next he sounded furious.

"No, it most certainly doesn't. And let me say that if you think you can practically force your way into people's homes in the early hours and expect to be asked to sit down, you can think again. Now, I repeat, what does the death of this *girl* have to do with me?"

Bidwell surveyed him impassively. Alison felt her nerves were being stretched like a thin rubber band to the verge of snapping.

Finally: "We think you may be able to help us in our enquiries," Bidwell said slowly.

Stephen gave a sigh. "Oh, for heaven's sake, drop the clichés! You mean you suspect me of being somehow involved in her death?"

"Frankly, yes."

"Why?"

The question came crisply and quietly. Alison looked at her husband closely. He seemed to be reverting to his usual self—cooler and more in control. She wondered, though, how much effort it was taking.

Bidwell hesitated for a moment. Then he said,

"Because of a statement by a witness."

"Who says what—precisely?"

"That she saw you kneeling by the body and then running away."

"Saw *me,* you say? You mean she identified me by name?" Stephen's voice was incredulous.

"No."

"What you mean is that she gave you a description which I fit."

"That's correct."

"Something like 'thirty-eight, five feet eleven, slim, dark haired, clean-shaven' and so on."

"More or less."

"And how many men in Fermouth do you suppose that description fits?"

Bidwell shrugged. "Quite a lot."

"Then I repeat my question: why come to me?"

"Because another witness followed you to your car, saw you get in, took down the number and passed it on to us."

There was a sudden silence in the room. Stephen licked his lips. "Well obviously, he—she—made a mistake. Look, what time was this?"

"A little after 9:30 P.M."

"In Fermouth?"

"Yes."

"That proves your witness got the number wrong. I hadn't reached town at that time. I was still on my way from London Airport."

"The witness also described the car—a Ford Sierra Ghia Estate."

Again there was silence. Alison took a deep breath. "Where exactly did this accident happen?" she asked.

The chief inspector looked at her and raised his eyebrows. "Who said anything about it being an accident, Mrs. Grant?"

Alison's eyes widened. "Well, surely you're not saying anybody would run this poor girl down on purpose?"

"I think you're under some misapprehension, Mrs. Grant," Bidwell said. "Linda Matthews wasn't run down by a car. She was strangled in her apartment."

Alison gave a gasp of horror. "You're not seriously suggesting my husband *murdered* this girl!"

"I'm not suggesting anything at the moment, Mrs. Grant—just asking him to assist us in our enquiries."

Stephen said helplessly, "I don't know what more assistance I can give. I've never known a Linda Matthews and at nine-thirty I was driving down from London. I reached Fermouth about ten. I'll submit to a search or to any kind of forensic test. Apart from that I can only repeat that your witness is mistaken."

"Nevertheless, sir, we'd like you to come along to the police station and answer a few more questions—"

"No," Stephen said firmly.

"Now, look, Mr. Grant—"

"I know the law, Chief Inspector. You cannot compel me to come to the police station. I'll answer your questions here or not at all. You can only force me to go with you if you actually arrest me. Now, are you prepared to do that?"

Bidwell didn't reply immediately. He was clearly indecisive and Alison felt a twinge of hope.

Then she seemed to see a sudden new glint in his eye. He said, "You mean that—about submitting to a search?"

Stephen nodded. "Of course."

"Here and now?"

"Certainly. Do you want me to undress? Shall we go to the bedroom?"

"That won't be necessary. If you'll just empty your pockets and let the sergeant frisk you."

"As you wish."

Stephen moved to the table and started to empty his pockets and place the contents on it. From his left-hand trouser pocket he took a handkerchief and from the right a handful of copper and silver. From his hip pocket he took his cheque-book in its folder. Then he started on his coat. It was as his fingers went into the right-hand outside pocket that his face changed. For perhaps half a second Alison saw cold fear in his eyes, and for that moment he froze. Then he brought his hand out. It contained his key-ring. He put it on the table.

Without any hurry or indication of especial interest, Bidwell picked it up. There were seven or eight keys dangling from it. Bidwell ran them through his fingers, his face remaining expressionless. Eventually he replaced the ring on the table.

Stephen meanwhile was continuing to empty his coat pockets—of a penknife, a packet of mints, a fountain-pen, a ball-pen, a pencil, a notebook, a comb, a second handkerchief, and finally, from his inside pocket, his leather wallet.

"That's it," he said quietly.

"Right, sir, if I may . . ."

Primrose began to run his hands rapidly and expertly over Stephen's body.

But Bidwell didn't watch. He picked up the wallet and opened it.

Stephen said, "Look, I didn't give you permission to go through my private papers—"

Bidwell glanced up. "Are you now saying I *cannot* examine the contents of this wallet?"

Then, as Stephen hesitated, he added, "Because, if so, I warn you I shall obtain a search warrant for this house and you will not be given an opportunity to remove anything from it in the interim."

"Oh, go ahead then, curse you."

"Thank you, sir."

But Bidwell did not start emptying the wallet. Instead, holding it in both hands, he began bending it slightly in different places. Alison watched him, transfixed. Suddenly Bidwell discovered an area of the wallet that would not bend. He marked the spot with one hand, and with the other located a zipped compartment. He opened it and his fingers slipped inside. A second later they drew out a shiny brass Yale key. He held it in his hands, gazing at it for several seconds, then placed it on the table. The click as it came in contact with the surface seemed like a tiny gunshot in the room.

Bidwell slowly raised his head and looked at Stephen. "Well, Mr. Grant?" he said quietly.

"Well, what?"

"Could you identify this key for me?"

"I'm not sure. It's a spare—perhaps for this house, perhaps for my office. Or maybe even for my last office. I'd forgotten it was there."

"It looks quite new, Mr. Grant."

"Well, I doubt if it's ever been used—or even out of the wallet since I bought it."

"I see." Bidwell reached into his pocket and brought out an envelope. He opened this and took from it another Yale key. It was darker and rather more worn-looking than the one from Stephen's wallet. Bidwell picked the first one up again and brought the two keys together. He held them in front of him, turning them over in his hands, squinting at them from every angle. When he raised his head he was wearing an expression of intense satisfaction.

Primrose said, "Well?"

"Identical." Bidwell didn't take his eyes from Stephen's face as he answered.

"Look—what's going on?" Stephen's voice was unnaturally loud.

He knows what's going on, thought Alison. He knows as well as they do.

"This key"—Bidwell held the older one up—"is the key to Linda Matthews' apartment. Yours is a duplicate. Perhaps you would care to explain that."

For maybe five seconds Stephen did not react at all to the invitation. He stood staring at the chief inspector, his face quite devoid of expression. Then, without the slightest warning he made a dash towards the door.

Taken completely unawares for a moment, Bidwell gave an angry gasp. "Get him!"

Primrose dived in pursuit. But already Stephen was in the hall. He ran towards the front door. It was as he was scrabbling at the knob that the sergeant reached him. Stephen turned and struck out wildly. Alison gave a scream as Primrose closed with him. The struggle was brief and inglorious. Bidwell joined the sergeant and a few seconds later Stephen was standing white-faced and panting, his hands manacled behind his back.

Alison stood by in a daze. She told herself that this couldn't be happening. It was a nightmare.

She said desperately, "No, please, you mustn't take him."

Bidwell turned to her. There was compassion in his eyes as he said quietly, "I'm sorry, Mrs. Grant. I have no choice."

"Then I'm coming, too."

"I'm sorry—but no."

Stephen looked at her. Suddenly he seemed calm and quite composed. He said, "Darling—phone Innes Lloyd. Tell him exactly what's happened. Ask him to get along to the police station at once. Will you do that?"

She gulped and nodded, quite unable to speak. She knew she wasn't going to wake up. Stephen had been arrested for murder. And whatever the outcome things were never going to be the same again.

CHAPTER TWO

It was advisedly that Fermouth was described earlier simply as a south coast town and not as a seaside resort. Although a comfortable fifty minutes' journey from central London by rail, and an hour and a quarter by road, it is the absence of a good sandy beach that has always prevented it becoming another Brighton or Eastbourne.

This is a deprivation for which the majority of residents are today extremely grateful. In fact, most of them would not be residents at all if things were different; for there are not very many third-, or even second-generation Fermouthites now living in the town, the greater part of the population consisting of commuters to London, retired persons and the professional and tradespeople who cater to them.

Most of the residential building is comparatively modern, many of the older middle-class terraces having been replaced by detached or semidetached houses or by large apartment blocks. Some arty, renovated fisherman's cottages near the harbour and a few Victorian villas—now mostly divided into flats—is about all that survives of the old Fermouth, though the rolling, wooded downlands around the town are dotted with some fine eighteenth- and nineteenth-century country seats. Within the town there are no slums, the relatively small working-class section of the population being accommodated in a few blocks of rather superior terraced houses near the station, and an equally superior council estate on the outskirts of town. The council has for years set its face firmly against any development that would spoil the "special character" of the town—particularly against road-widening or the provision of more than the bare minimum of public parking space. This, more than anything else, and with the full approval of all but the most avaricious of the shopkeepers, has largely succeeded in keeping trippers at bay. People do go to Fermouth for their holidays, but not in great numbers, for they have to be wealthy enough to afford one of the only two—both four-star—hotels. Consequently, the town is only a little more crowded in the summer than in the winter—though that is crowded enough, for it is a very popular place in which to live. This is not surprising, as in addition to its favourable geographical situation relative to London, the town has a lot going for it: three or four expensive restaurants, all of which have appeared in various good food guides; excellent shops; the picturesque natural harbour, home of a thriving sailing club; and, just out of town, a fine golf course. There is a permanent, subsidized repertory theatre, many well-organized social activities and a number of good schools. The air is bracing. There are no caravan parks, fun fairs or amusement arcades; and only one bingo hall—tucked rather shamefacedly away in a side street. Industry is nonexistent. Property prices and rents are a source of constant delight to the local estate agents, but there is no shortage of buyers or tenants. Fermouth is prosperous, comfortable, goodhearted, generally well behaved and perhaps a little smug. It is one of the six safest Conservative seats in the country.

At the time of Linda Matthews' death, Bertrand Innes Lloyd was the most successful solicitor in Fermouth. A stocky sandy-haired, pugnacious-looking individual of forty-eight, he had the appearance more of a prosperous builder or haulage contractor than a lawyer. In addition to his being their solicitor, the Grants had known him and his wife Marjorie socially for a number of years. While by no means close personal friends, all four belonged to the yacht club, while Alison and Marjorie were both stalwarts of the dramatic society, and the two men members of the golf club. Innes Lloyd was therefore the natural person for Stephen, at his arrest, to have told Alison to contact.

She could not, however, keep wondering, as she faced him in her sitting-room on the Tuesday morning, whether he was the *best* person for the job. She imagined that he handled very little criminal work and it was possible he would be somewhat out of his depth in defending someone accused of murder. He certainly appeared embarrassed by the situation; though in the circumstances that was perhaps natural enough.

"I don't have to tell you, Alison, how very, very deeply I feel for you in this awful situation," he was saying. "It's appalling, really, appalling."

"Thank you, er, Bertrand," she said. She didn't think she had ever addressed him this way before (had she ever called him anything?). "It's Stephen we ought really to feel for, though," she went on. "Held in prison for a murder he didn't commit."

"Er, yes—yes, of course." He cleared his throat.

"Did he tell you last night just what happened?" she asked.

"He gave me his story, yes."

"Can you tell me what it is?"

"You haven't heard it yet?" For a moment he sounded surprised. "No—naturally—you wouldn't have done. Well, it may be better if he tells you himself."

She wondered if this was some point of professional ethics, or whether he meant the story was so improbable that he couldn't bring himself to repeat it.

"He *was* having an affair with that woman, though." She said it flatly, as a statement of fact, not as a question. It had to be said. It was going to be said a lot, by all sorts of people. Let her be the first to say it.

"Well." Again came that nervous little cough. "We didn't actually discuss that aspect of things—only really what happened last night. But, I can assure you he said nothing to me about ever having been to her apartment before."

"I see. Then let us by all means preserve the niceties and say he called there on business, or to beg some water for his radiator, say. Have they actually charged him?"

"Not yet."

"Why is that?"

"Well, they don't have to for thirty-six hours."

"So—they can keep him there until tomorrow morning without charging him?"

"Yes. Then they can go before the magistrates and ask for a further thirty-six hours detention."

"But can't you object to that?"

"I could, but it would be unwise."

"Why?"

He hesitated. "The situation here is rather unusual. The police themselves cannot be absolutely certain of Stephen's guilt. They cannot, on the evidence, be sure of a conviction. If they were, they would charge him immediately. That they haven't done so is a good sign. So in this case Stephen's best policy is not to complain, but just be quiet and patient and answer all their questions calmly. They can only hold him for a maximum of ninety-six hours, anyway."

Alison made a quick calculation. "Till Friday night?"

"That's right; and the last thing we want to do is pressure them into charging him before they absolutely have to."

"But why not?"

"Because until that time they will not divulge his name to the press. Of course, if a paper can discover his name from another source, they *can* print it. But it's unusual. Obviously, the longer we can avert that the better. Then, if by any chance he should be released, nobody need ever know about it."

"I see. In that case, let's just keep as quiet as possible."

"I thought you'd agree."

"When can I see him?"

"Now, if you like."

"Now?"

"Well, in as long as it takes to get down to the station. I have cleared it with the chief inspector."

"Oh, that's wonderful!" Alison got hurriedly to her feet.

"Can I drive you?" he asked.

"No, really, thanks. I've got my Mini."

"I thought perhaps you could do with some moral support."

"That's a kind thought, but I honestly don't think so."

He bowed his head. "If you're quite sure. In that case I'll leave you to get ready."

He stood up and she went with him to the hall.

In the front doorway he turned. "One more thing, Alison. Persuade him to tell you—and me—the full and complete truth. That's vitally important."

"Are you saying he hasn't, so far?"

He hesitated. "Very few people do the first time," he said vaguely.

Alison and Stephen sat facing each other across the table in the small, bare high-ceilinged room. To her it seemed incredibly unreal—a scene watched hundreds of times in movies or read about in books. One never conceived of it happening to oneself. She forced herself to try to talk normally.

"How are you, Stephen?"

He shrugged. "All right, I suppose."

It was true he looked all right, pale, but more relaxed than the previous night. "I didn't sleep well," he added.

"I'm not surprised. Do you have a roo—er, a—"

"Cell is the word."

"A cell to yourself?"

"Yes. Law-abiding place, Fermouth. At the moment there's only one d. and d. and myself here."

"D. and d.?"

"Drunk and disorderly."

"Oh, I see."

"Seems a very decent bloke, actually."

"How are they treating you?"

"Very well, on the whole. No rubber hoses or bright lights. Scrupulously fair. But not exactly chatty."

"What about the food?"

"Oh Alison, for heaven's sake!" He banged the table with his fist, and she gave a start. "Stop talking about trivia. There are rather more important topics to discuss than my breakfast sausage."

"I'm sorry."

He suddenly slumped back in his chair. "No, *I'm* sorry. I had no right. Alison, I'm sorry for everything."

She said softly, "There's only one thing you have to be sorry for, Stephen."

He looked down at the floor. "I know."

"Oh Stephen, how *could* you?"

He shook his head. "I honestly don't know. A kind of madness."

"Had you known her long?"

"No."

"How long?"

"Oh, I don't know—"

"Stephen—*please.*"

"About four months."

Her eyes widened. "You call that not long?"

He looked wretched. "It didn't seem long."

"Doesn't time fly when you're having fun?" she said bitterly.

"I didn't mean that!"

"It's true, though."

"No, I wasn't having fun. I've been desperately miserable—and worried sick."

"Then why go on? Why even start?"

"I honestly don't know."

"You were in love with her?"

"No. Well, I thought I was. But it was just infatuation, I realise that now. I was going to break it off, I swear, when I could find the right time."

"So you're not grieving for her?"

"No—not in that sense. It was a ghastly thing to happen. I can't bear to think of it. But I can't bear to think of *anybody* being killed that way. I'm not glad she's dead—that would be awful—but I *am* glad she's not around anymore. If I knew she was in—in Australia, say, this morning I'd be as happy as a lark. But while she was here I just couldn't break away. It was a sort of enchantment, I suppose."

"Was she very beautiful?"

He thought for a moment. "No, not really. Not beautiful. Obviously, I found her attractive. If I said otherwise you'd know I was lying. She was pretty. Glamorous, if you like. But the more I think of her now, the more superficial a prettiness it seems. In ten years time she would have had nothing."

"Where did you meet her?"

"Alison, please—I don't want to talk about her anymore. Not now. Do you mind?"

"No. No, I suppose not."

"There's only one thing that's important to me now. Us. One thing I've got to know: can you forgive me? That's the question which has been haunting me all night—not whether I was going to be charged with murder—but whether you would—could . . ." He tailed off.

Alison was silent for a few moments. Then she said,

"Probably if things had happened differently the answer would be no, I couldn't forgive you. I mean, if I'd found out about her some other way, while the affair was going on, I'd have almost certainly left you immediately and got a divorce. But what's happened—well, somehow it's changed everything. For one thing, I can't hate *her.* I can only pity her. That makes a difference. And, of course, I love you, Stephen. I always have."

She paused before saying, "So the answer is—yes, I forgive you."

The relief in his eyes was indescribable and removed any lingering doubts she might have had that her decision was the right one. What they had *was* worth preserving—worth fighting for. And the fight was on.

She sat up, coughed and assumed a businesslike attitude. "Now, that's enough of that. Tell me about last night."

"You really want to know?"

"Of course. I *must* know."

He looked unhappy. "As you wish. Well, I arrived at the flat about nine and let myself in. The sitting-room light and the television were on but there was no sign of her. I called out, looked in the bedroom and the bathroom and came back to the sitting-room. Then I noticed that there was very little Scotch in the bottle on the cocktail cabinet; and it occurred to me she'd probably slipped out to buy some more. I poured myself out what was left, turned the TV off and sat down to wait for her. I finished the drink. And then—well, I'd had a long and tiring day and I fell asleep. I don't think I slept long—perhaps twenty or twenty-five minutes. I was woken up abruptly by the front doorbell. I was disorientated for a few seconds. I couldn't answer the door, of course. But I thought that when Linda got back she might like to have a description of the visitor. Also, it occurred to me that it might actually *be* Linda—that she'd somehow locked herself out and was ringing on the off chance I'd arrived. So I moved over to the window to see if I could get a glimpse of the caller without being seen, when he, or she, left. Stupid, really, because if I looked out with the light on, I'd certainly be seen myself; but I wasn't fully awake. Anyway, to get to the window I had to go behind a couch that stood in front of it. And then I saw her."

"Linda."

He nodded. For a moment it seemed he couldn't carry on. But then he made what was clearly a great effort, gulped and continued with barely a tremor in his voice.

"She—she was lying on the floor, on her side. There was a silk scarf round her neck—pulled tight. I just stared—I couldn't move—couldn't think. At last I heaved the couch out of the way, dragged her to the middle of the room and knelt down by her. Then, without any warning, there was a horrible scream behind me."

"Scream? From whom?"

"This old woman—well, not very old, really. Just lined and gaunt. I know now she was Linda's char. Mrs. Hopkins her name is. I'd never met her but Linda had mentioned her a few times—usually grumbling, when she'd found something the woman had failed to clean."

"But what was she doing there then?"

"It had obviously been her at the door. She'd come back for some reason, rung the bell, then, when there was no reply, she'd assumed Linda was out and let herself in with her key."

"I see. What happened then?"

"I stood up and tried to say something. I must have looked pretty ghastly, because she just went on screaming and backing away from me at the same time. The noise was appalling."

"What did you do?"

Stephen didn't answer at once. He looked down at his hands and seemed to be studying his nails, as he said quietly,

"I lost my head."

"What do you mean?"

"I panicked. I just pushed past her and ran out of the flat."

"Oh Stephen, you fool!"

"I know. Don't rub it in. The worst of it was that she came after me."

Alison stared. "Chased you, you mean?"

"Not exactly. But she followed me to the street door and started yelling out after me, 'Stop! Murder! Police! He's killed her!' "

"Oh no!" Alison momentarily closed her eyes in despair. Then she asked, "Wasn't there anybody else about?"

"Well, nobody to speak of. There was a kid on a bike, I think. Anyway, nobody tried to stop me. I just sprinted to the car—it was parked about a hundred yards away—and came home. The rest you know."

Alison regarded him silently. If anyone had forecast that a few minutes after her husband had admitted to an affair with another woman she would feel sympathy for him, she would have said they were crazy. But, in fact, that was the only emotion she could feel. That, plus a growing resolve that somehow she was going to get him out of this mess.

She asked, "When you went into the sitting-room, did you see any sign of somebody else having been there?"

He frowned. "How do you mean?"

"Well, cigarette stubs, used glasses—things like that."

"Oh, I see. I didn't examine the ashtrays. I think I should have noticed used glasses. You mean, had she been entertaining someone else—was the murderer someone she knew?"

"Exactly. What do you think?"

"I don't know. Frankly, Alison, I haven't given it much thought. My mind's been on you—and myself."

"Well, we're going to have to start thinking of things like that. How was she dressed?"

"Oh, let me think." He closed his eyes. "Blue dress—satiny kind of material."

"Smart?"

"Yes, I would say so. You might not have liked it."

"And she was made up attractively, and her hair done?"

"Yes. But I mean, she nearly always was. And she invariably dressed well. She never went around in cardigans and skirts or slacks."

Alison flushed slightly. "You mean like I do?"

"No!" The word came out sharply. "But I mean, as a model, she had to look her very best all the time."

"Is that what she called herself—a model?"

"That's what she was. Only she hadn't done much modelling lately. But I suppose it had become habit to keep herself up to the mark. Look, what's the point in this?"

"Well if you say she was a real glamour-puss, always dressed up to the nines, it's irrelevant, but I was just trying to find out if she might have been *expecting* somebody."

"Well, she was, of course. I—" He stopped short.

Alison stared at him, puzzled for a second. Then she got the point. "Oh. You mean *you?*"

He nodded, his eyes avoiding hers.

She said slowly, "That's why you came home from Dublin yesterday. You'd never intended to stop over there last night. It was a good opportunity to spend some time with her, without having to think up an excuse for me for not coming home. I was imagining you'd dropped in on her unexpectedly."

"No; I phoned her from the airport." He wriggled awkwardly. "I'm sorry darling, I've been a rat—"

She waved him down. "Shut up about it. We've discussed that. It's over with. I'm only going into it again from the point of view of the murder."

"Alison, you're wonderful, really—"

"Be quiet, Stephen. I want to think. Now: she was expecting you. Did she know what time you were arriving?"

"Not precisely, but roughly."

"And she seemed quite happy about your coming?"

"Yes—very happy."

"So she's unlikely to have been expecting *another* lover last night. Did she *have* other lovers?"

"I would have said definitely no, at one time. Now . . ." He didn't finish.

"But you don't know of any for a fact?"

He shook his head. "She never spoke about anybody else."

"So let's say that—unless she was incredibly reckless, or just didn't care about your finding out—she *didn't* invite anybody else to her flat last night. Suppose, though, that somebody turned up unannounced—somebody who didn't know she was expecting *you*—didn't even know she was *seeing* you. Then something she says, or something in her manner, gives the game away. They have a row, he loses his temper and kills her. How about that?"

"It's certainly the most likely sequence of events."

They were both silent for a few moments. Then she said, "If somebody saw *you,* they might have seen *him.*"

"I doubt it. I imagine his departure was rather less conspicuous than mine."

"Yes, if only you'd stayed and phoned the police yourself."

"I would have if it hadn't been for that horrible screaming char."

"All the same, you should have realised what running away like that would look like. You must have known they'd catch up with you."

"I didn't *know* they would. And even if they did I thought I might be able to bluff them."

"With the key to the girl's flat in your pocket?" She spoke more sarcastically than she had meant to.

He flushed. "Yes, that was stupid."

"Why on earth didn't you get rid of it?"

"I forgot all about it."

"But you'd just let yourself in with it!"

"But I'd put it away again. You see I kept it in the wallet because it was new and looked conspicuous on the ring. I thought you might spot it one day and ask what it was for. Well, what I'd always do when I got to Lin— to the flat—was take out my wallet, remove the key, open the front door, then put the key away immediately—actually as I was going through the door. It was automatic. It wasn't until I was emptying my pockets last night and felt my key-ring that I remembered the other key in my wallet. I knew then that it was all up."

"Stephen—it is *not* all up. We are going to get you off. And not only off —but cleared beyond a shadow of a doubt."

He looked at her with admiration in his eyes. "Sounds wonderful and I know you believe it. But how?"

"I don't know yet. But the killer must have been someone she knew. I mean, she couldn't have surprised a burglar, or anything like that, or there'd have been *some* trace left of a break-in or a struggle. And I can't see a girl, living alone, admitting a stranger to her flat after dark. So what I've got to do is find out everything I can about her life and her other friends. And that's where you can help. You've got to rack your brains to remember every conceivable thing you can that she ever told you about herself."

He looked doubtful. "I'll do my best, of course. But it's not going to be easy. She really said so little."

"Maybe. But in four months there must have been *something.*"

"I suppose so." He looked more unhappy now than at any time since she had come in.

She said, "You don't want to think about her, do you?"

"Not really."

"Well, you're going to *have* to. But"—she shrugged—"I suppose we can leave that for the time being. There are some other things we must talk about."

He brightened fractionally. "Yes, of course. Well, first the business. Luckily, Phyllis won't have expected me in this morning, so I won't have been missed yet. Will you please phone her?"

"What shall I say?"

"Oh lor, I don't know. Perhaps we needn't tell her yet. Did Innes Lloyd explain about there being nothing in the papers till I'm charged?"

"Yes."

"Then for now you'd better just tell her I'm ill and hope for the best. As to the work, tell her she's in charge. She'd better take on a temp as receptionist and typist and use her discretion about everything else. I think she's quite capable of handling things—in fact, it's the opportunity she's been waiting for, for some time. Send her Brannigan's typescript. She'll know just what to do with it. Obviously she mustn't take on any new clients, but otherwise I leave everything to her. If any real crisis comes up tell her to phone you, but I don't anticipate anything."

He paused, then said, "Heaven only knows what effect it'll have on me professionally, if I am charged."

"A very good effect, I'm certain, once you're cleared."

"You think so?"

"I'm sure of it—think of the free publicity. And I guarantee all your mystery writers will be clamouring for inside information on what it's really like to be a murder suspect. I bet everyone of them will immediately start planning to collaborate with you on a book about the case."

He smiled. It was a shadow of his old cheery grin, but it was a genuine smile.

"Anyway," she went on, "it's not going to come to that. I'm going to see you're *not* charged—even if I've got to go out and track down the real murderer myself."

He said quietly, "Alison, thank you."

"What for?"

"Everything. Being so wonderful about all this. Not just going off and leaving me—as you'd be perfectly justified in doing. For being willing to fight for me. And something else."

"What's that?"

"Not once asking me to swear I didn't kill her."

CHAPTER THREE

"Well, boss, what d'you think?"

"For heaven's sake, Freddie, don't call me 'boss.' Makes me feel like a Mafia godfather."

Detective Sergeant Primrose looked hurt. "You told me not to bother with 'sir' when we were on our own—that you didn't want things too formal. When I called you 'Chief Inspector' you said that was too much of a mouthful. What do you want me to call you?"

"Oh, anything. Use your imagination."

Detective Chief Inspector Bidwell spoke irritably. He slumped back in his office chair and rubbed his eyes. He'd had a short night and was tired. "Go and get us some coffee," he ordered.

"Oh right."

Primrose left the room. When he returned a minute or so later, carrying two plastic cups gingerly by the rims, Bidwell hadn't moved, though now his eyes were closed. Primrose placed the two cups on the desk and sat down himself.

Bidwell opened his eyes, picked up the cup, took a sip from it and gave a sigh of satisfaction. "Ah, I needed that."

Primrose tasted his own coffee and grimaced. "You know, I can't understand your liking this stuff."

"Well, I do. I like coffee from machines. And I know it's hygenic. I won't find a dead fly in it or lipstick on the cup. What did you say?"

"Nothing."

"You asked me a question—before you went for the coffee."

"What I should call you?"

"No, no—before that."

"Oh, just what you thought."

"About what?"

"Grant. Have we got the right man?"

"Oh yes, I should think so."

"He's very vehement he didn't do it. I just thought what he said had the ring of truth."

"When you've interrogated as many suspects as I have you'll realise that most people can put your average professional actor to shame—when they've really got to. Bring tears to your eyes, some of them. You feel like not only letting 'em go but giving 'em a fiver into the bargain. Guilty as sin, all the time."

"Yes, I know that. I mean, I'm not a rookie, I've seen some of them myself. But I did have doubts about Grant's guilt. Besides, there isn't really much evidence against him, is there?"

"Found kneeling over the body? Then running away. Not reporting it?"

Primrose shrugged. "It *could* have happened as he said."

"Theoretically."

"But you don't think so?"

"No, not really."

"So you're going to charge him?"

"Don't know. Haven't spoken to the chief super yet."

"But he'll ask you what you want to do?"

"I daresay."

"So, what will you tell him?"

"Haven't made up my mind."

Bidwell sipped at his coffee again. Primrose sighed inwardly. His chief was maddening in this mood. He opened his mouth.

"Then when—"

"When will I know? Perhaps by this time tomorrow. After all we've got over twenty-four hours before we have to charge him or go before the magistrates. We might as well spend at least part of that time finding out what we can about the girl. If we turn up somebody else who had a motive to kill her the situation could be changed. I mean, she might turn out to be a Bulgarian defector, or something. Who knows?"

"OK, where do we start?"

"We only know of two people who knew her—Grant and the cleaning woman. Let's start with her."

Mrs. Hopkins was a thin, bony woman of about sixty. She lived on the town's single council estate. She had obviously been expecting the police, for she opened the front door and stood waiting expectantly as they walked up the path.

"Come in, come in," she said standing aside. "Go straight into the lounge."

They went into a spotless little room. Mrs. Hopkins bustled in after them, closing the door behind her.

"Have you got him?" she asked eagerly as she did so.

"We've got the man you described, yes, ma'am."

She gave a sigh of satisfaction. "And what I told you helped?"

"Yes indeed," Bidwell assured her. It wasn't true. Her extremely vague description would have been useless had the schoolboy cyclist not taken Stephen Grant's car number. However, she *had* phoned the police, so she'd played her part. "You did very well," he added.

She tried unsuccessfully to look modest. "Then you'll be wanting me to come along to one of the identity parades?"

"No, that won't be necessary, ma'am."

Her face fell. "Why not?"

"Well, you see, the man we've picked up has admitted he was the one you saw kneeling down by the body."

"Oh." It was clearly a bitter blow to Mrs. Hopkins. "So you won't be wanting me to give evidence in court either?" she went on slowly.

"Afraid not. You see, there's no conflict of evidence. He admits he was there. That's that."

"He's pleading guilty, then?"

"Well, we haven't got to that stage yet, but we hope he will."

She looked so disappointed that Bidwell felt quite sorry for her. He decided to cheer her up. "Still," he said, "I'm sure the press will want to hear your story."

She brightened at once. "And the telly, d'you think?"

"Don't know about that. But the *Advertizer* certainly. Tell you what, I haven't had a press conference yet, but when I do I'll give them your name and address, shall I?"

"Oh well, I dunno, I'm sure." The show of reluctance was not convincing. "I shouldn't really let you. What'll my old man say?"

"He'll be proud of you, that's what he'll be," Primrose told her heartily.

"Oh well, if you're sure they'd be really interested." Unconsciously she patted her hair into place and smoothed down her dress.

These pleasantries completed, Bidwell got down to business.

"Now, Mrs. Hopkins, perhaps you can help us in another way."

"Oh yes." Instantly she was all agog. "Oh, please sit down," she said.

"Thank you."

They all sat. "What is it you want?" she asked.

"Well, first of all, you said something to the first policeman who arrived last night about a ring missing from Miss Matthews' finger."

She gave a decisive nod. "That's right. Third finger, left hand," she added meaningfully.

"This was an engagement ring?"

"In a way."

"How do you mean exactly?"

"Well, for one thing she had to go and get it by herself. Not that she minded that too much."

"When was this?"

"Few weeks ago."

"You commented on it, did you?"

"Didn't get a chance not to. She shoved it under my nose. 'What d'you think of that, Hoppy?' she asked. Always called me 'Hoppy,' she did. Well, course I admired it. Lovely it was, too—big diamond with little rubies all round it. 'You engaged, dear?' I asked her, and she laughed. 'It's highly unofficial,' she said, 'but, yes, I think you could say I am.' So, o'course I started to congratulate her, like, but she stopped me. 'Don't say anything to anybody about it, please,' she said. 'I shan't wear this out of doors, 'cos I don't want people asking questions, so you'll be one of the very few in the know.' And she wore it all the time indoors after that. I never saw her without it."

"And she had it on yesterday?"

"I didn't see her yesterday. But she had it on last Friday—definite."

"Wouldn't know where she bought it, would you?"

"I couldn't rightly say. But it was somebody local. I'm sure she'd just bought it when she showed it to me, and she hadn't been out of town."

"Then it should be easy enough to find out. Er, do me a favour—don't say anything about the ring to the reporters. Maybe the murderer doesn't know it's been missed, so it'll be our secret—for the time being. OK?"

"Oh yes. Course. Yes, sir, I won't say a word." Mrs. Hopkins adopted the air of someone In The Know.

"Fine. Now, tell me, Mrs. Hopkins, how long had you been, er, obliging Miss Matthews?"

Bidwell brought this word out with the slightly self-conscious air of the layman who wants the professional to know that he understands the jargon.

"Since just after she moved in—last July."

"Over a year, then? You went every weekday?"

"No—three afternoons a week—Monday, Wednesday and Friday. That was quite enough to keep a place that size looking nice."

"And you were there yesterday?"

"That's right—two till five."

"By the way, why did you go back last night?"

"I left my purse behind. You see, I made a telephone call. My sister's in hospital and I rang up to find out how she was. Now, I always pays for my phone calls. So I gets my purse out of my bag, takes the money out and puts it by the telephone. Then someone comes to the door and I puts my purse down to go and answer it. It was only a man come to read the meter, but it puts my purse out of my mind. When I gets home I finds I haven't got it. Well, there was about fifteen pound in it that I knew I'd want today, and as today wasn't one of my days fur Miss Matthews, I decided to go back and get it last night, after bingo. Well, I saw the light through the curtains and thought she was in. So I rang the bell, but she didn't come. So then I let myself in with my key. And . . . well, you know the rest."

"Yes, of course. Very nasty. You've had your own key for long?"

"Since about three months after I started. She said she knew by then she could trust me. You see, she liked to go out in the afternoons. At first, she used to wait in for me, but since then as often as not I haven't seen her when I've been there."

"And you didn't see her yesterday—alive, I mean?"

"No, she weren't in at all."

"So Friday was the last time you saw her?"

"That's right. She paid me then. That was the day I mostly saw her. Not always. Sometimes she'd go out and leave the money in a envelope. But *usually* I'd see her on a Friday."

"And last Friday her manner was perfectly normal?"

"As far as I could tell. Bit quiet. Thoughtful, like."

Bidwell nodded. "What sort of a girl was she, Mrs. Hopkins?"

"Oh, very nice. Real polite and considerate always, and always appreciating of what you done. Very fond of her, I was. Course I don't say her"—Mrs. Hopkins lowered her voice slightly—"her morals was all they might be."

She gave a sniff, but Bidwell felt it was merely a token gesture towards conventional morality and that Mrs. Hopkins didn't really give two hoots about Linda's private life. However, it gave him an opening.

"Have lots of men friends, did she?"

"Well, she'd *had* lots, from things she let slip."

"Did you meet any of them?"

"Not exactly." Mrs. Hopkins spoke reluctantly. "They'd always left by the time I got there. Reckon that's why she didn't want me there in the mornings. Spoke to some of them on the phone though, I did."

"How many did you speak to on the phone?"

She thought. "Can't rightly remember. Just the two lately. Course, there were probably others. I'd often hear her talking, but course I wouldn't know who to."

"What did these men sound like?"

"Oh, very nicely spoken. Gentlemen, you know."

"What sort of things did they say?"

"Just ask for Miss Matthews, and I'd either call her or tell 'em she wasn't in. They'd just say they'd try again later, or something like that. Never left a message nor nothing."

"And what sort of things did *she* say to them?"

"Oh, just canoodling sort of stuff—in that special *kind* of purring voice she'd use."

Bidwell smiled. "Canoodling sort of stuff? Can you be a bit more specific?"

"Pardon?"

"Can you give me an example of the sort of thing she'd say?"

"Well, things like 'Oh, darling, you mustn't say things like that,' or 'You're sweet' or 'You're too good to me.' She listened a lot and always made herself sound very admiring. She knew how to get a man, all right. They're all the same. Just want to be told how wonderful they are. No offence."

"None taken, Mrs. Hopkins. Did you ever hear their names?"

She hesitated. "Not really."

"What does that mean?"

"No surnames."

"First names?"

"Just the one. Steve."

"Oh, I see." He might have guessed.

"He was the newest and I think she was fondest of him. I got the idea it was him I saw last night."

"What makes you think that?"

"Well, for one thing you weren't very interested when I said his name. But besides, he looked like I thought Steve might. Was it him?"

"Afraid I can't tell you that, Mrs. Hopkins. He hasn't been charged yet. When he is it'll be in the papers. And you never heard the names of anybody else?"

"Not so as I'd remember."

"This Steve was the newest, you say. But she was in touch with at least one other as well?"

"Yes, he phoned her last week. Wednesday it was. 'Bout two or half past. I didn't hear much she said. I was cleaning the bathroom."

"And to your knowledge there were just these two current men friends: Steve, and the man who called last Wednesday?"

"That's right. But there must have been dozens of others over the years. You don't get a wardrobe of clothes like that on a working girl's wages. You seen them?"

"Her clothes? Not yet."

"Well, you take a good look. Eye-opener it'll be."

"But she was a model, wasn't she? I mean, she'd earn good money—and she'd *have* to dress well."

"Called herself a model. But I never saw her picture nowhere. I mean, I get lots of magazines from the ladies I oblige and ever since I came to Miss Matthews I been looking through 'em all regular, trying to find a picture of her. Never one."

"So what you're saying in effect was that she let men keep her?"

"Now, don't get me wrong. She wasn't no—well, you know what I mean: one of *them* girls. But she was a pretty girl and she knew what side her bread was buttered and she made sure she only went out with men what could afford to buy her nice things. And why not, I'd like to know?" Mrs. Hopkins added pugnaciously, "After all, a girl's looks don't last long. A few more years and they'd lose interest in her. She's got to do the best for herself she can, while she can."

Bidwell refrained with some difficulty from entering into a debate on the morality of what he considered a highly cynical point of view.

He said, "Well, that's as maybe. Fact is, Miss Matthews *didn't* do too well for herself in the end, did she?"

"That's part of the risk she run. She was unlucky."

"Yes, you could say that. Actually, though, you're only guessing at all these wealthy lovers, aren't you? You only know of two men in the last few months."

"You take a look in that there address book, and you'll see if I'm right."

"What address book's that?"

"Little red one. Well, I say little, but sort of thick. Never without it, she wasn't. Always flicking through it. It slipped off the arm of her chair one day and fell on the floor open. I picked it up. Must have been hundreds of names in it."

"You didn't notice any of the names?"

"No, I did not." Mrs. Hopkins spoke firmly. "I do not pry into other people's private things. Couldn't help seeing there were lots of names, that's all."

"We'll make a special point of looking for it."

"You do that."

"Now, what about her family—know anything about them?"

Mrs. Hopkins shook her head. "She never mentioned them."

"Friends? Girl-friends, I mean?"

"Don't think she had any. At least not in Fermouth."

"Did she have any hobbies—interests? Play any games—tennis, for instance?"

"Not that I knew of. Can't see her running around playing games, somehow."

"No, perhaps not."

Bidwell got to his feet, Primrose following suit. "Well thank you, Mrs. Hopkins, you've been very helpful. Now, is there anything else you can tell us that might prove useful?"

"Can't think of nothing."

"Well, here's my card. If anything occurs to you, give me a ring."

In the car, Primrose said, "What an awful woman."

"Oh, I don't know. She's loyal, at least. And no fool, either. Some of the things she said were quite astute."

"Where to? Linda's flat?"

"Yes. I'm looking forward to having a read of that address book."

Bidwell gazed round the large, airy sitting-room of Linda Matthews' flat. There was nothing now to indicate that a murder had been committed here not much more than twelve hours before. And with the removal of the girl's body virtually nothing to show she had ever lived here. The room was expensively furnished in the most up-to-date style. The decor, carpet and curtains were in the height of modern good taste. Yet, there was something lacking.

"Like a showroom at an exhibition isn't it?" Primrose remarked.

"Yes; that's the trouble. It's utterly impersonal. No books, no photos, no knick-knacks or souvenirs. Not even a travel poster. Difficult to believe a girl has been living here for over a year."

They went into the kitchen. Everything was spotless and looked almost brand-new. Not a thing was out of place.

They moved on to the bedroom. This was a little less tidy than the other rooms, with a hairbrush, comb and various make-up articles on the dressing-table, a nightdress thrown carelessly over the back of a chair and a pair of kicked-off slippers on their sides near it. But apart from this, it was as bare of any personal touch as the rest of the flat. One wall was completely taken up by a cupboard with sliding doors. Bidwell went across and opened it. Both men whistled.

Primrose said, "I see what Mrs. Hopkins meant."

The cupboard was packed with clothes. Bidwell started counting. There were two full-length fur coats, plus a cape; eight other coats; twenty-nine dresses, including seven evening gowns; and half a dozen suits. There were nearly a score of hats and over thirty pairs of shoes, as well as innumerable skirts, slacks, blouses and sweaters. None of the garments was soiled or much worn. Nor, to Bidwell's inexpert eye, did they look at all out of date.

"Right," he said, "let's have a look for this address book. You start in here. I'll take the living room."

He went back and began his search. The room was so unnaturally bare and tidy that for once this was an easy job. The solitary cupboard seemed to be the only place to look. Bidwell opened it. On a shelf inside was a large box file. He took it down, laid it on the table and started to go through the contents. These consisted of a passport; the registration document and insurance certificate for an MG Metro; a rent book for the apartment (rent paid up to date, he noted); bank and building society documents showing total assets of a little over £5,000; a medical card; and a large sealed envelope. Bidwell opened the latter and extracted a sheet of heavy paper. He unfolded this and read it impassively.

Next, he turned his attention to the handbag that it was plain Linda had been using most recently. But this contained only a handkerchief, make-up, a few pounds in notes and coins, a bunch of keys and a driving licence. That was it.

Bidwell stood up and continued his search. But nowhere in the room did he find any personal papers. There were no letters, no photos—and no address book.

Bidwell picked up the paper that had been in the envelope and returned to the bedroom. Primrose, who was going laboriously through the pockets of the coats and suits in the cupboard, looked round with a grimace. "What a hateful job. You feel such an intruder."

"Got to be done. Anything interesting?"

"No. The dressing-table drawers only contain lingerie and stuff. I found her jewel box. Four or five quite nice pieces—worth a few hundred quid, I'd think—nothing special."

"Well, I've been going through her papers. Seems she had some stuff deposited at the bank."

Primrose nodded at the piece of paper. "What's that?"

"Believe it or not, her will."

He held it out. Primrose took it. "Oh, it's one of those do-it-yourself ones you can buy in stationer's."

"Quite legal though."

"Looks short enough. Last will and testament . . . blah, blah, blah . . . everything of which I die possessed to my brother and next of kin, Roger Peter Matthews of 15 Erskine Gardens, London W.2. Witnessed by Sidney Harris, John Street, Fermouth, window cleaner, and Kevin Dooney, Church Terrace, Fermouth, also window cleaner. Dated—oh, only last Thursday."

Primrose looked up. "Interesting. Do you reckon she thought her life might be in danger?"

"It's possible, but I doubt it. Hopkins said her manner was normal on Friday."

"At least now we know who her next of kin is."

"Yes, we must get in touch with him at once. And those witnesses."

"No sign of the address book, obviously?"

"No. You nearly finished?"

"Just these few coats and things."

"I'll give you a hand. Then I suppose we'd better try the bathroom and kitchen—just for completeness."

But twenty minutes later Bidwell had to admit that the address book was nowhere in the flat.

"Means the killer took it, doesn't it, Chief?" Primrose said.

"Seems so." Bidwell was looking reflective.

"Doesn't that look good for Grant?" I mean, he didn't have time to take it after Mrs. Hopkins burst in on him—anyway she'd have seen him—and he'd hardly have lifted it *before* killing the girl, would he?"

"Doesn't follow. He could have killed her earlier, then pocketed the address book, and just gone back to the body when Mrs. Hopkins came in."

"But why?"

Bidwell shrugged. "Perhaps he was going to shift her into the bedroom —hoping to delay discovery of the body. And, after all, he didn't know who was at the door. The callers might have seen the light. If they kept ringing, Grant might have been forced to answer, rather than raise their suspicions. Obviously, he'd have to move the girl out of this room first."

"I suppose so. Wonder if he took anything else—letters or photos? I've never seen a home so bereft of things like that."

"He might have. But even if he did he'd have hardly taken *all* her stuff —only those things showing *his* involvement with her—and I shouldn't think there could be many of those. No, I reckon she just travelled light— didn't really look on this as her home at all. Apart from the clothes— which you could call the essential tools of her trade—she kept the bare minimum of stuff here. She was ready to move out at a couple of hours' notice."

"Into another apartment, handy to the house of some other wealthy man?"

"Probably. I wonder how many times she'd done it in the past."

"Doesn't a girl like that ever want to settle down? Have a permanent home—with a husband and kids?"

"I wouldn't know, Freddie. Why don't you ask one of them?"

He glanced round the room and his eyes alighted on the couch, which stood with its back to the window. He stared at it silently. Then he said, "Go and lie down behind the settee."

It was one of Sergeant Primrose's great attractions as an assistant that he never questioned instructions of this kind. He didn't even look remotely surprised—just crossed the room, squeezed past the end of the couch and got down on the floor.

Bidwell said, "I can see your head."

Primrose gave a wriggle and his head disappeared from the chief inspector's sight. Bidwell moved a yard to his right.

"Now I can see your feet."

"Sorry, can't be helped. Course I'm a good bit taller than Linda Matthews."

"Can you double yourself up a bit?"

"Not really. There isn't room."

"And the couch has always stood in just that place—marks in the carpet show that. OK, get up."

Primrose did so.

"How tall was the girl would you say?"

Primrose considered. "Five feet seven."

"Well, I'm just five eight and a half. We can make allowances for that. Here, help me pull the settee right out."

When the couch was in the centre of the room Bidwell lowered himself onto the same section of carpet on which Primrose had been lying. "Right, push the settee back—make sure you get it in exactly the same spot."

When Primrose had done this, Bidwell said, "Now, I'm going to wriggle down until my head is just out of your sight. Say when."

He edged his way awkwardly along the floor until Primrose said, "That's it."

"Sure?"

"Yes."

"OK, then move to one side and see how much of my feet and legs are showing the other end."

Primrose took a couple of steps to his right and gazed at Bidwell's lower extremities for a few seconds. "Hang on a minute," he said, "I'd better measure it."

He took a tape from his pocket and knelt down. Then he said, "Eight inches."

"Good. Now before I get up, just draw the curtains and turn the light on —make sure you could still see as much at night."

Primrose did as he was told. "Yes, if anything you're even more visible now."

"OK, that's it. Pull the sofa away."

When Bidwell was on his feet and the room had been restored to normal, he said, "Eight inches of my legs were sticking out. We're estimating the girl was an inch and a half shorter than I am. We can check precisely later. But let's say for now that she's two or even three inches shorter. Now, the gap between the settee and the wall is too narrow for the body to be doubled up at all. So whichever way you look at it, at least five, possibly six, inches of her was protruding behind the settee—either her head one end or her feet the other."

"You're saying Grant should have seen her in less than twenty minutes —before he went to the window?"

Bidwell gave a snort. "Should have! He'd be bound to have seen her! According to his own story, he came into the room looking around, expecting to see her. He poured himself a drink. Then he turned off the television on the other side of the room. Next he sat in that chair. He couldn't possibly do all that without once spotting her."

"Perhaps if he was very tired, as he claimed . . ."

"Tired! He'd have to be in a coma. No. Grant was lying through his teeth. I must admit that until now I thought he just might have been telling the truth. His story was *possible.* Now I know it wasn't."

"Could be difficult to prove, though, Chief. I mean, the jury would have to come in here, with somebody lying behind the sofa, in order to be convinced."

"Well, it could be arranged. That's a long way ahead, though. The important thing is that we *know* Grant wasn't telling the truth. That makes all the difference in the world when you're conducting an investigation."

"You going to put it to him that you know he's lying?"

"And give him and Innes Lloyd a chance to cook up some story to account for it? 'Oh, but you see Chief Inspector, I got a speck in my eye as I was going into the building. I was holding a handkerchief to it the first five minutes I was in the flat. After I'd closed my eyes for a while it was better and I was able to see properly . . .' No, we'll keep this to ourselves —for the time being, at least. Come on, let's get out of here. Bring that file along, will you? Might be helpful to have a look through those bank statements some time. Oh, and put the will back in it."

When they had returned to the car, Primrose asked, "Where to?"

"You can drop me off at the station and go chase up those window cleaners."

"What'll you be doing?"

"Press conference first."

Primrose grinned. "That means a ten minute chin-wag with Charlie Phillips of the *Advertizer.*"

"Press conference sounds better. I promised I'd see him at ten-thirty and it's nearly that now. He'll be fuming to catch his first edition, so better get a move on."

"Right, Chief."

"Oh, and Freddie, stop calling me *chief,* will you? Makes me feel like Sitting Bull."

CHAPTER FOUR

It was only occasionally that Alison bought a copy of the *Fermouth &
District Advertizer,* but on the Tuesday afternoon she was standing outside
a newsagent's shop at three o'clock, waiting for the first edition to be
delivered.

At last the newspaper van roared up, drew briefly to a halt and ejected a
big bundle of papers, which landed with a thud on the pavement. The
newsagent emerged to lift the bundle inside. Alison was beside him, holding out her money before he had even got the string off. Her eyes searched
the front page. Yes, there was the story. Not the lead item—which concerned a row in the council over bus service cuts—but quite prominently
displayed down the right-hand column, under the headline FERMOUTH
GIRL FOUND STRANGLED.

Alison took the copy which the man handed her and hurried outside,
forcing herself not to read the story then and there; it wouldn't do to let
anyone see she was too interested in that particular item. She hurried to
the car—she was using the Sierra today, as her own old Mini had not been
too reliable lately—and got in before starting to read. The report, under
the by-line *Charles Phillips, Crime Reporter,* ran:

> The body of a beautiful blond Fermouth girl was found in her
> luxury apartment last night. She had been strangled.
> Linda Matthews, who was about 28 years old and described as a
> model, had occupied the flat in Albany Court for a little over a year.
> Her body was discovered at about 9:30 P.M. by her cleaning lady,
> Mrs. Vera Hopkins, 59, of 10 Redlands Road, Fermouth. Mrs. Hop-
> kins had returned to the flat unexpectedly to fetch a purse she had left
> behind earlier in the day. On entering the sitting-room, she surprised
> a man who was kneeling down by the body of Miss Matthews. He ran
> from the flat when Mrs. Hopkins screamed.
> Nigel Jones, 14, of Eleanor Street, Fermouth, who was passing the
> building on his bicycle at the time of the incident, told me, "I heard a

lady scream and shout 'Stop—murderer.' I saw a man come running out the front door. I followed him on my bike till he got into a car and drove off. Later I was able to give the number of the car to the police."

Mrs. Hopkins today described Miss Matthews as a lovely girl. "You couldn't work for anyone nicer," she said. "I shall miss her a lot."

Detective Chief Inspector H. Bidwell, who is in charge of the enquiry, announced today that a man had been detained and was helping police with their enquiries. Charges are expected to be made in due course.

Alison breathed a sigh of relief. No mention of Stephen's name. Innes Lloyd had told her the police wouldn't divulge it, but the *Advertizer* might somehow have got hold of it. Now she had at least a short respite. But for how long? Unless further evidence was forthcoming they were bound to charge Stephen soon. And that would mean his name in the papers, everybody knowing. She thought of his mother and father. She would have to notify them before everything became public. They were retired and living in North Wales. It would shatter them. Her own parents were dead, and her only close relatives were a brother in Canada, and her sister, who lived in Birmingham. She needn't notify Tim, but Janet would have to be told. Alison fancied that her sister had never really liked Stephen; and although Janet would be full of sympathy—and would probably want to insist on coming to stay—Alison could almost sense already the very slight air of "I told you so" that she would exude.

Then there were their more distant relatives, friends, neighbours, professional associates of Stephen . . . Even if he eventually got off (what did she mean *if*? *When* he got off), they would all know, at the very least, about his affair with Linda. It was a humiliating thought.

If only she could *do* something! Something *now* to stop him being charged. But what?

She knew Stephen was innocent. There was not the slightest doubt in her mind about that. But the police knew the girl *had* been murdered. Which meant that they wouldn't let Stephen off the hook until they had another suspect. They wouldn't be looking for that suspect now. So—it was up to *her* to look. But where? Well, the girl had known plenty of other men; that was certain. And it was surely most likely—Alison tried to look at the case as the police would—that she had been killed by one of her lovers.

It was, therefore, Alison realised, *her* job to put a finger on one of those men. She didn't have to *prove* anyone's guilt—which, for her, would be impossible. All she had to do was sow a doubt in the mind of Chief Inspector Bidwell.

But how on earth to find the right man?

Then an idea came to her. This Mrs.—what was her name? She looked down at the paper. Yes—Hopkins. She had apparently known Linda well. And charladies were unrivalled experts in the art of finding out about their employers' affairs. Surely *she* would know if Linda had been seeing anyone —apart, of course, from Stephen. One name: that was all Alison needed in the first instance. Just to get her going.

She hesitated for only a few seconds. Then she looked down again at the paper. Ten Redlands Road.

She started the engine.

CHAPTER FIVE

At three-thirty that afternoon Sergeant Primrose put his head around the door of his superior's room. "The N.O.K.'s here," he said cheerfully.

Bidwell looked up from his desk. "The what?"

"Linda Matthews' next of kin—the brother."

"So soon?" Bidwell gave a groan. "Very well—show him in."

"Righty—oh." Primrose started to withdraw.

"And Freddie."

The sergeant came back. "Yep?"

"While he's here give the 'yeps' and 'righty-ohs' a rest, will you. Try the occasional 'very good' or 'certainly,' eh?"

"Will-co."

He went out to return a few seconds later, saying, "Mr. Roger Matthews, sir."

Bidwell got to his feet and held out his hand to the man who came into the room. "Do come in and sit down, sir."

"Thank you."

Roger Matthews was about thirty-five. He was tall, thin and rangy, with black curly hair and wore black horn-rimmed glasses. He sat down across the desk from Bidwell, and crossed his legs. He seemed quite at ease. Primrose meanwhile had closed the door and seated himself at the side of the room.

Bidwell cleared his throat. He hated meetings such as this. However, at least on this occasion he did not have a sorrowing mother or husband to deal with. Nevertheless, it was always difficult to know what to say, and he often found himself falling back on the sort of platitudes which in normal times he despised.

"You haven't wasted any time, Mr. Matthews," he said.

"No. Fortunately I was home at lunch-time when the constable called—which is quite unusual for me. I phoned my chief, got immediate leave of absence and caught the two-fifteen train."

"I see. Well, I'm sorry we have to meet on such a very sad occasion."

"Yes, indeed." Roger Matthews did not, though, look or sound particularly grief-stricken and Bidwell began to hope that this interview might not be too painful, after all.

"First, sir," he said, "let me offer you my sincere sympathy."

"Thank you. However, before you get into the habit of calling me 'sir,' perhaps I'd better show you this."

He reached into his pocket, took out a small object and laid it on the desk. Primrose, leaning forward, raised his eyebrows when he recognised it. Bidwell stared down at it. When he lifted his head his expression was subtly different.

"Detective Chief Inspector Matthews, Metropolitan Police," he said slowly. "I'd no idea."

"There was no way you could have."

"It's quite a coincidence."

"Not really," Roger Matthews said. "I mean, thousands of police officers have sisters. And the number of girls murdered these days is tragically high. It's not too surprising that occasionally one young woman should fall into both categories."

"I suppose not." Bidwell pushed the card back. "Well, Matthews—er, Mr. —" He broke off. "Dammit, I don't know what to call you now."

"As we have the same rank, why not make it Roger?"

"Oh, if you like." Bidwell looked a little disconcerted. "My name's Horace."

"And I'm Freddie," Primrose said.

Bidwell shot him a venomous glance and he fell silent.

The inspector cleared his throat. "Well, now, er, Roger, I expect you'd like to hear the whole story."

"I would indeed."

Bidwell paused to collect his thoughts, then clearly and concisely related the bald facts of Linda Matthews' murder, as well as what he'd learned from Mrs. Hopkins.

Roger listened intently until he'd finished, then said, "Right, let me get this straight. There's no indication of violence or force of any kind being used against Linda prior to the strangling. As there was no struggle she was apparently attacked from behind and taken by surprise; nobody heard any sound of a quarrel. The flat wasn't broken into, and apart from the ring and the address book, nothing seems to have been stolen."

"That's about the score."

"What about this ring?"

"We've checked with the police surgeon and he confirms that there are abrasions on the third finger of your sister's left hand—as though the ring had been jerked off with some force—probably just after death. Now, naturally, your sister paid for it by cheque. So we've been able to speak to the jeweller. It's a small exclusive shop and he remembers the ring quite well. He's given us a description, which is being circulated in the usual way, and if it's found he will be able to identify it."

"That's something. How much did she pay for it?"

"Eighteen hundred pounds," Bidwell said.

Roger whistled. "My word. She must have been doing very well for herself. So—could the motive have been robbery?"

"Hardly seems likely. For one thing, she was wearing another ring on her right hand. Not the quality of the missing one, but very nice—worth three or four hundred. Why wouldn't he take that?"

"So the other one had some special significance?"

"She called it an engagement ring—even though she'd bought it herself."

"But presumably the man didn't consider they *were* engaged. Tearing the ring off was a sort of gesture."

"It makes sense."

"By the way, what time did she die?"

"We can't be as precise as we'd like to be. The police surgeon was at the scene of a car crash when the call came in and his deputy was out of town. As a result the first medical examination didn't take place until ten-thirty. They estimated then she'd been dead between one and three hours."

"Roughly between seven-thirty and nine-thirty, then. No, not a lot of help, is it? What about prints?"

"Again, nothing helpful. Apart from your sister's own, Grant's and Mrs. Hopkins', there are naturally quite a few dotted around. But none of them are on file. They could be casual visitors—decorators—anybody."

Roger was silent for a few seconds. Then he said, "Now—what about this man Grant? What can you tell me about him?"

"Well, he's thirty-eight, a successful literary agent—whatever that may be—with a small office in Bloomsbury. Married—happily, apparently—to a very nice wife called Alison. No kids. Quite active in the town socially— sailing club, golf club and so on."

"Wealthy?"

Bidwell pursed his lips. "I wouldn't think so. Comfortable, I imagine, that's all."

"No form?"

"Not a thing. Not even a speeding ticket."

"Hm, quite a paragon. But he *was* my sister's lover?"

"Yes, he admits that."

"And this Mrs. Whatsername, the cleaner, has identified him as the man she surprised kneeling by the body?"

"She hasn't needed to—Grant acknowledges it was him."

"Did the charwoman know him?"

"Not by sight."

"Then you got him through this schoolboy's evidence?"

As Bidwell looked a little surprised, Roger added, "Oh, I bought a copy of your local paper at the station." He tapped his pocket.

"I see. Yes, that's right. He's a bright, reliable sort of lad. He heard Mrs. Hopkins screaming blue murder and saw Grant come running out. So he followed him on his bike till Grant got to his car. Then he made a careful note of the number and rode straight here with it."

Bidwell extracted a sheet of paper from a folder on his desk and pushed it across. "Here's his statement." Roger glanced over it swiftly.

"Thrilled to bits, he was," Bidwell went on. "Day in his life—" He stopped suddenly. "Oh, sorry—didn't mean—"

"That's OK." Roger slid the paper back. "And Grant doesn't deny he was that man?"

"No, claims he'd been in the room for half an hour or so, not knowing the body was lying behind the sofa and had just discovered it when Mrs. Hopkins came in. Then he panicked and ran away."

"Could that be true?"

"Could be—if that's all there was to it. But it's not. He's lying. He couldn't have missed seeing your sister's body almost as soon as he went into the room." He briefly described the experiments he and Primrose had made.

When he had finished, Roger said, "So you *are* going to charge him?"

Bidwell nodded. "I can't see any reason not to. I've got my chief super's approval. There's enough to go on now. Even without anything from forensic."

"Yes. Oh yes, I'm sure there is." For a moment Roger spoke absently. His manner irritated Bidwell slightly. He said shortly, "But?"

Roger stared. "What do you mean?"

"You seem doubtful."

"No, no," Roger assured him hastily, "I've got no right to be. *You're* the one who's interviewed Grant. *You've* examined the scene of the crime. It's just that I'd like to be as sure as humanly possible that we haven't got the wrong man."

"Yes, I can appreciate that. I wondered at first about other boy-friends —or ex-boy-friends. There *were* others—and at least one other current one, according to Mrs. Hopkins."

"So you said."

"I haven't tried to do any tracing yet. For one thing there hasn't been time. But chiefly because, frankly, I don't think there's any need. If you heard Grant's story and then saw your sister's flat you'd know he was lying."

"Oh, no doubt. But does that necessarily mean he *killed* her? It seems he was her favourite at the moment. Now jealousy can be a pretty strong motive. There might be somebody around who can put a name to this other man. Are you *sure* it's not worth trying?"

Bidwell did not reply at once. The situation was highly unusual and he was finding it an awkward one.

Not being a member of a big city police force he hadn't, during his long career, dealt with a great many murder cases—perhaps a dozen all told. In addition, though, there had been a number of deaths caused by hit-and-run drivers; and so in one way or another Bidwell had gleaned a fair amount of experience in dealing with grieving relatives. Although he did not realise it, he always did this with tact and sympathy. He believed, moreover, in answering all questions as patiently and fully as possible.

In the past, however, the questions asked him had nearly always been the same: "Do you know who did it?" "You'll catch the swine, won't you?" "You'll see he doesn't get off?" Never once in all his thirty-two years on the force had any victim's relative asked him specific questions about the course of his investigation—the nature of his evidence, the existence or identity of additional suspects.

These were the sort of queries that only another police officer (or perhaps a crime reporter) would ask. But in normal circumstances it would be unthinkable for an officer from another force to come into his station and start cross-questioning him about his conduct of the case. If it had ever happened he would have unhesitatingly put in an official complaint. The only persons authorised to ask such questions were his superior officers; and they rarely had, being content 99 percent of the time to let Bidwell conduct investigations in his own highly successful way, without interference.

Now, though, the situation was quite different: the next of kin, who had the right to ask, but not normally the knowledge or inclination to ask the right questions; and the police officer, who had the knowledge, but not normally the right, coexisted in the same person. As Linda Matthews had fallen into two categories, so did her brother.

And Detective Chief Inspector Horace Bidwell didn't quite know how to react to the situation. He felt irritated by the questions, yet at the same time guilty *because* he felt irritated; and frustrated because he couldn't display his irritation. So for some moments after Roger's last question he remained silent, staring down at his desk, pointlessly straightening the things on it.

Fortunately, at that moment the strangeness of the situation and the uniqueness of his own position and behaviour seemed suddenly also to strike Roger for the first time.

He sat up. "Look," he said, "I'm sorry. Officially I've got no right to do this. This isn't my case. I'm just an outsider. Heaven forbid I should sound as if I thought you weren't handling it properly. I know you are. When I had the message to contact you, I phoned John Ashford at the Yard. I remembered he'd been down here on a case a few years ago. You remember him?"

"Very well. The Twyman murder case. We worked on it together. Good man."

"Well, he certainly remembers you. He was very impressed with your work—says he's never known better. And he's a man whose opinion I respect."

Bidwell shifted in his chair. "Nice of him. Exaggeration, I'm sure. But appreciated."

Roger leaned forward. "So, please don't think I'm criticising or interfer-

ing in any way. It's just that—well, Linda *was* my sister and I suppose I'm
looking for a greater degree of certainty than I'd normally seek. I feel I've
got to know everything there is to know. Really, though, you've got every
right to send me off with a flea in my ear."

This speech certainly had the effect of clearing the air. Bidwell gave one
of his rare smiles. "Oh, I wouldn't do that," he said.

He picked up a battered old pipe from a rack on his desk and slowly
started to fill it from a pouch in his pocket.

"I'll answer any questions you may wish to ask," he said. "But I must
warn you now that you're probably not going to like what I've got to say.
In fact, it may make you very angry. You see, we've been told certain
things about your sister—things I wouldn't normally pass on to next of
kin. But if you want to know everything there is to know, well, there's no
way of keeping this from you."

Roger gave a slight smile. "I suppose what you've been told is that
Linda was a mercenary little gold-digger, who was kept by a succession of
rich men."

Bidwell stopped dead in the act of striking a match. "So—you knew."

"No, I didn't *know*. Let's just say I'm not a bit surprised. You see, I
hadn't seen or heard anything of Linda for over five years. That was at our
mother's funeral."

"I see. I was thinking perhaps you were very close."

"Far from it—unfortunately. You'll have noticed I'm not exactly con-
sumed with grief at her death. It would be hypocritical to pretend I were.
Which doesn't mean I'm not very sad and angry about it."

Bidwell nodded thoughtfully and at last struck his match. "And you feel
guilty, I suppose?" he said.

He applied the match to the bowl of his pipe and began sucking hard,
his cheeks going in and out like bellows. Primrose got to his feet and rather
ostentatiously opened a window. Bidwell ignored him.

Roger hesitated. "No, I don't honestly think so. I don't see I could have
acted differently towards her. In the first place, there was over six years
between us. That's quite a gap when you're growing up. I mean, she was
only twelve when I went away to university."

Bidwell glanced at him over the bowl of his pipe. "Oh, so you're a
college boy?"

Roger smiled. "Do I detect a note of disapproval? Are you one of the
old school which doesn't approve of graduate coppers?"

"No, no, I wouldn't say that," Bidwell replied. "University doesn't do
all that much harm, really. I've known a few graduates who were turned

into very good policemen, eventually. But go on—didn't mean to interrupt."

"Well, when I came down, Linda was fifteen or sixteen. And that was the first time that we were close enough in age really to talk. But, in fact, there was very little point of contact. I could see we wanted very different things from life."

"What did *she* want?"

"I think you know. Money."

Bidwell raised his eyebrows. "Even at that age?"

"Yes, even at that age. Oh, I don't mean she was a little miser. She'd spend her allowance the day she got it. What she wanted were the things money could buy. She talked of little except clothes, jewellery, furs—the sports car she was going to have one day. Mind you, she wasn't nasty with it. She was full of all the things she was going to buy Mother, too—even me. There was a sort of engaging, happy naïvety about it all that stopped it being really objectionable. At that time Mother kept saying she'd get over it."

"But she didn't?"

"No. And I know that over the next couple of years Mother grew more and more concerned about her. Our father had died several years previously and Mother found it harder and harder to cope on her own. I wasn't a lot of help, as I'd joined the Met by then and only got home occasionally —we lived in Norfolk. But we spoke on the phone pretty regularly. Mother had hoped Linda would follow me to university, but it turned out that she had no academic aptitude at all, and didn't even get a single O level. She left school and got a job in a supermarket. She started going out every night and staying out later and later. Mother could do nothing with her at all, and it worried her sick. All the same, Linda never went completely to the bad—never got in trouble with the police or involved with drugs, or anything like that."

Bidwell drew on his pipe. "What a few years ago we'd have called a good-time girl."

"Exactly. And she had developed into not a bad looker. Though, mind you, she'd worked on it. Then, one day she just left home. Told mother she was going to try and make it as a model in London—and simply went. Mother rang me, desperately worried, but of course there was nothing I could do, except go and spend a few days at home myself. Then, after a couple of weeks, Mum got a card from Linda, giving her new address. She immediately phoned me and begged me to see Linda and try and persuade her to go home. Well, I did my best. I found Linda had taken a seedy little bed-sitter in Bayswater. She seemed quite pleased to see me, but refused point-blank to go home. Obviously I couldn't force her. But I got her promise to keep in touch with Mother. I called there again a couple of weeks later, but she'd moved and left no forwarding address. However, she did keep her promise: she phoned home regularly—even though she would never again give out her address or phone number. The calls grew rather less frequent as the years passed. But she never forgot Christmas or birthdays. Every year there'd be presents for both of us. And they gradually became more expensive. Once for Mother there was a mink stole, and another time a diamond brooch that she had valued, for insurance purposes, at five hundred pounds. For me there were gold cuff-links and a Rolex watch that I still wear—trying not to ask myself how she got the money to pay for it."

Roger held out his wrist for Bidwell to see.

The chief inspector nodded. "Very nice. Go on."

"There's not a lot more. The year after I got this, Mother died very suddenly. I had no means of contacting Linda but I put an announcement in every paper I could think of, and at the last minute she did turn up for the funeral—in a chauffeur-driven limousine, dressed up to the nines, dripping with jewellery. There's no doubt, though, that she was genuinely upset."

"She came alone?"

"Yes. She informed me afterwards that she was off to the States almost immediately. I told her it would be nice if we kept in touch. She agreed. That year—or rather midway through the next January—I had a Christmas card from her in New York. And that's the last I heard of her, until about four hours ago. I'd imagined she was in America all this time."

"No. According to her passport—on which, incidentally, her occupation *is* given as model—she arrived back in England nearly three years ago. Then just over a year ago she moved here."

"As long ago as that? I wonder what made her pick Fermouth."

Bidwell shrugged. "Plenty of wealthy men live here."

"Yes; but not so many as in London. I mean, I can't see Linda just coming here on spec as it were."

"You mean somebody brought her here and installed her in that flat?"

"It seems more likely," Roger said.

"Yes, I suppose it does. Though Grant claims only to have met her four months ago."

"And you believe him?"

"Not necessarily. But having admitted he knew her, I can't see why he should lie about how *long* he'd known her."

"I see what you mean. Besides, you say that Grant isn't particularly wealthy?"

"One can't be sure, but he doesn't seem to be. Just a reasonably prosperous professional man, I'd say."

"Then could he afford to keep her? I mean, what about her flat? What sort of place is this Albany Court?"

"Oh, it's very nice," Bidwell said. "Not exactly in the luxury bracket, but certainly pretty pricey."

Roger spread his hands. "So—there we are. Back to the other man: the one who brought her to Fermouth and has been paying her rent."

Bidwell suppressed a sigh. "I agree, it's pretty obvious such a man does exist. But there's not the slightest indication that he killed her. We have a perfectly good suspect. He was found kneeling down by the body. He ran away. When located and questioned he threw a punch at Primrose and tried to escape again. And we know he lied about not seeing your sister's body until he'd been at her flat nearly half an hour. *Why* he killed her we can't say. There could be a dozen reasons, unconnected with money. You know as well as I do that when someone is murdered by a lover or a spouse, you really don't have to worry too much about looking for a specific motive."

"You're being very tactful, but what you really think is that Linda was making herself a nuisance to Grant—threatening to tell his wife about the affair?"

"I think that's possible—yes."

"I don't say it's impossible," said Roger, "and I'm not going to be such a fool as to say I don't believe Grant is guilty. You've seen him. So . . . well, it's your case." But he didn't seem happy.

Bidwell puffed thoughtfully on his pipe for a few seconds. Then he took it from his mouth and said, "Look, I understand how you feel. I'm sure I'd feel the same. And I want you to be satisfied beyond all reasonable doubt. So I'll tell you what I'll do. As I said, I've talked to my chief superintendent. Frankly, he's in favour of charging Grant straight away. But ultimately he'll leave the decision to me. I don't have to decide until about noon tomorrow. And even then, as you, of course, know, I can always go before the magistrates and apply for another thirty-six hours detention without charge. I don't think Innes Lloyd—that's Grant's solicitor—will fight us. From the point of view of publicity alone it's plainly to his client's advantage to have the charge postponed as long as possible. And he'll realise that in the present circumstances we certainly aren't going to *release* him. But even if he does object I'm sure we'll get it, anyway. So—spend the rest of the day looking into the case yourself. Interview Grant. Speak to the cleaning woman. Do anything you like. You can have full use of our facilities—for what they're worth. I'll fix it with the chief superintendent. I'll arrange for you to have a car. Come and see me tomorrow morning and if you then think there are grounds for doubting Grant's guilt, I'll apply for that extension and investigate your suspicions exhaustively. That's a promise. If not, I'll charge Grant. How about it?"

Roger gave an eager nod. "That'll be fine. And I appreciate it. Don't get me wrong: it's not that I doubt your judgement. If you say Grant is guilty he very probably is. It's just that I feel I want to do one last thing for Linda. Heaven knows, I was never able to do much for her when she was alive."

"I understand. So—what would you like to do first? Look at the flat—confirm what I said about the size of the sofa in relation to the body?"

"No, no, I'll take your word for that. I'll have to go there some time—I suppose it's up to me to go through her things. First, though, I'd like to talk to Grant—then to Mrs. Hopkins."

"As you wish. I'll fix it for Grant—and give you Hopkins' address. Oh, and by the way, talking of your sister's things—"

He broke off, stood up, went to a shelf and took down the box file from Linda's flat. "These are the only papers we found there. I thought it might be interesting to look at her bank statements, but I haven't had time yet. Now you can do it."

He handed the file to Roger. "And here are her keys," he added. "Now come along with me and I'll take you to see Mr. Stephen Grant."

When Bidwell came back into the room a few minutes later, Primrose looked up. "Was Linda's will still among those papers, gaffer?"

"It was."

"That'll be a nice surprise for him."

"Let's hope so. Anyway, we've got him out of our hair for a bit, so we can concentrate on something else. Oh, and Freddie—not 'gaffer.' Makes me feel I've got straw in my hair."

Stephen Grant had hardly bothered to raise his head when Bidwell introduced Roger. When the chief inspector had left the room Roger sat down and eyed the other closely. Grant looked haggard. He still didn't return Roger's gaze, just spoke wearily, his eyes on the table top.

"I made it quite clear I have nothing further to add to my statement."

"Don't decide that just yet," Roger advised him. "Listen to what I have to say first."

"I thought I had the right to have my solicitor present when being questioned."

"As far as I'm concerned, you're very welcome to have him—or anybody else—present. But I hoped this wasn't going to be that sort of conversation. It's quite off the record. Nothing you say will be taken down and used in evidence, I assure you."

For the first time Stephen eyed him with a glimmer of interest. "You're a funny sort of policeman."

"So I've been told quite often at Scotland Yard."

Stephen frowned. "What's a Scotland Yard man doing here? Has the Yard been called in, as they say?"

"No, I'm here privately."

"I don't understand."

"I don't think you took in my name when Chief Inspector Bidwell introduced me. It's Matthews."

Stephen gave a start. He said sharply, "Roger Matthews? Her brother?"

It was Roger's turn to look surprised. "You've heard of me?"

"Yes. She spoke of you several times. She was very proud of you."

Roger stared at him. "Linda was proud of *me?*"

"Yes. You found that little girl who was snatched, didn't you? You were on TV. Linda was thrilled."

"Well, I'm blowed." Roger was silent. The interview was not going at all as he had expected. "What else did she tell you?" he asked.

"About you? Very little."

"About herself."

"Virtually nothing. I don't even know if she had any other relatives. She was a—" he stopped, before finishing—"a private sort of person."

Roger nodded. "Secretive. That's what our mother used to call her."

"Mind you, I'm not criticising her," Stephen said quickly. "It's not a bad thing to be—to a degree. Most people gab too much about themselves and their families."

They were both silent for a few seconds. Then Stephen said quietly,

"I didn't kill her, you know."

"No?"

"I couldn't kill anybody—let alone a girl. Let alone Linda."

"You telling me you were in love with her?"

Stephen hesitated. He moistened his lips. Then he slowly shook his head.

"Well, you're honest, anyway," Roger said.

"I'm trying to be. You see, I'm in love with my wife. And no matter what they may say, I don't think you can be in love with two people at the same time. At least, I can't. But I was enchanted by Linda. Bewitched, in a way. I couldn't stop seeing her. Even though the whole situation was making me feel quite wretched in my better moments." He paused, then added, "My *few* better moments, you'll no doubt think."

"But why did you feel like that?" Roger asked. "I mean, provided your wife didn't suspect anything . . ."

"Well, it was so unfair to Linda."

"But she was quite content, surely? So long as you carried on paying the rent."

Stephen's head jerked up. "What do you mean? I didn't pay her rent!"

"You must have," Roger said sharply.

"I didn't, I tell you! Think I could afford the rent on a place like that?"

There was an undeniable ring of truth to his words. Roger said, "All right, but you *were* helping her towards it—making her an allowance."

"I never gave her a penny." Stephen was vehement. "I never even gave her a present—except flowers, chocolates, things like that. She wouldn't take anything. There was a brooch once—in a shop. I wanted to buy it for her. She refused it. Said she had all the jewellery she needed."

"What did you suppose she was living on?"

"I imagined she'd made a packet out of modelling."

"If she wasn't getting anything from you, why did she carry on seeing you?"

"Why? Why do you think? She was in love with me. She wanted us to be married."

"And how did you feel about that?"

"I—" Stephen stopped, gulped, then said quietly, "I told you: I'm in love with my wife. Believe it or not. I don't want a divorce."

"Yet you let Linda buy herself an engagement ring."

"I didn't *let* her. She did it without telling me."

"You let her go on wearing it."

"I couldn't stop her."

"You let her go on thinking you were going to marry her."

"I never said 'Yes, I'll marry you.' "

"You just let it be tacitly assumed?"

"I didn't—" He broke off before saying, "Well, perhaps I did. But only for a little while."

"How long?"

"I don't know. A week—two."

"Then what?"

"Well, I told her it was something we'd have to think very carefully about before coming to any decision. That it would mean a complete change in both our lives and—"

"You made it clear it was no go."

"I wouldn't say that. I just asked her to think about it. Did she really want to—?"

"When was this?"

"Towards the beginning of last week. Tuesday, I think."

"And that was the last time you spoke to her before yesterday?"

"Yes—until I phoned her from the airport, that is. I thought it was best to let things cool off for a few days."

"So you left her in a pretty depressed state."

"No, not depressed. Thoughtful, perhaps."

"You'd shattered her dreams, hadn't you?"

"No! I'd never given her to understand we could be married."

"But that's what she thought."

Suddenly Stephen shouted, "That wasn't my fault!"

About to make an angry retort, Roger got a grip on himself. He paused. Then: "No," he said quietly. "Maybe it wasn't."

"I felt very bad about the whole business. I knew the wise thing would be not to see her again. But I couldn't just leave things like that. So I phoned her from the airport yesterday evening. And she was over the moon when she heard me. She wasn't in the least bitter. She said she'd love to see me."

He paused, then added softly, "But, of course, she never did."

"So you say."

"It's the truth."

"Well, let's not argue about that just now. What were you intending to say to her when you went to the flat?"

Stephen made a gesture of hopelessness. "I honestly don't know. I like to think I would have had enough guts to break it off. But it would have depended on her attitude. Frankly I was hoping she might be losing interest in me. But if she'd been just as—just as intense about me as ever I might not have been able to do it."

Roger frowned. "You keep talking as if she were absolutely besotted by you."

"Well, frankly, she was—or had been."

"Oh, come on—"

"Come on, nothing! I know it sounds an appallingly conceited thing to say but I can prove it."

"How?"

Stephen hesitated. "There are some letters."

"Love letters? From her to you?"

"Yes. Look, I don't want anybody to see them. Especially not Alison. I won't let them be used in evidence. But—but if it's really going to help, I'll let you see them—in confidence."

"Where are they?"

"In my office safe—in a locked deed box. I'll give you the key—oh, you've got my keys already—and a letter to my secretary, Phyllis, authorising her to give you the box."

"I may take you up on that later. But I don't suppose you'd be such a fool as to offer to show me something that doesn't exist. So I'll believe you."

He was tempted to add, "And I'm very glad." But he couldn't quite go that far. Though it was a relief to know that at the end Linda had become something more than a mere gold-digger. Even if she had wanted to steal another woman's husband, she had at least proved she had feelings for something other than money.

Instead: "Tell me exactly what happened last night," he ordered.

"I've already told Bidwell."

"Never mind. Tell me."

Stephen sighed. "I got to the flat shortly before nine o'clock . . ."

When Stephen finished speaking, Roger eyed him silently for about ten seconds. Stephen shifted uneasily in his chair but resisted the impulse to say anything further.

Eventually Roger said quietly, "You're lying."

Stephen shook his head hopelessly. "I am not lying; I've told the truth."

"Listen to me. Chief Inspector Bidwell has proved that your story is impossible."

Stephen seemed to go slightly pale. "Proved? I don't believe it! How can he have?"

"I'm not at liberty to tell you that. But he's convinced me. And he'll convince a jury."

Then, as Stephen opened his mouth to give another angry retort, Roger raised a hand to silence him.

"I said just listen. Your only hope is to tell the complete truth. I don't mean I expect you to change your story here and now. But think about it.

Talk it over with your solicitor. Tell me a story that hangs together, and I just might believe you didn't kill my sister. There *is* an explanation I would believe. That's what I expect you to come up with. If you do, you might convince me."

"And what good will that do me—*your* belief? You're only a private citizen, after all."

"It may not do you any good. But as things stand the case against you is very black. And there are no other suspects. Convincing me may be your only hope. Chief Inspector Bidwell has promised at least to take my views into account. So think about it. All right?"

Stephen nodded. "All right." He paused, then added, "And thanks for giving me at least a little hope."

Roger stood up. "Don't bank on it. You haven't convinced me you're innocent yet—far from it. The right story—a story that makes sense—may just sow a big enough doubt in my mind to let you keep that hope alive."

CHAPTER SIX

The first time Alison rang Mrs. Hopkins' front doorbell there was no reply. She went away, wondering what would be the best time to go back. She didn't want to irritate the woman by interrupting her preparation of the evening meal; on the other hand, Mrs. Hopkins probably rose early, so it wouldn't do to call too late. And if she went between times she risked interrupting some favourite television programme. In the end she timed her second attempt for a little after five-thirty. She could only hope for the best.

She drew up forty yards short of the house—it wouldn't do to look too affluent—and walked along the road. She was just about to open the gate of number 10 when she saw that a young man was sitting on the front step, his back against the door. Alison hesitated. Momentarily she wondered if this could be Mrs. Hopkins' son, but she quickly rejected the idea. He didn't look the part. Then it came to her: a reporter, of course. Blast! Well, she certainly mustn't let him identify *her*. She started to turn away.

But she was too late. The young man had spotted her hand on the gate. He uncurled long legs and got to his feet. Alison began to walk away, but now he was hurrying down the path, and she heard him call, "Oh, excuse me!" He had a pleasant voice.

Reluctantly she stopped. It would only arouse suspicions if she didn't. She turned back, managing a smile of interrogation. "Yes?"

He had reached the gate. "Good evening. Er, you wouldn't be Mrs. Hopkins, I suppose?"

Then before she could reply, he added, "No, of course not; you couldn't be. Stupid of me."

She realised he was regarding her quite inoffensively but in a definitely approving manner.

She said, "No. And you're obviously not Mr. Hopkins."

"Afraid not. Were you looking for him?"

"*Mrs.*, actually."

"She should be home in about ten minutes. At least, she usually gets home about a quarter to six on Tuesdays, according to the lady opposite, who is now watching us interestedly through her lace curtains. Charming woman, though somewhat troubled with her feet, she tells me."

The young man gave a cheerful wave in the direction of the house across the street. "Ah, she's gone now. I had quite a long chat with her. Apparently, Mrs. Hopkins is not very popular at the moment. She's become rather uppity on account of having witnessed this murder and being interviewed by police and press."

"She didn't actually witness the *murder,* surely," Alison said quickly.

"Perhaps I should say witnessed the murderer."

"Are *you* a reporter?" she asked suddenly.

He put his head on one side. "Now, why should you suppose that?"

"I—I don't know. I just thought you might be. She's been interviewed by one reporter already. Presumably there'll be others."

"I see." He nodded. "A reasonable supposition."

But he didn't answer her question. Instead he asked, "And are you a lady of the press?"

"No. I—" She broke off, annoyed with herself. Now he knew something about her that she didn't know about him. It might have been quite a good cover too. "I'm nothing to do with the press," she said. "I wanted to see Mrs. Hopkins about quite another matter."

"I see."

There was silence for a few seconds. He glanced along the road to where Alison had parked the Sierra. "Nice car," he remarked.

"Er, yes."

"Had it long?"

"About eighteen months." She glanced at her watch. "I must be getting along."

"I thought you wanted to see Mrs. Hopkins."

"I did—do. But you were here first, and I can't really wait until you've finished your business with her."

"But couldn't we speak to her together? I mean, I don't suppose she grants private audiences, like the Pope or the Queen—no matter how uppity she's become since yesterday."

"No, it's a private matter. I must speak to her alone."

"Very well. Can I give her a message—tell her what time you'll be calling back—make sure she keeps time for you in her crowded schedule?"

"No, really, thanks. I must go. Goodbye."

Again Alison started to move away.

"Goodbye, Mrs. Grant," he said.

She froze. Then she turned slowly and looked at him.

"How did you know?"

"The registration number of your car. I saw that schoolboy's statement to the police."

She flushed angrily. "They had no right to go showing that to reporters. It's an abuse of privacy."

"Ah, but they didn't. You see, I'm not a reporter."

"Then do you mind telling me what and who you are?"

"Is there any logical reason why I should?"

"You know who *I* am."

He frowned. "I can't see that as a logical reason."

"Oh, all right," she snapped. "Have it your way."

"Suppose I were to say I was just selling insurance or double glazing?"

"You're not. You're here about the murder of that girl. Well it's no business of mine. Will you do me one favour?"

"If I can."

"Don't tell Mrs. Hopkins that Mrs. Grant wants to see her. I don't think she can know the name of the man she saw, and once she does it'll be all over town."

"Very well. I promise."

"Thank you."

Again she turned away, and again, with perfect timing, he froze her in her tracks.

"My name's Roger Matthews."

After the second it took for the penny fully to drop Alison spun round. "Matthews?"

He nodded. "Linda's brother."

She stared at him. "Of course," she said slowly, "I might have guessed."

"I don't see how you could."

"I—I'm terribly sorry—about your sister."

"Thank you. Though you have no reason to think of her fondly, I'm afraid."

"No. All the same, I couldn't wish *that* on anybody."

There was a pause. Alison began awkwardly, "Well—"

He interrupted her. "I spoke to your husband not long ago."

"What?" Alison looked astounded. "They let the victim's brother—her next of kin—talk to the chief suspect? I don't believe it!"

"It's true. But then I'm in a unique sort of position. I also happen to be a detective chief inspector in the Metropolitan Police."

Alison was taken aback. All she could think to say rather stupidly, was, "Oh." Then she rallied.

"So, you're in charge of the case now, are you?"

"No." He spoke firmly. "I came in a purely private capacity. However, I have come to an arrangement with Chief Inspector Bidwell." He briefly explained the understanding they had reached.

It didn't take Alison long to grasp the significance of what he was saying. Her face lightened. "You mean—*you* think Stephen is innocent? That's fantastic! I—"

"Now hold on," he said quickly, "I don't say that. I just think there's an element of doubt. I could almost accept his story. But the trouble is he lied."

"Yes, at first. He panicked. But he's told the truth since."

"I don't think so. And Chief Inspector Bidwell is certain of it. He's an experienced officer, and not likely to be mistaken."

"But I don't understand." She shook her head in bewilderment. "You believe he's lying—even if you think he may not have actually killed her. Lying in what way?"

"I can't tell you that. It's Bidwell's ace. All I can say is that *if* Stephen is innocent, then things must, I think, have happened in a certain way. I advised him to talk to his solicitor, and then tell the full truth. If he does so, and his story then coincides with my mental reconstruction of what happened—well, in that case I'll be much more inclined to believe in his innocence. So—if you have any influence over him, for heaven's sake try to persuade him not to lie *in any particular.* If he tells the truth now, his false statements won't count against him. But if it comes to court, they certainly will."

Alison was silent for a few seconds, digesting this. At last she said,

"Well, I don't pretend to understand just what you're getting at. But I'll trust you. I'll advise Stephen to do as you say."

"Good. He won't regret it—if, as I say, he is innocent."

"He is."

"Why are you so sure?"

"I know him. He couldn't kill anybody."

He gazed at her thoughtfully. "You obviously believe that 100 percent. I must say that carries more weight with me than any other factor."

For some reason Alison found herself embarrassed by this. She started to cast around for a sensible reply. Seeming to sense her unease, he glanced at his watch and said briskly, "Well, our Mrs. Hopkins should be home any time now. Will you stay and see her with me?"

"Do you really think that's a good idea?"

"Yes, I do. I think she's more likely to talk freely to a man and woman together than she is to me alone."

"Even to the wife of the murderer—as she believes?"

"Well, it may not be a good idea to tell her *who* you are. She's never seen you, I suppose?"

"No, but what story can I possibly tell her—?"

"Don't you worry. I'll think of something."

"What do you hope to get out of her, anyway?"

He smiled. "What do *you?*"

"The names of any other men friends Linda might have had."

"Chief Inspector Bidwell has already asked her about that. Seems she doesn't know of any."

Alison's face fell. "Oh. Well, in that case there doesn't seem much point in asking her again."

"Ah, but do we believe her?"

Alison stared at him. "You think she might be lying?"

He shrugged. "Let's say I find it rather surprising that she'd been working at my sister's three days a week for a year and never heard or read the name of any man other than Stephen."

"But if she *has,* why should she hide it?"

"Could be a number of reasons. A natural reluctance to get anyone into trouble with the cops. An unwillingness to give the impression of having snooped. Both combined with a firm belief that the real killer is already in custody. However, I think that when it comes to talking to Linda's brother she might be a little more forthcoming."

"You won't tell her you're also a policeman?"

"I think not. It'd only confuse the poor woman. She wouldn't know *who* she was talking to."

He stiffened slightly as his eyes alighted on somebody coming along the road behind Alison's back.

"And here, Watson," he said softly, "unless I'm very much mistaken, is our client now."

Alison turned round. As she did so, Mrs. Hopkins obviously spotted the two people by the gate, and increased her pace. She was carrying a bulging carrier bag and was panting a little when she arrived. But there was an eager, enquiring look on her face.

Roger was all charm. "Mrs. Hopkins, I believe." In some strange way, without actually having one on, he gave the impression of mentally doffing a hat.

"That's right, sir."

Mrs. Hopkins' eyes were hungrily taking in every detail of her two visitors' appearance.

"We were wondering if you could kindly spare us a few minutes."

"Why, yes, I reckon I can."

"Oh, fine."

"You'd be reporters, I take it."

Roger blinked. Alison could almost read his thoughts: not another one? In spite of everything, she had to suppress a sudden giggle.

Roger said gravely, "I'm afraid not. Actually, my name is Matthews. I'm Miss Matthews' brother."

If Mrs. Hopkins was disappointed at not having a chance to give another interview to the press, the disclosure of Roger's identity was plainly compensation enough. She stared at him, an expression of intense interest coming over her face. Then she seemed to recollect herself and said, in her best party-manners voice, "Please accept my deepest sympathy, sir." She looked rather pleased with herself at having got this out, then cast an inquiring sideways glance at Alison.

Roger said hastily, "Oh, this is my wife, Alice."

How Alison prevented herself from giving a gasp of indignation and amazement she never afterwards knew. But somehow she managed to control herself, nodded to Mrs. Hopkins and said graciously,

"How do you do?"

"Pleased to meet you, ma'am. Would you both like to come inside?"

"That would be very kind, if it's not too much of an intrusion." Roger was positively effusive.

"Not at all, sir. Please follow me." Mrs. Hopkins started up the path.

Roger said, "Here, let me take that." He deftly relieved her of the carrier and followed on behind, saying over his shoulder to Alison, "Come along, my dear."

Inwardly fuming, Alison brought up the rear. However, by the time they were all seated in the sparkling little lounge she had recovered her temper a little and decided to make a contribution to the conversation. "I hope we're not holding up your meal, Mrs. Hopkins."

"Oh no, my old man's gone off with his darts team tonight, so I won't be getting much."

"That's fine," Roger said. "Anyway, we hope not to keep you long."

"You know, sir, I never knew she had a brother, or any family. She never spoke of you."

"Well, she did speak of you, Mrs. Hopkins."

"Of me, sir?" She looked surprised.

"Yes, indeed. Oh, I mean in her letters, of course. I hadn't actually *spoken* to Linda for some time. But she wrote regularly. And I remember in one of her letters she said you were a real treasure, and how good it was to have someone she could absolutely rely on."

"Well, really, I'm much obliged, I'm sure." Mrs. Hopkins positively preened herself. "It's true I did me best never to let her down."

"I'm sure you did. And I think she regarded you more as a friend than anything else—a confidante."

"Er—a—?" Mrs. Hopkins' expression was a cross between gratification and puzzlement.

"Oh—someone she could confide in—talk to seriously."

"Ah," Mrs. Hopkins nodded sagely. "It's true we had some very nice little chats."

"And what can you tell me about her last days, Mrs. Hopkins?"

"What exactly did you want to know, sir?"

"Well, chiefly—was she happy?"

"Oh, I think so, sir."

"You see, it's so difficult to tell from letters—people are able to hide their real feelings—but I got the impression she was worried about something."

Mrs. Hopkins looked doubtful. "I don't think so, sir. She certainly said nothing to me."

"I see. No boy-friend difficulties—anything like that?"

"Not that I know of, sir."

"This man you saw, kneeling down by her—" He broke off. "Incidentally, that must have been a terrifying experience for you."

"Oh, it was that, sir. Nearly fainted I did when I come in and he looked up at me with his mad, staring eyes. Then I screamed and he came right at me. Thought my last moment had come. I did, really. Had palpitations for half an hour after."

"I'm not surprised! I think you were remarkably brave." He turned to Alison. "Don't you, darling?"

Alison nodded, tight-lipped. "Yes, indeed." She was furious over the woman's absurd remark about Stephen's eyes.

Roger went on. "That man had been Linda's boy-friend, hadn't he?"

Unconsciously, Mrs. Hopkins lowered her voice a fraction. She looked round conspiratorially. "Well, I think he must 'ave been the one."

"You'd never seen him before?"

"No, and the police won't tell me his name. If I knew it I could say for certain. Tell me, sir, you don't happen to know: was it Steve by any chance?"

Roger hesitated only for a second. "Yes, I believe it was. The police accidentally let it drop."

A look of intense satisfaction spread over Mrs. Hopkins' face. "Then I was right. He *was* her boy-friend, all right. In love with him, she was. I could tell. She changed after she met him."

Alison gave an involuntary wince. Fortunately Mrs. Hopkins did not notice this.

Roger said, "Changed in what way?"

"She was sort of happier."

"I see. Anything else?"

"Well, for one thing I think she was looking for a job."

Roger raised his eyebrows. "Really? You do surprise me."

"I dunno how serious she was, mind you. But she started having the *Advertizer* delivered in the afternoons. Soon as it came she'd start looking through the—the situ—what do they call it?"

"Situations vacant."

"That's right. She'd read right through it. And she went up to London a few times, too—looking for modelling work, I think. Course nothing came of it. But it was all for this Steve."

"Yet, all the same, you think he killed her?"

She stared at him. "Course he did. Didn't I see him kneeling down by her?"

"It seems he claims he just found her dead."

"That's a likely story."

"Couldn't it be true, though?"

She thought. "I suppose it could be—but in that case why'd he run away?"

"Says he was frightened."

"He wasn't the only one."

"Well, then . . ." Roger spread his hands. "I mean, why should he kill her? She wasn't going to do him any harm, was she? Not if, as you say, she was so fond of him."

It was a weak argument, he knew, but it served his purpose for the moment.

He paused, then added, "But perhaps you were mistaken about that."

She shook her head decisively. "I was not. There was something about her when she spoke to him. To her, he was different from the others."

This gave Roger the opening he'd been waiting for.

"You really think so? What about the previous chap, though? I thought she seemed very fond of him. What was *his* name, now? She did tell me, but it's slipped my mind. Oh dear, my memory."

"You mean Phil," said Mrs. Hopkins.

Alison drew her breath in sharply between her teeth. Was this the name she was seeking? Luckily once again Mrs. Hopkins didn't seem to notice her reaction. Roger showed no surprise at all.

"Phil?" He screwed up his eyes. "Yes—yes, I believe that was it."

"Or Bill," Mrs. Hopkins added. "My hearing isn't too good these days, but it was one or the other."

"Yes; I'm sure you're right. Did you know his surname?"

"No, I never heard it."

"Do you know if she was still seeing him?"

Mrs. Hopkins shook her head reluctantly. "I couldn't say if she were actually *seeing* him, sir. I know he used to phone her. But she was definitely not so keen as she once was."

"Really? What makes you say that, Mrs. Hopkins?"

"Well, once when she'd been talking to him—about ten days ago, it'd be —after she rang off I heard her mutter to herself. 'Unreasonable.' That's what she said. Then she sort of noticed me and gave a kind of smile. 'Some people think they own you, Hoppy,' she said. And that's very true, sir. Why some of my ladies . . ."

She embarked on a long anecdote. Roger didn't interrupt. He was glad of a short respite, to think. So was Alison.

Phil or Bill. It was a slim enough lead. On the other hand, it was at least a start. Where she went from here she didn't know. She could only take things a step at a time. But with Chief Inspector Roger Matthews looking for an alternative suspect there surely had to be a chance.

". . . and the next time your dog's sick on the kitchen floor you can clean it up yourself. That's what I said, straight out. Don't you think I was in the right, now?"

"Absolutely, Mrs. Hopkins," Roger said heartily. "Perfectly justified. Don't you think so, darling?" he said to Alison.

"Oh—yes—certainly."

Mrs. Hopkins seemed suddenly to recollect the circumstances of the meeting. "Oh, I'm sorry, sir, this is hardly the time to talk about such things."

"That's all right, Mrs. Hopkins, life must go on. By the way, you didn't mention this man, Phil or Bill, to the police?"

"No, sir. I did not. Only just that there was a man. What'd be the point in saying more? Tell the police as little as you've got to, that's what my old man says. Never know what it might lead to, if you say too much."

"Name, rank and serial number only, eh?"

"Pardon?"

"Oh nothing. And you don't recall the names of any other of her men friends?"

"No, sir, I'm afraid I don't. You want to look in that little address book of hers."

Alison pricked up her ears. "What address book is that, Mrs. Hopkins?"

"Little red one. Miss Matthews always had it with her. I told that there inspector about it."

"Yes, he mentioned it to me, Mrs. Hopkins," Roger put in. "Unfortunately, it's vanished. He thinks the murderer must have taken it with him."

They remained talking for another ten minutes or so, but learnt nothing more of interest. Then they took their leave. From her front door, Mrs. Hopkins watched them go.

When they reached the street, Alison made to turn left in the direction of her car. But before she could do so Roger took her by the arm and marched her smartly the other way.

She began to protest. "My car's down there—"

"My car's up here. And don't you think la Hopkins would consider it a little odd if we went off in opposite directions? I'll bring you back to get yours later."

"Why can't *I* bring *you* back to get *yours* later?"

"In the first place I don't like being driven by *anybody,* but especially by strangers and more especially by strange women. OK, OK, don't say it. I know. I'm just funny that way. Secondly, my car is not really *my* car. It's the property of the local police and I feel an obligation not to get it stolen."

"Oh, and it doesn't matter if *mine* is stolen?"

"Did you lock yours?"

"Of course."

"I may not have locked mine. Besides, we're nearly there, so it's not worth arguing about it now."

He walked up to a dark blue Montego parked by the kerb and tried the door. "Ah, I did lock it."

"Surprise, surprise," Alison said.

When he had unlocked the doors and they were both inside, he said suddenly,

"Would you like a drink?"

Alison hesitated. She found the man infuriating, but she knew he could be useful to her.

"I'd prefer a cup of tea," she said.

"Fine by me." He started the engine. "Tell me where to go. All right, don't say the obvious thing."

"I never say the obvious thing." She thought for a moment. "I don't want to go anywhere where I'm likely to be recognised by someone. But I think I know of a place. Turn left at the end of the street."

Ten minutes later they were seated in a small, dimly lit café. A tired-looking waitress and three customers were the only other occupants. They were silent until the waitress had brought tea for Alison and coffee for Roger. Then he took a sip of coffee and said,

"You say your friends don't come here?"

"I don't think so, no."

"I'm not surprised. I thought this town had a reputation for fine cafés." He pushed the cup away.

"This tea is very good," she said frostily.

"I'm pleased for you. But I'll take your word for it."

She gave him a disgusted look. "Is this really the time to worry about the quality of the coffee?"

"Oh, I'm not *worried* about it."

"For heaven's sake! My husband is in gaol for a crime he didn't commit. And your sister was murdered last night!"

His face hardened. "I'm well aware of that fact, Mrs. Grant."

"You don't give much evidence of it."

"Because I seem to you flippant?"

"Frankly, yes."

"I assure you that impression is false. I could easily adopt a gloomy countenance and sepulchral tones. What good would it do? Whatever my manner, the fact is I am very angry about my sister's death and determined to get to the bottom of it."

"Angry—but not exactly bowled over."

"No; because as I've explained once today already, I hadn't heard anything from Linda for five years. And never really expected to hear from her again."

Alison, in the act of lifting her cup, stopped with it half-way to her lips. "But you told Mrs. Hopkins she wrote to you regularly."

"That's right."

"But why lie?"

"Because she was very fond of Linda. If I'd told her my sister and I hadn't been in touch for all that time, she'd have assumed we'd quarrelled —become estranged. And she'd have also assumed it was my fault. That would have made her slightly hostile, and less likely to talk freely."

"You couldn't *know* that."

"Agreed. But it was a possibility. One that it was better not to risk."

"Do you lie about everything?" she asked coldly.

"No, only when it's strictly necessary in the course of an investigation."

"You lied about locking the car. That was strictly necessary?"

"No, but I knew you'd find out in a few seconds, so it hardly counted."

"You lied about my being your wife. What on earth was the point of that? I've never been so embarrassed in my life."

"I'm sorry about that, but I had to think quickly. You didn't want her to know you were Stephen's wife. But I had to introduce you somehow. If I'd said you were my secretary, or just a friend, Mrs. Hopkins would have immediately started speculating on the relationship between us, and not given all her attention to thinking about Linda. It seemed far better to tell her you were my wife."

Alison sniffed. "You fancy yourself as quite a psychologist, don't you?"

"Well, as a matter of fact I did take a degree in it."

She stared at him. "Do you have an answer for everything?"

"No, not quite."

"Well, I just hope I don't run into her in my capacity as Mrs. Stephen Grant. Heaven knows what I shall say."

"Oh, you'll carry it off with aplomb. Say the other girl was your twin. Or, if you like, that I forced you into the masquerade with horrible threats."

"Serve you right if I did say that. Anyway, I hope it rebounds on you. I hope your wife hears you've been going around with another woman, passing her off as Mrs. Matthews."

"I haven't got a wife."

"I'm not surprised."

Alison was glad at this opportunity to throw the phrase back at him, but then he added quietly,

"I *had* a wife. She was killed four years ago. In a car crash."

Alison felt her cheeks grow scarlet. She opened her mouth to say something but before she could do so he went on,

"And in case you're wondering: no, I was not to blame. She was driving —at her own wish. I was a passenger. I wasn't scratched."

Very softly Alison said, "I see. I'm very sorry. And, of course, that's why you don't like being—"

He interrupted. "Look, let's not talk about it. Do you mind?"

"No. No, of course not." She sipped her tea silently for a few seconds. Then without looking up she asked, "What would you *like* to talk about?"

He smiled. "Phil, perhaps."

"Phil or Bill remember."

"Yes, but I shall call him Phil. He sounds more a Phil. Phil I see as having long greased hair, a toothbrush moustache, sideburns and lots of very white teeth. Bill would be large and fresh-faced—rather like Sergeant Primrose."

"Have it your way. Are you going to try and trace him?"

He shook his head. But it was not the firm shake of refusal, but rather an indication of uncertainty.

"I don't know. Without any other sort of lead, it's an almost impossible task. I really don't know where to start."

"But surely Linda must have had some friends—girl-friends—somebody she would have talked to—apart from her cleaning woman."

"I'm not at all sure she would have. She was a single-minded sort of girl, who kept herself very much to herself. She'd have acquaintances—but I doubt very much she'd discuss her love life with them."

"Everybody has got to have *somebody* to talk to," Alison said stubbornly.

"Maybe you're right. If so it would be an *old* friend—probably in London. Not here in Fermouth, anyway."

"Couldn't you put out a police message for anyone who knew her to come forward?"

"I'm not sure Bidwell would be too happy about that. He's quite satisfied he's got the right man in custody."

"Oh, but that's absurd. You know it is!"

"Now, hang on. I don't *know* anything of the sort. All I say is that there's an element of doubt."

"But surely, after what Mrs. Hopkins said, there must be more than an *element.*"

"Mrs. Hopkins told us Linda had other men friends, apart from Stephen. Which I was already certain was the case anyway. She mentioned two very common Christian names. And that's it."

"But it's not!" Alison said fiercely. "Phil is 'unreasonable.' He thought he owned Linda. Remember?"

"Of course. That is suggestive. Interesting. But it's no more than that at this stage." He paused. "Do try to understand, that if Stephen had not panicked—run away—told lies—he'd probably be at home with you now. Still under suspicion, probably, but no more. All those other things would be going on: appeals on TV and in the press for those who knew Linda to help; police records being searched for Phils and Bills with convictions for violence against women; door-to-door interviews; visits to all the London model agencies—the works. And it might go on for weeks. As things stand, however, it's just me with an uneasy feeling."

"And me," Alison said.

He bowed his head. "And you, of course. I'm quite certain you'll do all in your power. But what *is* in your power? Or *do* you have any suggestions? I'll gladly consider them."

Alison thought hard. "What about Linda's neighbours?"

"Well, of course that is really the only starting point: the other residents of the block. She *might* have got friendly with one or two of them. Or somebody might have caught a glimpse of Phil calling on her. I'm not too hopeful, because as I understand it, that's a pretty exclusive sort of place— the kind of place where people mind their own business. But as I see it, it's that or nothing."

"What will you do? Just go round from door to door, asking questions?"

"That's it."

"Can I help?"

"I don't think so, thank you."

"But I could cut the time it takes in half."

"Not really—*I'll* have to speak to everybody in any case; I'll need to satisfy myself about them. Besides, I've got a warrant card to wave. Nobody will be surprised at a policeman coming round asking questions after a murder in the block. *You* have no authority. I mean, how would you pass yourself off? Would you tell people you were the wife of the man who's been arrested?"

Then, as she hesitated, he added, "If so, will you give your right name? If not, what excuse will you give for wanting to know? It would be very awkward, either way."

Alison gave a sigh. "I suppose so. It's just that people speak more freely to a private citizen than to a policeman."

"Well, I'm not sure that's not a myth—at least where the respectable middle classes are concerned. But of course, I can't *stop* you going round, asking questions if you want to."

Alison shook her head hurriedly. "No—no, I don't want to get in your way. You're Stephen's best chance. Perhaps his only chance."

"I'll tell you what," he said. "There'll be an awful lot of dead ends. Most of the tenants will have nothing useful to tell us at all. Many of them will have never set eyes on Linda. It's amazing but that's the way it is in these big blocks; people have fixed routines—go out and come home at regular times—and just never come in contact with people living only a few yards away. It'll be a long boring job, weeding them all out. When I find the ones who *did* know her, and have got all I can out of them, I'll give you their names and, if you want to, you can follow up."

She looked pleased. "OK. I must do *something,* you see."

"Of course. I feel the same."

"When will you start?"

He looked at his watch. "Tonight, I think. No doubt a lot of people will be out at work all day, so if I *can* catch them this evening it'll save time."

"Then I mustn't hold you up."

She wriggled awkwardly out from between the fixed table and chair and he followed suit. He paid at the cash desk and they went out to the street. He said,

"I'll drive you back to pick your car up now."

Shortly afterwards he drew up a few yards behind the Sierra.

Alison turned to him. "Thanks. Look, you *will* let me know how it goes?"

"Of course. I'll phone you."

"Well, I'll be out most of tomorrow. I have to go up to London to deliver the manuscript of a novel to Stephen's secretary. I should have posted it today, but I forgot, and the publishers are waiting for it. But I'll be home in the evening."

He took a notebook and pencil from his pocket. "And the number?"

"208721. And if anything really important or hopeful crops up tomorrow, will you phone our solicitor, Innes Lloyd—so he can tell Stephen—cheer him up?"

"Sure. Do you know his number?"

"Yes—his private line at the office. You don't need to write it down—it's the easiest to remember in town: 234567."

"Right. But you mustn't expect too much—in fact, don't expect *anything.*"

"Then I won't be disappointed—I know. That's what my mother used to say."

She started to open the door, then stopped. "Oh, by the way, where are you staying?"

Roger stared at her blankly. Then he said, "Believe it or not, I've no idea."

"Haven't you booked in anywhere?"

"No. I was in a hurry to get to the police station when I arrived. I meant to do it immediately after I left there. Then I didn't give it a thought."

"Well, there are only the two good hotels. They're both very expensive —and nearly always booked well in advance. There are some little boarding houses, but not many."

"I hate little boarding houses, anyway."

She hesitated. "Well, I'm sorry I can't offer you our spare room. But I think it might seem a little odd, if anybody found out, don't you?"

He smiled. "Yes, I can just see the *Sun*'s headlines."

There was silence for a few seconds, before Roger said slowly, "Of course, there is one obvious place to stay."

"You mean Linda's flat?"

"Yes."

"I didn't like to suggest it. How would you feel about that?"

He grimaced. "Well, I can't say I fancy the idea very much: sleeping in the very place where—where it happened."

She gave a little shiver. "No, so I can imagine."

"On the other hand," he said, "it would be extremely convenient for questioning the residents. Then again, I *do* have to go through her things sometime. *And* it would save me a lot of time searching for another place. So I really think I'm going to have to be coldly rational and force myself."

"Well, I suppose it is the commonsense thing to do," she said. "Do you know how to get there?"

"No, but they'll tell me at the police station. I have to go back there—I left my suitcase there. And a file of Linda's papers that Bidwell thought I might like to look at."

"Oh, right."

She opened the door, got out, then looked back in through the window.

"Well, I'll wait to hear from you, then."

"Sure. Oh, by the way, sorry I was a bit overbearing earlier."

"That's all right. And thanks."

"What for?" he asked.

"For helping. I was getting desperate."

"I'm only doing it because I want to make sure the right man gets put away."

"I'm only doing it because I want to make sure the wrong man doesn't. Good night."

"Good night, Mrs. Grant."

Alison walked to her car and went home. Roger drove to the police station.

CHAPTER SEVEN

"Stephen, I want you to listen to me carefully. It's utterly vital that you tell me the truth. You understand, of course, that anything you tell me is absolutely privileged and cannot damage you in any way."

Bertrand Innes Lloyd paused, not really waiting for a reply, but just giving his words time to sink in.

But Stephen answered all the same, "Yes, I understand."

"Good. Then let me ask you again: did you kill Linda Matthews?"

"No."

"Very well. Now another question: are the police right? Did you lie about what happened in the girl's flat last night?"

Stephen took a deep breath. He looked away for a moment, then met the lawyer's eyes again.

"Yes," he said quietly.

Innes Lloyd raised his eyes heavenward. "Just as I feared! Oh, why will people never learn?"

"I'm sorry," Stephen muttered.

"You don't have to apologise to *me*. It won't harm me at all."

"Only myself?"

"That remains to be seen. I'll give you my opinion when I know the exact extent of your untruths. You had better tell me now—at once—exactly what did happen."

He sat back and listened while his client talked.

It was only about two minutes before Stephen said, "Well, that's about all," and fell silent.

Innes Lloyd drummed with his fingers on the table top.

Stephen waited a few seconds, then said anxiously, "Well—how much harm have I done myself?"

"That remains—" Innes Lloyd remembered he had already used that phrase, and amended it. "That depends. What you've told me doesn't materially alter the facts of the case. It depends on whether the police believe your new story. If so—well, it's certainly not going to make them *release* you. It might convince them even more firmly that you did it. On the other hand, it may, if you tell the new story convincingly, create a slight doubt in their minds about your guilt. It's impossible to say at this stage."

Stephen opened his mouth. He wanted to say, what a load of waffle. Instead he swallowed and said, "So, what's the next step?"

"I'll see Bidwell first thing in the morning and tell him you want to make a new statement—in my presence, of course. He will no doubt wish to question you further. It may be politic to agree, and to answer all his questions as fully as possible, even if they are repetitive."

"And then? Tell me what you really think."

"Very well. Frankly, I'm very much afraid that then they are going to charge you with the girl's murder."

CHAPTER EIGHT

"Good night, Mr. Hodges."

"Night, Tracy. Straight home now. No messing about."

"OK! See you tomorrow. Night."

Tracy Bartlett grinned to herself as she pulled the pub door closed behind her and hurried away along the street. Every night exactly the same words. What did they mean, anyway? What did he think she might do? Still, he wasn't a bad sort, old Hodges. She'd had worse bosses.

She quickened her pace still more. She rather wished she'd told him that she wasn't meeting Myra tonight.

Myra was the barmaid at the *Anchor,* a hundred and fifty yards away. They always met on the corner and walked home together—Myra lived in the next street, so Tracy had company right to her own front door. But Myra had rung up to say she was off work, sick. So Tracy had to walk home alone.

She didn't mind, really. After all, it was only half a mile or so. And Fermouth was a nice, law-abiding sort of place. Not like London or Birmingham, with all those muggers—even though a girl *had* been murdered here the other night. After all, they'd got the bloke who'd done that. And *she'd* been no better than she should be, it seemed. In spite of her posh address. Yet she'd have probably looked down on a barmaid in a little back street pub.

At least, I'm alive, thought Tracy, somewhat smugly. All the same, she would mention it to Mr. Hodges tomorrow. Perhaps he or Bert the cellarman would walk her home. Though she wouldn't trust Bert all that far, if he got her on her own in a dark street. Not that he'd *kill* her, of course. She giggled at the ludicrous thought of Bert murdering anyone.

Perhaps she'd tell Dad instead. He'd come and walk home with her. But it was hardly fair, with his bad leg. And he didn't like her working evenings in a pub, anyway. He'd try and persuade her to get a job in a nice shop or something. Which would be easier said than done. Apart from the fact that she *liked* working in a pub. It was more cheerful than working in a shop, any day.

Though, all the same, she didn't want to make a habit of going home alone at this time of night. She was beginning to feel definitely jumpy. Not a good idea to let her mind run on muggers and murderers—

Tracy's heart gave a sudden lurch and she stopped abruptly. Had that been a footstep behind her?

She strained her ears. No, nothing. But perhaps *he'd* stopped too . . .

She longed to glance over her shoulder. But she couldn't bring herself to do so. She started walking again—now just about as fast as she could. She was determined not to run. It was absurd to be scared. She was in her own town, only a quarter of a mile from home. There were houses all around her, full of people. She wasn't in the heart of the country.

All the same, there weren't many people on the streets tonight. Surely, when she walked home with Myra, there were normally quite a few other folk about? She and Myra were usually talking; so perhaps she didn't notice too well what was going on around her. But that was the impression she had.

Now, though, she couldn't see a living soul. Where *was* everybody? Were they all staying indoors—because they didn't really believe the murderer of that Linda girl *was* behind bars?

Tracy shivered and told herself not to be a silly little twit. Only a few minutes now and she'd be home.

The next second she gave a gasp of fear, as this time she did hear what were without doubt footsteps behind her. What's more, they were approaching in a rush. She started to swing round. But she had left it too late. She saw a kind of blur before her eyes. Then there was a sudden hard pressure against her throat and she felt herself being jerked backwards. She was prevented from falling by two hands at the back of her neck. She tried to scream but the rapidly tightening band round her neck stifled the sound at birth. She raised her hands and clawed wildly at the material which was biting into her skin. She threw herself desperately from side to side. But it was hopeless. Her assailant was just too strong.

Gurgling sounds came from Tracy's throat. Everything was going black. She felt her legs buckling beneath her and then her knees hit the pavement. She dimly realised that it was only the stuff round her neck that was holding her body upright. Her head was bursting, her throat on fire. She was choking—choking—choking . . .

Abruptly Tracy felt the pavement rise up and hit her a sharp blow on the cheek. It was cool against her face. Blessedly cool. She realised she was breathing. The effort was tremendous, but air was again getting through to her lungs. The band had gone from her neck. The hands that had been holding it were there no longer . . .

Tracy lay on the pavement, gasping, retching, wheezing; too paralysed with shock even to try and get up.

It was thus she was found a few minutes later by a man and his wife from a nearby house, who had heard the sounds of the scuffle. Twenty-five minutes after that Tracy Bartlett was in hospital.

CHAPTER NINE

"How's the girl?" Primrose asked.

Detective Chief Inspector Bidwell threw himself into his chair and rubbed his face with both hands. He sighed.

"Not too bad, I suppose. Her throat's terribly bruised, of course, and she can only croak. But they say she'll be right as rain in a few days."

"Oh well, that's something. Could she give you a description of the assailant?"

"No. She says he was big, but I don't set a lot of store by that. She's quite a small girl. Being set on from behind like that a man of my height would seem tall to her."

"And what exactly was the form of the attack?"

Bidwell said tonelessly, "He approached her from the rear, threw something like a silk head square or scarf around her neck, crossed his hands and pulled."

Primrose gave a whistle. "Exactly the same M.O.! You think . . . ?"

"I think: copycat," Bidwell snapped.

"But surely," Primrose began. He was frowning. "The *Advertizer* piece said nothing about a silk square being used in the attack on Linda. How could a copycat know to do it the same way?"

"Plenty of people knew. Apart from our chaps, the stretcher bearers, medical assistants—and above all, the charwoman. I bet she told a couple of dozen people at least. Let them all tell just two each, and each of *them* tell two, and hundreds would know within hours."

"Yes, I suppose so." But Primrose was still looking doubtful.

"Listen, Freddie, I am not prepared to believe in a mad strangler, going around attacking girls at random. Linda Matthews was much too streetwise to have admitted a stranger. Besides, there's one big difference between the two attacks."

"What's that?"

"Tracy Bartlett wasn't killed."

"Oh, I see what you mean. But maybe her attacker was scared off."

"The girl didn't hear anybody. It was several minutes before she was found."

"Well, she wouldn't be likely to hear, would she? Besides, it could have just been a light going on in one of the houses—headlamps in the distance. Something like that could be enough to panic him."

"I know, I know. And maybe you're right and he *did* intend to finish her off. But I still say there's no connection with the Matthews case—except that that gave him the idea. We've got Linda's killer. Which doesn't mean there isn't a very disturbed and dangerous young man out there, who's got to be found."

"Think he'll try again?"

"I just don't know." Bidwell spoke wearily. "Probably not immediately, or not in this way. But sometime, somehow—maybe. He's a nutter, so who can say?"

He gave a groan. "This is just about all we needed!"

Primrose coughed. "Oh, by the way, Innes Lloyd's been in. Seems Grant wants to change his statement."

"What?" Bidwell looked up sharply. "You mean—confess?"

"He didn't say. But I didn't get that impression. 'Amend' was the word he used, I think. Anyway, Innes Lloyd wants to be present. Says will you phone him?"

"Oh, I suppose so." Bidwell reached for the telephone. "Might as well get it over with." He lifted the receiver. "Lawyers! Has it ever occurred to you, Freddie, how much easier police work would be if it wasn't for lawyers?"

Stephen said deliberately, "I wish to correct something I put in my original statement. I *did* find Linda Matthews dead. That was perfectly true. What wasn't true was that I only discovered her *after* Mrs. Hopkins rang the doorbell. Actually her body was lying in the middle of the floor and so, naturally, I saw it as soon as I arrived."

He paused. Bidwell, looking furious, muttered under his breath. Innes Lloyd glanced at him sharply, but said nothing.

Stephen continued. "I was horrified, of course—well, I needn't go into that. I made sure she was dead. Then I was going to phone the police. But I was scared. I knew I'd probably be suspected of killing her, and at best my wife would find out about my affair. I reasoned that I couldn't help the police in any way. I could give them no clue as to who might have done it. I made up my mind to leave, and then phone the police anonymously and report what had happened. But it was still light out, and I didn't want to risk being seen. I decided to wait there until it was dark. I went into the kitchen and just sat there—I don't know for how long.

"Then somebody rang the front doorbell. I was petrified. I decided just to sit tight and wait for them to go away. But I realised they might have seen the light. They might *not* go away. Suppose eventually I *had* to let them in? Well, obviously, I couldn't do that with Linda's body on the sitting-room floor. The only thing to do seemed to be move it—her—into the bedroom. It was a mad thing to think of. But I was in a state of utter panic. I got down to put my hands under her shoulders. And that was when I heard Mrs. Hopkins scream behind me. The next part you know. Afterwards I was ashamed of just having stayed there all that time with the body—not doing anything. So I said I hadn't seen the body—that it had been behind the sofa and I'd only just discovered it. That's all. Everything else I said was the truth."

"What made him do it? That's what I want to know," Bidwell asked twenty minutes later. There was a scowl on his face.

Primrose didn't attempt an answer. He didn't think one was really wanted.

"What made him change his story?" Bidwell went on. "Did Innes Lloyd put him up to it?"

He was prowling round his office like a caged lion. Suddenly he stopped and stared at Primrose. "Well," he snapped, "say something."

Primrose gave a little start and thought hurriedly. "Could it just be this story's the truth, governor?"

"What? Oh, it *could* be. I'm a fair man, Freddie, so I'll admit that. It could also be he realised his original story of not seeing the body couldn't be true and came up with this more feasible one. If so, it's mighty clever. But it smacks more of Innes Lloyd than Grant."

He threw himself down into his chair. "You realise one thing? The situation's almost exactly the same now as when we arrested him—before we went to the flat and messed about behind that settee. The only difference is that now Grant's admitted making a false statement. We didn't believe his protestations of innocence before that, so there's certainly no reason for us to believe them now."

The words were firm, but Primrose fancied he detected a shade less certainty in the tone in which they were uttered. He didn't reply, and it was his silence that seemed to draw the chief inspector's attention to him. Perhaps Bidwell sensed the sergeant's awareness of his first stirrings of real doubt and it was this that irritated him still further. "And Freddie," he said, "don't call me 'governor.' Makes me feel I ought to be running California."

It was shortly after this that Roger Matthews returned. Bidwell's greeting was polite enough, but there was a stiffness in his manner of which Roger, sensitive to atmosphere, was immediately conscious. He decided to try and dispel it by ignoring its existence.

"Well, any developments?" he asked easily as he dropped into the chair Bidwell indicated.

"You could say that. Grant's changed his statement."

Roger sat up. "Has he indeed? In what way?"

Bidwell told him. By the time he'd finished, Roger was wearing a satisfied expression.

"Why are you looking so pleased?" Bidwell demanded accusingly.

"Well, when you tumbled to the point about the sofa being too small to conceal the body, I realised that *if* Grant was innocent, the true facts had to be something along the lines of this new statement. I actually told Grant that his story was rubbish, but that if he came up with an account that hung together I might be prepared to believe in his innocence. It seems he took my advice to heart."

"Let me get this straight." Bidwell sounded grim. "You say you told him his story was rubbish. You mean you warned him what we'd worked out about the settee and the body?"

"No, no, of course not. What do you take me for? I simply told him you were convinced his story was false and believed you could prove it."

"I see," Bidwell said. He still didn't seem too happy.

"Well, there was no harm in that, surely?"

"I don't know. That must have got him thinking about his statement—wondering where it could be proved false. He could have realised where he'd gone wrong and come up with this new version in order to spike my guns."

"Oh, I think that's unlikely," Roger said. "I merely advised him to speak to his lawyer—and then tell the truth. I knew the sort of story that I, at least, could believe. Which is the story he now tells. I think that's significant. I'm sure if he'd been going for another lie he'd have come up with something quite different—something that would show him in a better light. After all, he's had plenty of time to think of one. He could have claimed—oh, to have surprised the killer: to have walked into the flat, seen the body, then been knocked over the head and only just been struggling to his feet when Mrs. Hopkins came in. We'd have had a job to disprove that at this stage."

Bidwell gave a grunt. "You sound as if you'd have made a pretty effective criminal yourself."

"Yes, I've often thought that." Roger paused. "Look, Horace, I'm sorry if I said anything out of place, but I honestly didn't give him a hint as to what aspect of his story you disbelieved. For all he knew it could be you had some forensic evidence regarding the time of Linda's death; anything at all."

"Oh well, you might be right, I suppose." Bidwell had decided to be magnanimous. Roger breathed an inward sigh of relief.

"Anyway, congratulations," he said. "You certainly proved your point. Grant was lying."

"But you still don't think he's guilty?"

"I never said that. I just don't know yet."

"You haven't made much progress, then?" Bidwell asked.

"Well a little. I've got a name—or rather two."

He related what he had learned from Mrs. Hopkins. "Now, I know that's not much," he said. "But at least we know there *was* another current boy-friend, who was possessive and unreasonable. The sort who wouldn't have been at all happy about Linda seeing Stephen Grant."

Bidwell looked dubious. "But without a surname, or a description . . ."

"Oh, I know. And there I've drawn a complete blank. I spent most of yesterday evening and the early part of this morning talking to the other residents of the block. Only about four of them had ever spoken to Linda, and then only to pass the time of day. I did get two descriptions of a man seen entering or leaving her apartment at various times."

Bidwell pricked up his ears. "Indeed?"

"Yes. Thirty-five to forty, tall, dark and slimly built."

Bidwell relaxed. "Oh, Grant, of course."

"Afraid so. I've got quite a few neighbours to see yet, but I'm afraid that road's going to be a dead end. However, I discovered a few interesting things. I was going through that file you gave me—by the way, I spent the night at Linda's flat."

"Oh, I'm sorry you had to do that."

"I didn't want to, of course, but it was convenient. And at least there was very little there to remind me of her."

"Yes, we were struck by how impersonal it was—how bare."

Roger nodded. "I think she must have stored a lot of her stuff—personal things: letters, photos, souvenirs—before she ever moved here. Heaven knows if we'll ever locate it. It could be anywhere."

"Still, as you say, there was that file."

"Yes, that was interesting." Roger paused. "Especially the will."

Bidwell looked a little embarrassed. "Ah."

"You saw it, of course? I suppose that's where you found my name and address?"

"That's right. It, er, must have been quite a surprise."

Roger shook his head in disbelief. "I was absolutely staggered," he said. "All those years without a word—and now this. I don't mind admitting I was very moved. I think my main reaction, though, was how pathetic it was. All those men. And not one she wanted to leave her money to. She made the will after Grant had virtually told her marriage was out. She must have suddenly realised she had nobody. I daresay she felt quite suicidal—" He broke off abruptly, was silent for a second, then said, "Oh, there were a couple of witnesses to the will . . ."

Primrose said, "Yes, sir, I tracked them down. They were cleaning windows there. This girl they'd never seen before came out and asked them to witness her signature. She showed them her passport to prove her identity, signed the form, they witnessed it, she thanked them and went back in. That was it."

Roger nodded.

Bidwell said, "We didn't find much jewellery at the flat. We thought perhaps it was at the bank."

"It is. I've just been along there now and had a look at it. Some very nice stuff. I'm no expert, but there must be five thousand pounds worth there."

"Is that so?" Bidwell seemed slightly at a loss for words.

Roger gave a wry smile. "Don't know whether to congratulate me on my good fortune, do you? I know how you feel."

Bidwell shrugged. "Well, it *will* be a nice little windfall, all put together.

Your sister wanted you to have it. So I should just try and make the most of it."

"I shan't keep it," Roger said decidedly. "I couldn't—thinking of the life she led to get it. It would be like living on immoral earnings. I'll sell everything and give the proceeds to charity."

"Well, that's your decision, of course."

"However"—Roger spoke more briskly—"so long as I'm down here I will use her car. I've had a look at it; it's a nice little job, only twelve months old. So I shall not require your official loan anymore."

He took a ring with two keys attached from his side pocket and laid it on the desk. "Many thanks."

Next he reached into an inner pocket and took out a sheaf of papers. "Now something else," he said. "I've been looking through Linda's bank statements and they're really quite intriguing."

He laid the papers in front of Bidwell and went round the side of the desk, so they could study them together. Primrose came up and stood on the other side.

"Right," Roger said. "According to her rent book she moved into her apartment on ninth July last year. She paid a month's rent in advance—cash. On the tenth she opened this account with a deposit of one thousand pounds. You'll notice that nearly every week thereafter until about the end of March there was a cash deposit. Up to the end of last year they were mostly over a hundred pounds, several times over two hundred. This year they were smaller—generally around forty to seventy. But they were still being made. Since April, though, there've been no deposits at all."

"So," Bidwell said, "this bloke Phil or Bill installed her in the flat last summer, giving her a thousand quid to get settled, and then kept her week by week. Until she met Grant, that is, and threw the first man over."

"It's an obvious scenario."

"He must have thought an awful lot of her," Primrose put in.

"Yes," Roger said, *"and* been very well off. Though, knowing Linda, that goes without saying. Seems he might have started to cool off a bit this year, though—if the reduced deposits are anything to go by."

"Perhaps he was feeling the pinch, sir. Maybe he wasn't quite as well off as he'd led her to think."

"Yes, that's possible."

Bidwell cleared his throat. "Yes, well, you've put together a very reasonable hypothesis to account for the situation revealed by these statements. I suppose there could be others . . ."

He tailed off, again seeming reluctant to say anything further.

Sergeant Primrose, however, had no such inhibitions. "Such as black-mail," he said happily.

"Sergeant!" Bidwell spoke sharply. "It's Mr. Matthews' sister we're talking about."

"No, no, the sergeant's quite right," Roger said. "It *is* another explana-tion and has to be considered. The man could have been paying large sums regularly until the end of the year. Then he managed to convince her he couldn't keep it up and she settled for smaller pay-offs. By the spring she'd either bled him dry and realised she couldn't get any more. Or she met Grant, had a change of heart and decided to let the other bloke off the hook."

He paused. "Or, alternatively, she was still getting money from him. She'd just stopped paying it into the bank. Perhaps she put all her cash into buying jewellery. Anyway, the blackmail was still going on. Yes, ei-ther way it's a plausible explanation of the facts."

"Maybe," Bidwell said, "but from what you know of your sister, is it likely?"

Roger returned to his chair and sat down before replying. "I honestly can't say, Horace. It's such a long time since I really knew her. My instant reaction is no. For all her faults, Linda was never remotely dishonest. But who can say how people change? If she saw the chance of really big money —even spread out, over a period—she might succumb. And let's face it, those deposits are almost certainly only a proportion of her income. She must have been spending the rest as it came in. She could have been receiving three hundred quid a week. It's difficult to imagine a man shell-ing out that amount on a regular basis, just for the occasional pleasure of her company."

"Oh, don't you believe it," Bidwell said. "Some of these wealthy blokes spend a lot more than that on their mistresses."

"I know that. But on *Linda?*"

"Don't forget you were her brother. No matter how fond a bloke is of his sister, he can never see she's got any sex appeal. I only saw her after—after it happened, but I think she must have been a remarkably beautiful young woman."

Roger screwed up his eyes. He seemed to be trying to remember. Then he nodded judicially. "Yes, I suppose you could say that."

Bidwell said, "Of course, the line between overt blackmail and simply being a kept mistress doesn't have to have been all that hard and fast."

"How do you mean, exactly?"

"Well, suppose she's being kept by some man—outwardly very respectable. She knows he's *really* nothing of the sort: perhaps it's merely the fact that he *is* keeping her that he'd want kept quiet; or maybe she knows something worse than that. Perhaps he's a crook. Whatever it is, she doesn't have to make any specific demands in return for her silence. He knows that if he wants to maintain his facade of respectability he's got to keep her sweet. She knows he knows it. There's a tacit understanding."

Roger nodded thoughtfully. "I see what you mean. And I *can* visualise Linda in that sort of situation. Or perhaps not even fully realising she did have this power over the man. You see, I don't think she ever *would* rat on a person. And I don't believe it would occur to her that anyone who knew her would even suspect she'd do so. I see her as just hardly able to believe her luck that he's so generous. And given that, she could find herself in an even more dangerous situation than if she were an outright blackmailer."

Bidwell frowned. "Now it's my turn to say how do you mean, exactly?"

"I think I know what Mr. Matthews means." Primrose spoke again. "She's only got to say 'Oo, honey-bunch, I saw the most heavenly fur coat in a shop window today. Only twelve hundred pounds.' To her it's just an innocent remark. Hopeful, no doubt. But if he doesn't cough up, well, as far as she's concerned, that's the end of it. But to him it's a veiled threat. So she gets the fur—and next week tries her luck again—admiring a diamond bracelet, or something. And so it goes on."

"That's it, Sergeant," Roger agreed. "She doesn't realise how it appears to him. A real blackmailer would know not to squeeze the man too hard, not to push her luck. Linda, say, thinks he's just besotted by her—and pushes her luck for all it's worth, while she can. The man thinks he's going to be bled dry—and he strikes back."

Bidwell gave a somewhat embarrassed cough. "Seems to me that for a girl not to realise how it looked to the man, she'd have to be rather, er . . ." He deliberately didn't finish the sentence.

"I know," Roger said. "And I have to admit it. Linda had a lot of good qualities. She was kind-hearted—generous—loyal. She was also mercenary, vain—and rather stupid. I'm afraid it was a fatal combination."

Bidwell shook his head. "I don't buy that."

Roger looked surprised. "You don't?"

"Not if by that you mean she was killed by a man she was blackmailing —even if she didn't realise she was blackmailing him. I believe your Phil was keeping her, quite voluntarily. Then she met Grant and broke with Phil. So the payments stopped. You see, you're forgetting one piece of information you gave me yourself not ten minutes ago: according to Hopkins, Linda'd been looking for a job. Now, that's the action of a girl who's planning a whole change in her life-style—not one who thinks she's got a nice permanent source of income from some wealthy sucker—be he blackmail victim or sugar-daddy."

Roger nodded slowly. "Yes, that's true I must admit, that hadn't occurred to me. Naturally, I'd love to believe she had changed for the better."

"I'm sure she had. The motive for this murder wasn't money. If she'd stopped getting cash from this man as long ago as April he had no motive to kill her. Besides, according to Hopkins, it was *he* who'd been pestering *her*—who wanted to see her. Not the action of a man who'd been paying through the nose to keep her sweet."

Roger was silent, mulling over Bidwell's words. Then he looked at the chief inspector. There was a new expression on his face—one of both respect and gratitude. "Thank you," he said. "I *will* buy that. And it's a weight off my mind. So, you still go for Grant as the killer?"

Bidwell didn't answer immediately. Then he slowly nodded. "On the balance of probabilities, yes. He says he phoned her from the airport on Monday evening and told her he was on his way to see her. Isn't it more likely she phoned him before he went away, demanding he call? As a result, he came back early, deliberately to see her. She told him she wasn't prepared to lose him—that unless he told his wife about her, she would do so herself. Grant couldn't risk that and killed her."

"I agree that version is quite possible," Roger said. "On the other hand, according to Hopkins it was Phil who was possessive and unreasonable, who didn't want to let Linda go. But suppose, after Grant told her the previous Tuesday that marriage was out, she agreed to see Phil again. Suppose he was actually at her flat Monday evening when Grant phoned. Suppose she then told Phil he would have to leave, because his rival was coming. Isn't it on the cards he would have seen red and killed her?"

Bidwell shrugged. "It could have happened—if he was the murderous type."

"Well, does *Grant* strike you as the murderous type? It may be a pose, but to me—well, he just seems too civilised."

Bidwell was filling his pipe. He said, without looking up, "Seems to me you've come right round to believing Grant innocent."

Roger shook his head. "No. There is a case against him. All I'm saying is that it's far from being cast-iron. There's a big doubt. I'd just like some additional evidence."

Bidwell struck a match and lit his pipe. "All right," he said when it was glowing red, "I will concede there's a doubt. I wouldn't personally say it's a big one, but it is there. So, our agreement stands: I'll apply for a further thirty-six hours detention, without charge." He looked at his watch. "And I'd better get a move on. However, you're going to have to bring me something really good before tomorrow night if I'm not to charge him then."

Roger smiled. "And just what would you like, Chief Inspector?"

Bidwell shrugged. "Tell me who Phil is. That'd be a start, at least."

CHAPTER TEN

Alison gave a start when the front doorbell rang. It seemed she always did these days. Fortunately, since Stephen's arrest, there had been few visitors, and those unimportant. Amazingly, news of it had still not leaked out. But every moment she was expecting to be confronted by reporters and photographers.

She hesitated, gnawing at a fingertip. She was tempted not to answer. But it might be important; she'd worry all night if she didn't know.

She went out to the hall, approached the front door and called, "Who is it?"

"Roger Matthews."

"Oh." She opened the door eagerly. "Come in—please."

He did so. "Sorry to call so late," he said, "but I did promise to report."

"That's all right. I'm glad you did. Come into the sitting-room."

She led the way in. The room was comfortable—conventional—somehow peaceful. Roger looked around him with satisfaction. Restfulness was rare.

"This is nice," he said.

But Alison wasn't in the mood for graceful small talk about the decor. She just asked urgently, "Any news?"

"Afraid not."

Her face fell. "Nothing?"

"Well, not as regards the neighbours. All like the three wise monkeys."

"Have you seen them all?"

"Except a few who are away. I finished this evening."

"Oh." She sounded flat. "Does this mean Stephen *will* be charged?"

"Well I think possibly Bidwell is beginning to be not quite so certain as he was, but he still goes for Stephen as the most likely suspect. So I'm afraid the answer's yes—probably within twenty-four hours. Unless one of us comes up with something."

Alison clenched her fists and punched the air with both hands in an act of sheer frustration. "One of us! I talked so big: 'We're going to get you off Stephen.' And what have I done? Absolutely nothing!"

"Now, take it easy. You've done all you could. You went to see Mrs. Hopkins, who was the only possible source of any clue. You helped persuade me there was a reasonable doubt of Stephen's guilt."

"There must be something more," she said.

"Well, frankly, as I said yesterday, I can't think of anything. If I could, I would advise you."

She gave a little shrug of resignation. "Thanks. I know you mean well."

"Oh dear," he said. "The most dampening words in the English language."

"Sorry. They weren't meant to be. Look, do sit down. Can I get you a drink?"

"I wouldn't say no to a Scotch and soda." He lowered himself gratefully into a leather easy chair. "Anything to delay going back to that horrible flat."

"Oh, I was forgetting. Did you find it very unpleasant?"

"Shall we say my thoughts were unpleasant? I didn't sleep much. However, it was *very* convenient. And having broken the ice, tonight will be easier."

She brought him his drink and sat down herself.

He asked, "Have you seen Stephen today?"

"No. I've been in London. I told you I was going—remember? I had to take that typescript to the office. Then Phyllis, Stephen's secretary, wanted me to hold the fort there, while she rushed it to the publishers. She hadn't had time to get a temp. It could almost have been like old times. If it hadn't been for—"

Suddenly she had to stop speaking. Her throat seized up and she felt tears pricking at her eyes. She groped for a handkerchief, hating her own weakness.

Being very careful to show neither embarrassment nor concern, Roger said casually, "You worked there at one time, did you?"

She nodded, without looking at him.

"Did you enjoy it?"

Alison gave a gulp and raised her head. She managed to speak brightly. "Yes, it was fun. An adventure. A—terrible risk of course."

"How do you mean?"

"Well, we'd been more or less kept alive by my earnings. The agency was bringing in hardly anything in those days. We were living in two ghastly little rooms, though even for them the rent was astronomical—or so it seemed then."

Alison paused and seemed to recollect herself. "Still, you don't want to hear all this."

"Yes, I do," he said. It was true. He wanted to sit here—just sit, sipping whisky and listening to her talk. It was restful. Domestic. Pleasant. And he wanted to know more about her. It was foolish, no doubt, to let himself feel such an interest. But you couldn't always be sensible. And besides, she had a lovely speaking voice. He didn't really care *what* she said, so long as he could just stretch out and go on listening.

"Please don't stop," he said. Then to give her a lead: "Stephen founded the business himself, did he?"

"Yes. Funny he didn't really want to. He was with this big, old, established agency, and doing very well. I had a good job in market research. We'd been married about two years, and we had this nice little flat. Everything was going fine. Then the agency changed hands. There was a big upheaval; nearly all the old guard resigned or were fired. Stephen could have stayed on, but he hated the new regime. So he decided to take the risk of setting up on his own. Fortunately, most of his authors agreed to go with him and he soon got a few more. But it was an awful struggle."

"Why? Weren't these authors any good?"

"Yes, but they were mostly young, and weren't best sellers. Stephen placed an awful lot of books, but they didn't bring in much money. And 10 percent of not much is practically nothing. He was working all the hours there were for a pittance. I did all the overtime I could, but we were living on a shoe-string, because, of course, he had to keep up an office in the West End. It was terribly worrying. But you know something? We were really happy."

Roger nodded. "I know what you mean."

For a moment her eyes were years away. Then she blinked and came back to the present. "It got to the stage, after about three years, where he just couldn't handle all the paperwork—but he still couldn't afford a proper secretary. That's when we took the second big risk and I gave up my job to work with him. The first year it was awful—some weeks after we'd paid everything we had literally to live on baked beans. The next couple of years were better. Then about four years ago we had the most tremendous break—he sold the film rights for two books in the space of three months. It was the sort of thing that could never happen twice—unless you happened to represent one of the six or eight really block-busting best-selling authors. But it put us on our feet. He was able to move into proper offices, get a decent car—*and,* best of all, move here."

"Not to mention hire a secretary."

"Phyllis? Yes. *I* hired her. She's extremely efficient, plain as a pikestaff, a workaholic, and just ambitious enough. She's not ever likely to set up on her own—though I imagine one day she'll have to become a partner. That is, if everything—if everything . . ." She tailed off.

"I know," he said hastily. "Er, what made you pick Fermouth to move to?"

"Well, I was sick of London. And I'd always wanted to live here, ever since I stayed here with an aunt when I was a little girl. It's a lovely town —and so solid and unchanging and—and English. It's a place that gives one a sense of security. And, of course, it's handy to London. Though I suppose coming here was a mistake, really."

"In what way?"

"Well, financially. The mortgage is terrifying. And Stephen's income didn't ever again match that one year. I spent about three months getting the house in order, but then I realised that to make ends meet I was going to have to start work again. I managed to get quite a good job as secretary to an estate agent. I stayed there nearly three years. However, all the time the agency was gradually doing better and better until about a year ago we calculated I didn't *need* to work anymore. Stephen wanted me to give up and I suddenly decided that I would *like* to be just a housewife for a bit. After all, I'd been working for about sixteen years, as well as running a home. So I decided I'd earned a bit of a rest."

"I'm sure you had."

"So for the last twelve months I've been a lady of leisure—or comparative leisure. I've been doing all sorts of things I never had time to do before. It's been lovely. Stephen's been working a little less hard. It really seemed that at last everything was beginning to work well. And now—this."

She raised her hands, palms upwards, in a gesture of helplessness. But there was more anger in her voice than there was of despair as she went on.

"It seems that any time we look like being able to take it easy and really enjoy ourselves, Somebody Up There says, 'Oh no, we can't have this.' "

Roger regarded her silently for a few seconds. Remembrance of happiness and a sense of present injustice had lent her face a kind of intense animation he had not seen in it before. Twin specks of colour had highlighted her cheeks and her eyes seemed to look out with a sense of hurt on an unfair world that she had ceased to understand. And, for the first time since Roger had known her, she looked beautiful. For a moment he stopped breathing.

She seemed suddenly to become conscious that he was staring at her in a different kind of way, and her flush deepened to one of embarrassment. She said quickly, "Oh, I know Stephen and I aren't unique. And I suppose if it wasn't this it would be illness. It just seems so horribly unfair."

"I know. But isn't it C. S. Lewis who says that sometimes our life has to be made less agreeable to us so that our illusion of self-sufficiency may be shattered, and that we're never supposed to feel completely happy and at home and secure on this earth."

"But why not?" she asked passionately. "It *is* our home; it's where we are—where we find ourselves. Why shouldn't we feel secure?"

He shrugged. "Because we're *not* secure, I suppose, and never can be. But when things are going well, it's very easy to forget that nothing is permanent—that it's all going to end."

"But what good can it do to think about things like that? It's just morbid."

"Is it? I suppose it can be morbid. But not necessarily. To think of eternal things can be quite exciting, once you get matters into perspective."

She stared at him. "You're talking about religion. I'm afraid I'm not very religious."

"Neither am I—not in the sense that I'm at all unworldly or mystical. It's just that—well, you said this misfortune seems so horribly unfair. Unfair of whom?"

Then, when she hesitated, he went on. "I'm not trying to catch you out. But unless you believe in Somebody Up There, as you put it, who orders things, if you believe in pure blind chance, how can you complain about life being unfair? You might just as well complain that a penny is unfair for coming down tails when you've called heads. And once you believe there is Somebody, it doesn't take much to believe He knows what's best for you in the long run."

Roger gave a sudden, rather self-conscious laugh. "Look, I'm no sermonizer. It's just that since my big tragedy I've had a long time to think about these things."

She nodded. "Yes, I can see you've thought about them a lot."

"At great length, but at very little depth, I'm afraid."

"You say that all this has happened to me to make me less self-sufficient. But I'm not self-sufficient. I never have been. I need Stephen. I'm half a person without him."

"Yes, I felt the same about my wife. Perhaps to too great an extent. Perhaps I was too dependent on her. You can idolise another person. Perhaps I needed to be forcibly separated from my idol for my own good—and for hers. Perhaps we both needed to be made less self-sufficient *and* less each-other-sufficient."

"But that's ridiculous!" she cried fiercely. "Stephen's my husband! Surely your religion teaches that we *ought* to be dependent on each other."

"Look, I'm not talking about you, specifically. I can really only speak about myself. But sometimes I believe a relationship with another person can be too intense—too all-consuming, and can get in the way of a more important relationship." He grinned. "I'm back to C. S. Lewis again."

"Never mind C. S. Lewis. You mean your relationship with God, don't you? You're implying God is trying to make me love Stephen less—so I'll love *Him* more! That's absurd! Believe it or not, we were actually married in church. We took certain vows before a priest. Were those wrong?"

"Naturally they weren't—"

"Was Stephen tempted into that affair, so that he and I should be forced apart?"

"No, of course not. But good can be brought out of evil. The affair was an evil. The murder was an evil. But if we can learn something from it . . ."

"Such as?"

"Well, I've learnt what a lousy brother I was. Stephen—well, it's obvious what he's learnt."

"And me?"

"I can't say for certain. Perhaps that no human relationship can be totally and permanently satisfying. Perhaps you've already learnt something—tolerance, forgiveness. Or maybe it's more a question of what others can learn from you."

"What do you mean?"

"I was thinking of loyalty. You've shown a loyalty towards Stephen that he conspicuously failed to show to you. It's impressive."

Alison looked a little taken aback at this.

"Well, I don't know about that. I didn't feel loyal or forgiving at first. But, you see, I know his good qualities—and his faults. I've been glad enough of the good ones over the years. So I have to accept the faults. And one of those is that in some ways he's—he's—oh, I don't know, too pliable —too malleable. He hates to say no to people. He likes everybody to like him. I've known him agree to handle a book that had no chance of finding a publisher just because he didn't like to tell the author so. He submitted it to three or four firms before I stepped in. It did his reputation no good at all. That's why, if a beautiful girl like your sister set her cap at him—and I'm sorry to be blunt and I'm sure she had her good qualities too—then he would be a pushover for her. Of course, it hurt—terribly—to learn what had been going on; but when I saw what was happening to him as a result of this failing, then I knew that I had to stick by him and see him through it. I had no real choice. Though sometimes now I doubt if things can ever be quite the same again."

As she said these last words her voice became so deeply sad that Roger felt a sudden hatred and contempt for a man who could cause so much hurt and deliberately undermine the foundations of a marriage like this one, with a wife like this.

And, as he did so, he felt himself also hating Linda for her part in it, and momentarily entertaining the frightful thought that perhaps what had happened to her had been for the best. Almost instantaneously then came a surge of guilt at this act of mental betrayal. But the thought remained: how many couples had she broken up? How many would she have broken up in the future?

Then Roger's reason returned to him. One thing became clear: Linda shouldn't have been killed—not for that. Thou shalt not kill. A life for a life perhaps. But not a life for a marriage.

Besides, as far as Stephen Grant was concerned, if it hadn't been Linda, wouldn't it have been another girl? Something Alison had said had been very significant. Speaking of her husband's secretary, she had remarked, "*I* hired her. Plain as a pikestaff." An unconscious slip, revealing that even as long ago as that, she had realised, perhaps without even admitting it to herself, that Stephen was liable one day to cheat on her. And if this was the case, could Linda have been his first affair? Would she, if he did get out of jail, be his last?

Alison interrupted his train of thought. "Do you know what hurts as much as anything?"

"What?"

"That he let her call him Steve. He always said he hated it. Even I never called him anything but Stephen."

"Ah, but you didn't know Linda. She *always* used abbreviations. She's the only person who ever called me 'Rog.' If a name wouldn't shorten, she'd think up a nickname—for women as well as men."

"Like Hoppy."

"Exactly. Don't give it a thought."

"I'll try not to." She was silent for a moment, then sat up and said more briskly, "Right—so what's your next move?"

He blinked. "Oh. Well, I really don't know. At the moment I'm out of ideas."

"But you're not giving up?" Her tone was accusing.

He felt a surge of annoyance. It was on the tip of his tongue to say, "Look, I'm not working for you. I'm not under any obligation to clear Stephen."

But then he knew there was an obligation. It was his sister who had been ultimately responsible for all this mess. Moreover, it was he who had talked blithely about making sure the right man was convicted. And he was still far from sure Stephen Grant was the right man.

He racked his brains for something encouraging to say.

"Well, we do have one—rather slim—lead."

"What's that?" She was suddenly alert with eagerness. He was reminded of a dog that hears the word "Walk."

"It seems Linda must have had at least one very wealthy man friend."

"How wealthy?"

"She was paid a thousand pounds by somebody when she first moved into the flat, and she was getting a regular weekly income—presumably from the same source. She could have received, oh, six thousand pounds all told."

"But that couldn't have been from Stephen! I mean, I know I said things had been going well, but he doesn't have *that* sort of money. Even if he did, I'd be bound to know: we have a joint account; everything we have is in both our names. You're welcome to speak to our accountant or bank manager, look at our tax returns—"

He cut her off. "No, I didn't think it *was* Stephen. For one thing, the money seems to have dried up at about the time she met him."

"So, we're talking about the man called Phil or Bill."

"It seems so."

She frowned. "Well, there can't be that many men in Fermouth rich enough to throw all that money away in a few months."

Again Roger felt a tinge of annoyance. The man in question had obviously not considered the money thrown away. He realised suddenly that he had been feeling a subconscious—and rather immoral—pride in the value someone had placed on his sister. Whatever else she had been, she hadn't been, in the literal sense, cheap.

He said, "No, not that many. But enough to make him still hard enough to trace."

"Yes—but a *rich* man named *Phil* or *Bill?* It can't be impossible. For one thing, surely someone must have seen Linda and him together."

"I doubt if he ever took her out—at least, not in Fermouth. To London, possibly, but I imagine they'd travel separately, or he'd pick her up outside town—something like that."

"Why are you assuming that he's a married man, who had to keep the relationship secret?"

"For one thing, because he must have taken great care not to be seen entering or leaving her apartment. Otherwise, in six months *somebody* would have spotted him."

"Yes. Yes, I suppose so." Alison fell silent.

Roger said, "The trouble is there's only me searching. With all their facilities and manpower, and a bit of time, I'm sure the local police could trace him. If I could just convince Bidwell that this man had a case to answer . . ." He left the sentence in the air.

"Bidwell's a fool!" she said bitterly.

"No, he's not. You must remember he has a very strong case against your husband. Stephen had motive and opportunity; he was found kneeling by the body; he ran away; resisted arrest; told a pack of lies to the police. I tell you, 99 percent of police officers would have charged him already. Bidwell's played along with us very fairly so far. And all we've got to go on is your knowledge of Stephen, and my uneasy feeling that it's all just too pat—a feeling I probably wouldn't bother to entertain if the victim was anybody but a member of my family."

Alison drooped in her chair. She felt spent of energy. She said flatly, "You're saying it's hopeless?"

"No; I'm saying that to save Stephen from being charged is a pretty forlorn hope. You will almost certainly have to face the publicity that will result from it. But—being charged isn't being convicted."

Before Alison could reply there came a peal from the front doorbell.

She said, "Oh, that'll be Innes Lloyd, I expect. He phoned just before you got here to say he wants to speak to me."

She got to her feet. Roger stood up, too. "Well, I'd better leave—"

"No, don't be silly. I want you to meet him."

She went out to the hall and opened the front door. To her surprise both Mr. and Mrs. Innes Lloyd were standing on the step.

Somewhat taken aback, Alison said, "Why, Marjorie, how nice. This is unexpected."

She stood aside and Marjorie bustled in. Bertrand followed at her heels.

"I simply had to come, my dear," Marjorie said. "I haven't spoken to you since this ghastly business started and I felt I must just see how you were and find out if there was anything I could do."

She was a short, plumpish woman of about fifty-five, with a double chin and blue-rinsed hair, and always seemed to be in a hurry. She talked a great deal and tended to gush, but she was good-natured and kindly. Alison was always rather amused by her, but in a mild sort of way quite liked her. Of course, it was a pity she knew about Stephen; but as it had been Marjorie who had answered the phone on Monday night, when a frantic Alison had rung up with news of the arrest, this had been unavoidable.

Now, seeming to read Alison's thoughts, Marjorie laid a reassuring hand on her arm.

"Don't worry, dear. I know I'm a terrible gossip, but when it's a question of Bertrand's professional secrets my lips are absolutely sealed. He positively put the fear of death into me when we were first married, and I've never once slipped up." She turned to her husband. "Have I, darling?"

"No, Marjorie, I can't say you have."

"Well, you needn't sound so grudging about it."

"I don't doubt it for a moment, Marjorie," Alison told her. "And you're very kind. However, I'm afraid that after tomorrow you won't have any secret to keep. Anyway, thank you for coming." She led the way towards the sitting-room. "I've got another visitor at the moment, as a matter of fact," she said over her shoulder.

"Oh well, we don't want to interrupt," Innes Lloyd began.

"No, you won't—I want you to meet him."

She ushered them through the doorway, saying as she did so, "Mr. and Mrs. Innes Lloyd—Mr. Roger Matthews. Or Chief Inspector Roger Matthews of Scotland Yard, I should say." There was the slightest hint of almost proprietorial pride in her voice. It was as if Roger's mere presence here was some sort of proof to Innes Lloyd that her words after Stephen's arrest had not been merely hot air.

Innes Lloyd's eyebrows went up. "Linda Matthews' brother?"

"That's right," Roger said.

"Well, well, this is an unexpected pleasure, Mr. Matthews." He held out his hand. "I'd heard you were in town, but I didn't anticipate meeting you here. Why, until yesterday I never even knew she had a brother."

"It seems not many people did," Roger said, as he shook hands.

Marjorie came forward. "Do please accept our sincere sympathy, Mr. Matthews."

"Thank you."

They both stood gazing at him, as if they didn't know what to make of him. Roger began to feel rather like an avant-garde painting at an exhibition.

Innes Lloyd gave his nervous little cough. "This is a rather unusual situation," he said awkwardly. "The defendant's wife. His solicitor. And the victim's brother."

"Yes, well, the circumstances are unusual." Alison stepped into the breach. "You're no doubt wondering what Mr. Matthews is doing here. Well he doesn't—" She broke off, then restarted. "I mustn't exaggerate. He's not yet convinced that Stephen is the man who killed his sister. He's been hoping to find some lead to whoever else she'd been seeing. I asked him to keep me informed of his progress."

"Indeed?" Innes Lloyd was now clearly fascinated. "Well, I find this most encouraging, from my client's point of view. May I ask if you are having any success, Mr. Matthews?"

"Some," Roger said.

"Do you know there *was* another man?" Marjorie asked.

"Oh yes. And we know that at the very least he was on the phone to her a few days before she died. Apparently he'd been making a bit of a pest of himself. We have a couple of clues to his identity, but they are rather vague."

"Of course, there's no indication that this man, whoever he may be, actually killed Linda?" Innes Lloyd asked.

"No, but if your client's story is true—and he tells it with considerable conviction—then this other man is the obvious suspect. Unless, that is, one can believe my sister admitted a strange man into her flat, when she was there alone—which I can't."

There was silence for some seconds while they digested this. Then Innes Lloyd said,

"Well naturally I wish you every success, Mr. Matthews. If there is anything I can do to help, please let me know."

"Thanks. I don't think there's anything at the moment." He paused. "Oh, there is one thing: my sister made a will shortly before she died."

Innes Lloyd nodded approvingly. "Very wise. I always advise everybody to make a will, however little they have to leave. The legal problems raised by intestacy—" He broke off.

"I'm sorry. I must not deliver a lecture."

"It may not be the sort of will you approve of," Roger said. "She got one of those do-it-yourself forms from a stationer's. It will be legal, though, won't it?"

The solicitor pursed his lips. "That depends. Is it properly signed and witnessed?"

"Oh yes."

"And is it simple?"

"Extremely: she merely says that she leaves everything to her brother—me."

"Then I would foresee no difficulties. If you'd like me to take a look at it . . ."

"Thank you. I'll bear it in mind."

Alison said, "Now, what can I get you both to drink?"

"Nothing for me at all, thank you, dear," Marjorie said. "We really mustn't stay long."

"Nor for me, thank you," Innes Lloyd added. "I really just wanted to speak to you for a couple of minutes to apprise you of the latest development. But perhaps Mr. Matthews has already done that."

Alison looked apprehensive. "What development?"

"About Stephen changing his story."

She gave a gasp. "No!"

"Sorry," Roger put in quickly. "I thought you knew."

Alison had gone pale. "Changed his story? But why—in what way? I don't understand."

"Now don't be alarmed," Innes Lloyd said soothingly. "I'll explain."

Alison listened intently while he did so. When he'd finished she just said quietly, "Oh, the idiot!"

"Don't be too hard on him. It *was* foolish but I doubt that it has done any real harm—not in view of the fact that he corrected his story so promptly. And I think we have to thank you for that, don't we Mr. Matthews?"

Roger shrugged. "I certainly told him that Chief Inspector Bidwell knew his original story couldn't be accurate and advised him to tell the truth. After speaking to you, of course."

"Well, he did both. And I'm much obliged."

In spite of the words, there seemed, however, a degree of coldness in the solicitor's voice, and Alison wondered if he was resentful of this stranger who had come to town and apparently had a greater influence on his client than he himself had.

It appeared that Roger, too, sensed this slight air of reserve. He said, "Of course, I'd had the benefit of being let into Chief Inspector Bidwell's confidence. Without breaking that confidence I was able to convince Stephen Grant that his original story was not going to be believed and would almost certainly lead to his conviction."

Alison said, "I really am very grateful." In *her* voice there was not the slightest coldness, but just the opposite; a fact that Marjorie clearly noted with interest.

There was a moment's somewhat awkward silence, which was broken by Marjorie saying, "You know about this attack on the barmaid last night?"

Again Alison stared. "No, I don't. In Fermouth?"

"Yes, it's in the *Advertizer.*"

"I haven't seen a paper this evening. What happened?"

"A man came up behind her as she was walking home and started to strangle her with some sort of scarf. He stopped and ran away, though, before he did any real harm."

"But, but that's exactly the same way Linda was attacked!" Alison turned excitedly to Roger. "Did you know about this?"

He nodded. "Yes, I'm afraid it's what we call a copycat crime. Someone —probably a disturbed teenager—who heard about the murder and tried to duplicate it. Though I doubt if he ever intended actually to kill. It's unlikely he'll try it again—or at least, not for some time."

Alison's eagerness subsided as he spoke. When he stopped she just said quietly, "I see."

"Cheer up," he said. "After all, you wouldn't really want there to be a homicidal maniac on the loose in town, would you?"

"No, of course not."

"It's just a question of any port in a storm, isn't it, dear?" Marjorie said brightly.

It was not an intelligent remark and seemed to embarrass her husband. As if to cover the silence that followed, he said hastily, "Well, let's hope the London papers don't link the two attacks. Once they get the idea that there's a mad strangler at large in Fermouth it'll be all over the front pages."

Alison stared at him. "I hadn't thought of that. I've been very relieved at how little there's been in the nationals—just short paragraphs on some of the inside pages. I'd been afraid they might splash it."

"Not a lot in it for them," Roger said.

She raised her eyebrows. "Beautiful blond model murdered? I should have thought they would lap it up."

He shrugged. "A model nobody's ever heard of. They'd obviously think the word was just a euphemism—especially given the way the *Advertizer* used it. There weren't actually quotation marks round it, but you could almost feel them hanging in the air above it, waiting to drop down each side of it, given half a chance." His voice was bitter.

Innes Lloyd said, "What's more, the press has been given to understand that the murderer is in custody. So there's no mystery element. To them it must sound just another sordid crime of passion, with no particular outside interest."

"Which I suppose is just what it is," Alison said.

There was silence for a few seconds before Roger drained his glass and put it down. "I must be getting along."

Innes Lloyd looked at his watch. "Yes, so must we."

"Oh, so soon?" Alison said. "You've only just arrived."

Though truth to tell, she wasn't sorry they were leaving; she was very tired and felt that tonight, in spite of everything, she might succeed in getting some sleep.

"Well, I've done what I came for," Innes Lloyd replied.

"But I haven't, yet," Marjorie put in. She turned to Alison. "My dear, I wanted to come with Bertrand, to ask you to spend the night, or as many nights as you like, with us. It must be dreadful for you here all alone by yourself. I should have asked you before, only like a fool it just didn't occur to me till today. As you know, we've got masses of rooms, so please say yes."

Alison looked at her in amazement. She was genuinely touched by the offer. She and Marjorie had never been close friends—friendly acquaintances would be a more accurate description—and there was absolutely no moral obligation upon her to do this.

She said, "Why, Marjorie, that's really very sweet of you. I do appreciate it."

"So you'll come?"

"No, I won't. Thank you all the same, it's a lovely thought, but at the moment I'm better off here on my own."

"Well, if you're quite sure . . ." Marjorie sounded doubtful. "The offer will stay open."

"I'll remember. And I may take you up on it later, if—if things get bad."

She showed them all out, said good night, waited till they drove off and then went back inside and locked the door. She returned to the sitting-room, poured herself another drink, sat down on the sofa and tucked her feet under her.

A pity, in a way, Roger Matthews had gone. She would have liked to talk to him some more. There were all sorts of things she wanted to ask him, ideas she wanted to put to him. However, it had obviously been better for him to leave with the Innes Lloyds. It was gone ten, and it would certainly have seemed strange to them if he'd stayed behind after they'd left.

No, it wouldn't have done at all. It would have been most unwise. No, not unwise—that was the wrong word. Indiscreet. Oh dear, that was worse. Inadvisable? Anyway, it would have looked bad.

The Innes Lloyds might have got absolutely the wrong idea of what was a purely working relationship between her and Roger.

Not that they could have been blamed if they had, because Roger Matthews really was rather attractive—in a way that grew on you quite slowly. He wasn't as handsome as Stephen, of course. But there was a lot of character in his face. And there was a strength about him, too, she felt sure, a moral strength which was rare. This was only a guess, really, but she was certain she was right. Of course, Stephen had a different kind of strength. She had told Roger that he was pliable. But that was really only kindness on his part—a reluctance to hurt people's feelings. It couldn't fairly be called weakness, whatever some people might think.

Oh dear, what was the matter with her? Why did she keep comparing Stephen with Roger? Such comparisons were absolutely irrelevant. Stephen was her husband. He was in jail for a murder she just knew he hadn't committed, and she had sworn to get him off.

Alison sighed. She had to face reality. There was at the moment nothing more she could do. And Innes Lloyd wasn't going to do anything. He might be entertaining more doubts about Stephen's guilt than he had at first. But he was quite content to let the case come to trial. Which was fair enough—he was a lawyer, after all.

However, it all meant that everything was now up to Roger. If he really put his mind to work tomorrow, there might yet be a chance of Stephen being saved.

Ironic if it was he, the brother of the victim, who brought about Stephen's release. Restored her husband to her and then went out of her life again for good.

Alison stretched, got to her feet, washed the glasses and went to bed.

CHAPTER ELEVEN

Roger slept better that night. But his sleep wasn't restful, for it was plagued by unpleasant dreams. They weren't nightmares, but they were eerie, imbued with a nebulous air of menace. Linda kept coming into them: she wasn't really dead, it had been a case of mistaken identity; then she was dead, after all, but she could still talk to him. "It wasn't your fault," she kept saying. Or perhaps: "It was your fault." He could never be quite sure.

He awoke at seven o'clock possessed by that vague sense of unreality that vivid dreams often induce. It was a glorious day, but this did nothing to dispel a deep depression that engulfed him.

It was as if for the first time he was really feeling Linda's death.

It was strange; he had been, as he had told Bidwell, angered by her murder. But it had been the dispassionate anger of a man who reads in the paper of some terrible injustice, and then turns the pages to laugh at the cartoons. He had felt detached—as though he were investigating the murder of a complete stranger. At moments he had felt quite light-hearted, had even managed the occasional wisecrack. He had denied—truthfully at the time—Bidwell's suggestion that he felt any guilt.

When it was that the change had started to come about in him he couldn't be sure; perhaps when he had read Linda's will. However, the change had gone so far that by last night he had come out—rather to his own surprise—with the confession that he'd been a lousy brother.

Well, at last he'd faced up to it—admitted his grief and his guilt. But this had had no cathartic effect whatever. This morning he felt absolutely wretched. He wouldn't be making any wisecracks today.

He washed, shaved, dressed, made himself some tea and sat at the kitchen table, drinking it and trying to decide on a plan of action for the day. However, no fresh ideas had come to him overnight. He needed a flash of inspiration, but inspiration had never seemed less likely to come.

Should he go and see Alison again? It was tempting. But he had no reason. What excuse could he give? Perhaps if he phoned her she would ask him over.

At that moment Roger heard the letter-box flap rattle and a second later came the faint thud of something landing on the hall mat. He got to his feet and went out. A nine by four manila envelope lay on the floor inside the front door. Probably only junk mail, he thought, as he bent to pick it up. There was something fairly bulky inside it. A free sample of toilet soap? Then he turned the envelope over and saw that the name, Ms. Linda Matthews, and the address were handwritten—in a large, careless, sprawling hand.

Roger got a fingernail under the flap and opened the envelope. He gave it a shake and the next moment was staring in amazed disbelief at the object that was lying on the palm of his left hand.

It was a small, fat, bright red, indexed notebook.

For long seconds Roger just stood there, staring down at his hand, unable immediately to take in what had happened. This, surely, had to be Linda's missing address book—the one Mrs. Hopkins had spoken of. But how—what . . . ?

In a fever of excitement he started flicking wildly through the pages. Then he got a grip on himself. This wasn't the way to do it. Besides, there might be something else in the envelope. He groped inside—and his fingers felt paper.

Gingerly, as though it were a wet tissue, Roger drew the paper out—two folded sheets of light blue writing vellum. Hardly breathing, holding the sheets by their corners, he opened them out. They were covered with the same large handwriting as on the envelope. His eyes began to fly over the sheets.

When he'd finished reading the letter, he drew a deep, deep breath. He was almost literally shaking with excitement. He went back to the kitchen, poured another cup of tea, sat down again and drank it slowly while reading the letter through more closely another three times. Then he turned his attention to the address book again and spent ten minutes methodically going through it. When he'd finished he got up, went to the telephone and put through a call to Scotland Yard. He spoke for about seven minutes, making notes much of the time. Having rung off, he put letter and address book back in the envelope, donned his jacket and left the flat in a hurry. His depression had vanished like a morning mist.

Detective Chief Inspector Bidwell was not in a good mood. There had been a break-in the previous night at the ostentatious home of a wealthy wholesale grocer, who also happened to be an influential councillor and ex-mayor of the borough. The sergeant who had taken his irate call at 1:30 A.M. had thought it important enough to ring up Bidwell. As the chief inspector had only got home at nine o'clock the previous evening, after a day spent mostly in a fruitless search for leads to the attacker of Tracy Bartlett, he was not best pleased. He got back to bed at three-thirty and was bleary-eyed, pale-faced and suffering from a headache when he arrived at police headquarters just after eight forty-five. He was not, therefore, especially delighted to be told that Roger was waiting to speak to him.

Nor were things helped when Roger's first words on seeing him were, "Oh, here you are at last. Thank heavens!"

Bidwell tightened his lips and reminded himself anew that Roger was the bereaved brother of a murder victim, who had been killed on his, Bidwell's, patch. He couldn't contrive a smile, but he did manage to say quietly and with reasonable politeness,

"Good morning. What can I do for you?"

"Nothing."

"Then if you don't mind, I'm really extremely busy—"

"It's what I can do for you."

"Oh?" Bidwell raised his eyebrows quizzically. He looked at Roger more closely. "You're different this morning. You're on to something, aren't you?"

Roger nodded. "You could say so."

"All right, let's have it."

For answer Roger took the manila envelope from his pocket and emptied the address book out onto Bidwell's desk.

The chief inspector's eyes bulged. "Great Scot! Is that your sister's?"

"It is."

"Where on earth did you get it?"

"It came through the post. In here."

Roger waved the envelope. Bidwell would have found his air of sheer self-satisfaction insufferable had it not been for the fact that it was somehow catching. He felt excitement growing within him. Something big was afoot.

"In the post?" he repeated, disbelievingly. "You'd better explain, p.d.q."

"This will explain."

For the second time Roger extracted the letter from its envelope. He unfolded it and laid the two sheets side by side on Bidwell's desk, moving various objects to hold the edges down.

"Better not touch it yet," he said. "You may want to dust it for prints."

Bidwell bent over and began to read. There was no address at the top and it was dated the previous day.

Dear Linda,

I was groping down between the side and arm of my settee last night, looking for an errant lipstick, when I came up with the enclosed. I remembered you had it out to look up somebody's number when you were here the other day and it must have slipped down there then. Hope you haven't been too lost without it.

It was lovely to see you, darling, and to hear all your news. May I take this opportunity to offer a bit of girl-to-girl advice? Forgive me, but I honestly don't think it's an awfully good idea to try and keep two men on the go at the same time—particularly when one of them has got a temper like you tell me Eddie Gilbert has—*and* is so jealous. All in all, he sounds quite a dangerous sort of character—madly attractive, no doubt, and exciting, but definitely not the sort of man who would take kindly to being played fast and loose with. It's all very well to keep pouring out your undying love to him, and all that sort of thing, but if he finds out you're seeing somebody else behind his back, you could be in real trouble. Steven sounds nice, but I'm sure he wouldn't be exactly pleased to learn about Gil, either. Fermouth's not a very big place, so just be careful.

No doubt you'll think it's rich for me, who's got her own love life in such a tangle from time to time, to be giving this sort of advice, but it's just that I don't want to see an old chum get in the same sort of mess as I have. So take it from One Who Knows. Sorry and all that, but have been wishing I could put my word in and this gives me a perfect opportunity. Anyway, hear endeth the first—and last—sermon.

Well, as you know, by the time you get this I'll be off in Foreign Parts. As I explained, not sure exactly how long for. You know how it is.

I'll be thinking about you, darling, and will phone you when I do eventually get back, to see how things have sorted themselves out.

Much love,

Toots.

Bidwell finished reading and looked up. All signs of tiredness had been miraculously wiped from his face. Instead, it was wearing an expression of almost beatific happiness.

He breathed just six words. "Eddie Gilbert . . . I might have guessed."

Roger nodded. "Not Phil or Bill. Gil."

"Yes. You know"—he tapped the letter—"this could be the break I've been looking for, for nearly four years—ever since Gilbert came to live here, just after he got out of Dartmoor."

"I thought you'd be pleased," Roger said modestly.

"You know all about him, do you?"

"Well, not *all*. I remembered the name, of course, but he went inside a bit before my time. So as soon as I'd read this I phoned the Yard and refreshed my memory."

Roger took out his notebook, opened it and glanced over the notes he'd made on the phone. "Not a nice man, Mr. Eddie Gilbert."

"Oh, but he is," Bidwell said.

Roger stared. "What's that? Armed robbery, GBH, demanding money with menaces—"

"I mean when you meet him, he's charming. Real gentleman. He's had most of the rich fools here eating out of his hand—especially the female ones. He contributes to all the local charities, gives Christmas parties for the orphanage kids, puts up silver cups for the golf tournaments and the school soccer teams. They're all quite sure he was wrongfully convicted. There was even talk of petitioning the Home Secretary to get his case reopened. But Gilbert himself put a stop to that. 'Very grateful, but didn't want to relive the horror of it all.' I ask you! He knows very well that a lot could come out now that never did at his trial."

"Let me see, how long did he serve?" Roger started to consult his notebook, but Bidwell answered him immediately.

"Ten years. His sentence was fifteen, but he got maximum remission."

"So he was convicted about fourteen years ago—when I was at university. How old is he now?"

Bidwell thought. "Forty-eight—nine."

"And they never recovered the proceeds of that bank job?"

"Not a penny. Four hundred and eighty thousand pounds they took. Gilbert must have had half of it. It was probably earning interest all the time he was inside."

Roger whistled. "He was lucky to get away with fifteen years."

"Well, they were never able to prove he had the cash—or that he'd planned the whole thing. He was only convicted of being one of the gang. I reckon the Yard were glad enough to put him away on that. He'd been a thorn in their side for years. I was friendly with quite a few of the Met boys. They knew Gilbert'd been behind at least five other big jobs. In addition, he was involved in the protection game—and every kind of racket you can think of since he was about eighteen. Started out as a persuader for Johnny Corelli. Good at his work—enjoyed it. Moved up in the organisation and branched out on his own when he was about twenty-three. For ten years if London had had a Public Enemy Number 1 he'd have been it."

"You've got it all at your fingertips, haven't you? I needn't have bothered to phone the Yard."

"I found out everything I could about him when he moved here. I didn't like having him on my patch. I've kept tabs ever since."

"I hadn't a clue he was in Fermouth. Is he still in the rackets?"

"Not to the same extent. He's made his pile. But he's keeping his hand in, all right."

"Examples?"

"The Pelican Club, our one and only gaming establishment. Nice place. Respectable. Owned for years by a chap called Willis. No archbishop, you understand, but not at all bad, on the whole. Never let the punters get in too deep. About three years ago Willis had an offer for the club, from a faceless sort of bloke called Brown. An accountant—who just happens to be Mrs. Gilbert's sister's husband's brother's cousin—or something like that. Also happens to be the accountant for a perfectly legitimate motor dealer's in London, which Gilbert owns. Willis turned down the offer—it was way below market value, and anyway he didn't want to sell. Then nasty things started happening to him. His office was broken into and wrecked. There was a fire at his house; oh, nothing too serious—the family was out at the time. The brakes of his car were put out of action; again no real danger—he discovered it almost as soon as he started moving, before he got up any speed—but he had a nasty little bump and was badly shaken. Then his daughter was terrified by a gang of louts on her way home from a disco. They didn't hurt her—didn't lay a finger on her—but for about twenty minutes they made her think they were going to. And at the same time as each of these incidents there came another offer from Mr. Brown—just increased by a tiny, nominal amount—a hundred pounds or so. At last Willis gave up. He sold out and moved away. I know all this, by the way, because he told me—unofficially. He didn't want any action taken: he just wanted me to *know*. There was no reason for him to lie, and besides I checked up on a few of the things he told me and found they tallied. Anyway, Mr. Brown is still titular owner of the Pelican; but he never comes near Fermouth. The club's run by a smoothie called de Sousa, who imposes virtually no credit limit—that is when the punter has any sizeable assets, or, say, is a youngster with a wealthy parent. And whose house do you think Mr. de Sousa calls on every week to make his report? No prizes for guessing right."

Roger nodded slowly. "Very interesting. It's the sort of thing we're used to in London—or any big city, I suppose. But Fermouth seems such a peaceful, law-abiding place."

"It always was."

"Where is this house of Gilbert's?"

"Called The Cedars. Big place, just outside town to the west. Oh, he's a real country gentleman, is Mr. Gilbert. Would you believe he keeps a domestic staff of four or five, full-time gardener, et cetera."

"Is Gilbert married?"

"Not now. His wife died at the end of last year. She'd been an invalid for years. In fact, that's the only good thing I've ever heard about him: he was a very devoted husband and looked after her extremely well. Of course, he wasn't faithful to her. But his girls didn't really mean anything to him, and he kept his affairs discreet."

"And Linda was one of those girls," Roger said grimly.

"Yes—the last."

"And you'd say he *could* have killed her—I mean from what you know of his character? Is he a possible strangler?"

"Well, he put a girl who'd been two-timing him in hospital once. This was before he came to Fermouth, but the leopard doesn't change its spots. *She* wouldn't bring charges—too scared. And you saw what your sister told this Toots girl about his temper and his being jealous. Yes, in a real rage he could have strangled her. No question."

Roger frowned. "There's only one thing: you said his girls didn't really mean anything to him—which hardly fits in with that sort of jealous rage."

Bidwell considered. "The answer to that is probably that he did genuinely love his wife. But, as I said, she was an invalid for years. So, he needed to go elsewhere for relaxation. Any pretty girl would do for that. But after his wife died, maybe he started looking round for a permanent relationship. Perhaps he genuinely fell for your sister. Or, it could equally be that he just couldn't take a girl throwing *him* over. I daresay that had never happened to him before."

"Yes, that's true—she *had* given him up, hadn't she?" Roger brightened noticeably.

"Certainly—if, Mrs. Hopkins is telling the truth. It was obviously *after* Linda visited this Toots girl that she decided she was in love with Grant—and told Gilbert so. She celebrated her decision by buying herself an engagement ring. But Gilbert wouldn't leave her alone. Yes, it all fits."

Roger smiled wanly. "Do I detect a slight change of emphasis in your approach to this case, Horace? The first real suspicion that we might have the wrong man?"

Bidwell shook his head slowly. "I'd love it to be Gilbert, I really would. But we've got to face it, the evidence against Grant is exactly the same today as it was yesterday. We already knew there was, or had been, another man in Linda's life. We just couldn't identify him. Now we can. But there still isn't an iota of evidence against him."

"Not yet," Roger said.

"Oh, agreed. We are most certainly going to look into this. It'll be lovely to give Gilbert a real grilling, even if it doesn't get anywhere. Wouldn't it be great if he lost his temper and attacked Freddie Primrose?"

For a moment Bidwell looked quite dreamy. Then he glanced down at his desk and his eye alighted again on the letter.

"What did you mean about dusting this for prints?" he asked.

Roger shrugged. "Well, it's a remote chance but if Toots should happen to have form, it may be the only way we could hope to trace her."

Bidwell scanned the letter again. "Oh, I see what you mean. Doesn't tell us much about her, does it?"

"Virtually nothing; not even her first name—'Toots' is obviously a nickname."

"What was the postmark?"

"Illegible—as they mostly are these days. Don't know if the lab boys could bring it out."

"We can try, if it becomes necessary. Not that I imagine it would be a great deal of help if we did get it."

"Probably not. Still, you never know, and if we *could* trace her she might be able to give us something useful. For instance, if Linda had told her Gilbert had actually threatened her . . ."

"Yes; of course, it seems she's out of the country by now."

"But she does intend to come back. I agree, it's no big deal, but it would be nice if we knew who she is, and I didn't want to risk obliterating any possible means, no matter how unlikely, of tracing her."

"Oh, I'm with you. I'll certainly get it dusted. Presumably she's not in the address book?"

"No—at least not under the name Toots. She might be there under her proper name—first or second—but there's no way of telling."

Bidwell peered at the address book closely, then picked it up, saying as he did so, "No point in trying to preserve prints on this sort of material. There won't be any."

"That's what I decided."

Bidwell started to flick through the pages. "Anything interesting in this?"

"Well, it *would* be interesting if it hadn't been so overshadowed by the letter."

"Gilbert in here?"

"Yes—under E. 'Eddie,' then 'Gilbert' in brackets. Just his number—no address. In fact, actually there aren't many addresses at all. She's used it mostly for phone numbers."

Bidwell turned the pages. "Ah—here we are: Eddie. That's great—additional proof he knew her."

"Odd, though, his fingerprints weren't anywhere in the flat," Roger said.

"Oh, Eddie'd take care about a thing like that." Bidwell continued to thumb through the address book.

Roger said, "There aren't a lot of Fermouth addresses or numbers in there. Apart from him, just Ma Hopkins, the doctor, and some commercial ones—hairdresser, beauty salon, garage and so on."

"What about Grant?"

"A London phone number—presumably his office. I imagine he didn't exactly encourage her to ring him at home. Actually the majority of entries are in London: model agencies, photographers, et cetera. There are literally scores of males known only by their first names. Not so many females. Oh, and no 'Phil' or 'Bill,' incidentally—which proves Ma Hopkins did mishear the name."

"Your number's in here, I see," Bidwell said.

Roger nodded. "And that's a number I only got three years ago. She must have looked it up in the directory and copied it into her book."

He turned away suddenly and looked out of the window. When he spoke it was almost to himself.

"Was she thinking of ringing me, I wonder? Why on earth didn't she? Was she ashamed? Did she think I'd despise her? Is that the impression I gave at our mother's funeral? If she'd just picked up the phone—just talked to me! Who knows? I might have been able to help her get sorted out. She might be alive today." He turned back to face the room.

"Now don't blame yourself," Bidwell said firmly. "It was she who cut herself off, not the other way round."

"I know that. It doesn't help a lot, though. She was my kid sister. Our parents are dead. I should have done more for her. As a policeman it would have been simple for me to have discovered her whereabouts, any time in the last five years. I could have phoned her, just asked how she was—shown I cared."

Bidwell pushed the address book back across the desk. "You could reconstruct her whole life over the last few years with that—given time. You'd probably find there was nothing you could have done."

Roger sighed. "Yes, daresay I could do that. Doubt if I ever will, though." Then he added quietly, "Unless it becomes really necessary."

He pocketed the book, then said more briskly, "Right, what's the next move?"

"Oo, I think a surprise call on friend Gilbert, don't you?"

"Count me in—if I'm welcome."

"The more the merrier. And let's make it as formal and impressive a visit as we can—you, me, Primrose, a uniformed driver and the biggest marked car I can get hold of. Might even use the siren going up the drive and skid to a halt outside the front door, like they do in the films."

Roger grinned. "Give him a fright, eh?"

"Oh, we won't frighten him. But we might make him feel a little uneasy."

CHAPTER TWELVE

Thirty minutes later, sitting next to Bidwell in the back of a three-litre Rover, Roger said,

"We'll look a bit silly if Gilbert's not in."

"He will be. I know he's not away—saw his Porsche in town last night, outside our best restaurant—and nobody drives that car but Eddie. Probably got in late, which means he'll sleep till about eleven."

Roger glanced at his watch. It wasn't yet nine-thirty.

"We'll be waking him up then," he said.

"Aw, what a shame," said Bidwell.

They left the town behind and were soon bowling along a winding country road flanked by tall hedges, heavy with foliage. It was a sparkling day with a fresh breeze, more like spring than late summer, and all the men felt their spirits rising. When hunting it was always exhilarating to feel you had the quarry—a worthwhile quarry, whom it would be an unalloyed delight to corner—in sight; and in the present case for Roger it would be even sweeter than usual. He wasn't deceiving himself that the hunt was over; Gilbert would undoubtedly take a lot of convicting. It might even turn out that, after all, he was innocent. Nonetheless this scent was a strong one; there was a chance that the end of the trail was in sight. For the moment that was enough.

Very soon Bidwell said, "This is it."

The car swept through a large pair of wrought-iron gates, standing open, and proceeded along a straight gravelled drive that bisected the well-clipped lawns of a neat but unimaginative garden of about half an acre. There were a few trees, but none of them cedars.

Roger was gazing at the house that lay ahead. He estimated it as late Victorian. It was of dark red brick and ivy covered. Although no mansion as to size, it was large enough to be impressive, probably having about eight bedrooms. It looked mellow, stable and secure. Outside the front door was standing a bright red Porsche.

"He *is* in," Bidwell said.

"Going to use the siren?"

"Better not." Bidwell sounded reluctant. "Still, a good blast on the horn wouldn't come amiss, Parsons," he added to the driver. "I mean, that *is* a cat I see in front of us, isn't it?"

In the mirror Roger saw Parsons grin. "Can't see it myself, sir, but I'm sure you're right."

And as he brought the Rover to a halt on the circular forecourt next to the Porsche he gave a long double blast.

"Right," Bidwell said, "let's make it nice and brisk and military looking. Slam the doors."

They jumped out and the doors slammed loudly in quick succession.

Bidwell cleared his throat and raised his voice almost to a shout. "Parsons—round to the back. Primrose—you come with Chief Inspector Matthews and me."

Parsons saluted and hurried round to the rear of the house. Bidwell led the others in a brisk march towards the front door.

Roger glanced up to the first floor and caught a glimpse of a dark face peering through the gap in some nearly drawn curtains. Then it was gone.

Bidwell mounted the steps to the door and exerted lengthy pressure on the bell-push. A faint and distant jangling could be heard.

When no reply was forthcoming in ten seconds Bidwell pressed again, even longer.

"Patience, patience," Roger murmured.

"Can't have the law kept waiting."

At last they heard the sound of a bolt being withdrawn.

"Ah, here we go," Bidwell muttered. "Better wait out here, Freddie. Stay near the door."

"Right, sir."

The door slowly opened and a woman stood there. In an acid voice she said, "Yes? What is it?"

Bidwell had his warrant card out and without waiting for an invitation marched straight in through the open doorway, saying, "Police officers," as he did so. Roger followed. The woman was forced to step back. There was a furious expression on her face.

Bidwell said sharply, "We wish to see Edward Gilbert."

"Mr. Gilbert is not available—"

Bidwell cut her off. "I said we wish to see Edward Gilbert, and I meant it. Now I know he's in. Get him. Tell him if he's not here within three minutes we'll come up and fetch him. Understand?"

She said icily, "This is intolerable behaviour."

Roger said soothingly, "It's very important we see Mr. Gilbert quickly. Now, will you please tell him?" She eyed him with fractionally less disfavour than Bidwell, and then said, "I will inquire if Mr. Gilbert wishes to see you. Wait here."

She turned, walked slowly and with an air of great dignity to the stairs, and disappeared up them.

Roger said softly, "Well, well, well. I'm seeing a new side to your character, Horace—tough, curt, overbearing. I didn't think you had it in you."

"You'd be surprised," Bidwell said.

"Enjoying yourself, aren't you?"

"Let's say I'm finding the experience not unsatisfying."

Roger glanced around him. The hall was square, high ceilinged and oak panelled. It had a highly polished parquet floor with several old but expensive-looking rugs scattered about. A grandfather clock stood against one wall. Above it was an oil portrait of a middle-aged man of forbidding aspect, attired in the uniform of a high-ranking Victorian army officer.

Facing him on the opposite wall was a mounted stag's head. On a low table stood an old-fashioned brass dinner gong. It all looked as traditional as if it had been created for a film set, but far more solid. Everything was spotlessly clean and there was a faint aroma of beeswax.

"Crime doesn't pay, eh?" Roger remarked.

Bidwell made a noise expressive of disgust. "Sickening, that's what it is."

"Does he own this place?"

"No; rents it from the heirs of old General Milburn, who died childless. Our friend Innes Lloyd is solicitor to the estate, and handled it all. I did hear, though, that Gilbert's been negotiating to buy the place, only they can't agree on a price."

"I see. Sad to think of it passing completely to a man like that."

"Sad? Makes me furious. When I think—"

Roger touched his arm. "She's coming back."

The woman descended the stairs and unhurriedly crossed the hall towards them. She said, "Mr. Gilbert's compliments, gentlemen, and he will be with you in *five* minutes. Will you kindly wait in the morning-room?"

She moved to one side of the hall, opened a door and stood aside. Bidwell hesitated for a second, then went into the room, Roger on his heels.

It would have been petty to cavil at the extra two minutes waiting time; nonetheless, Bidwell was conscious of suffering a slight defeat. But truth to tell he was finding it more and more difficult in these surroundings to maintain his overbearing manner. In a nightclub or a plush penthouse apartment it would have been different. But here the shades of innumerable Victorian and Edwardian butlers and footmen seemed to hover about him; here stout, red-faced village constables had stood and nervously tried to explain their failure to put a stop to the intolerable activities of the local poacher. Atmosphere in houses, Bidwell decided, was a very real thing.

The room he and Roger entered was filled with sunlight. It had a light grey carpet, chairs and a couch with cretonne covers. The woodwork was cream and there were a number of pot plants dotted around. Magazines were scattered about on low occasional tables. It looked a decidedly feminine room.

The woman was about to go out when Bidwell said to her,

"Wait, please. I'd like to speak to you for a moment." Even his voice was less peremptory in tone. After all, he told himself, he had nothing against this woman.

She turned back and regarded him impassively.

"Yes?" If a single word could be made to sound insolent she succeeded.

Roger regarded her closely for the first time. She was aged about forty-five, and was tall and angular. Her hair was black and drawn into a loose bun at the nape of her neck. Her features were good, the eyes deep, dark and watchful, her brows thick and straight, her nose rather long, her mouth and chin firm. Her skin, slightly swarthy, was unlined and seemed to be stretched tightly over high cheek-bones. She had something of the look of a gypsy about her, though her speech seemed educated. She was wearing a plain grey woollen dress with long sleeves, that looked as if it might have been worn any time in the last fifty years without appearing dated.

Bidwell said, "Might I know your name?"

"Trent."

"And your position in the household, Miss Trent?" He had already noticed she was not wearing a wedding ring.

"Housekeeper."

"I see. And have you worked for Mr. Gilbert long?"

"Since he moved here. I was previously employed by General Milburn."

Bidwell said, "I see" a second time. He was uncertain about the best way to proceed. Handled right, this woman might be able to give him useful information about Gilbert. The question was: just how loyal to her employer was she? If she had worked for the general, it might well be that she resented the new regime. It must be startlingly different from the old one.

Seeing his colleague's hesitation, Roger chipped in. "Would it be out of place to congratulate you on the condition of this house, Miss Trent? It's refreshing to see a place so lovingly cared for."

She didn't even look at him. "Thank you. But it is my job."

Roger felt snubbed. Bidwell said hurriedly, "General Milburn must have been a remarkable man."

Her eyebrows went up an eighth of an inch. "You knew him?"

"Not personally, but of course I knew *of* him. A fine soldier, I understand."

"No doubt. I did not serve under him in the army, so naturally I cannot say."

"No, no, of course not." Bidwell was finding this heavy going. "Was the general married?" he asked.

"His wife died ten years before he did."

"Oh, so both your employers have been widowed."

"Yes."

She was giving him not an iota of help. He decided to be a little bolder. "What sort of a woman was Mrs. Gilbert?"

"An invalid."

"Yes, so I understand. I'm sure she depended on you a great deal."

"Obviously. She depended on other people for almost everything."

"I imagine it was a burden to her husband."

"He gave no indication of considering it so. He was devoted."

"I'm sure. However, in one sense her death must have been a blessed relief."

"For her, do you mean, or for Mr. Gilbert, or for me?"

"I suppose I meant for him."

"You would have to ask him about that."

"Yes, of course. It's simply—well I may find it necessary to question him about that period and I was hoping to find out how he might react. I don't want to upset him unduly."

This was a patent lie, but Bidwell was becoming frustrated. There had to be a way to break down this woman's icy reserve. It wasn't vital that he did so, but he had a feeling there could be *something* here, if only he could dig it out.

"After all, you must know him better than anybody," he added persuasively.

She unbent fractionally. "Perhaps as well as anybody. I would not say better."

"Then can you help me?"

She considered. "I would say that Mrs. Gilbert's death was a great grief to him, but hardly a shock. He has got over it just to the extent you would expect a person to get over such an occurrence in eight months."

"So he's getting round and about again?"

"Naturally."

"Leading an active social life?"

He noticed the slightest tightening of her lips and there was a momentary pause before she answered. "H—he seems to. Not that he entertains a great deal."

"Out a lot, is he? In the evenings, especially?"

"It depends what you mean by a lot."

"Every night?"

"No."

"Five—six nights a week?"

"Not six—not often. Four perhaps, on average. I—I don't know. Ask him, not me. I can't help you. You shouldn't badger me in this way."

She was getting decidedly rattled. Bidwell ignored her protests and pressed on.

"So overall he'd be out more often in the evenings than in?"

"I suppose so. But—"

"What about last Monday?"

"I beg your pardon?"

"Last Monday. Was Mr. Gilbert out last Monday evening?"

"I don't remember."

"Oh, come on, Miss Trent! It was less than three days ago."

"Yes, come on, Katherine; tell the gentleman what he wants to know."

The voice came from the doorway. They all turned. A man was standing there—a tall man, wearing an exquisite blue silk dressing-gown and matching cravat.

So this was the notorious Eddie Gilbert; Roger surveyed him interestedly. Gilbert was big as well as tall, with shoulders square, like a prizefighter's—or an ex-prizefighter's, for he did not look healthy. Too much soft living was having its effect. He wasn't especially fat, but there was an indefinable flabbiness about him; there was a puffiness around the eyes, which were slightly bloodshot; his skin was pale. As for the rest, he had heavily greased black hair, brushed straight back from a rather shallow forehead. Lines were deeply etched into his face and he was heavily jowled. His mouth was large with the lips thick, and on his square chin was a stubble of black beard. The backs of his large hands were covered with hairs, and his fingers were short and stubby. There was a smile on his face, a smile that was trying hard to be casual, cynical and lightly amused, but only succeeded in looking decidedly menacing and wolf-like. He strolled into the room, sticking one hand into his dressing-gown pocket in a gesture of studied nonchalance, while with the other he drew on an exceptionally long cigarette.

Miss Trent addressed him in a flustered, agitated manner. "He's been asking all sorts of questions about you. I didn't know what to say."

"Oh, always tell the police the truth, Katherine. That's my policy."

He had a surprisingly cultured accent, with only the slightest east London twang in it. He had, Roger suspected, made a conscious effort to get rid of it and was obviously in every respect trying—with a fair degree of success—to live up to his new image.

Miss Trent was looking at her employer uncertainly. He nodded at her in an encouraging manner. "Go on: answer the inspector."

He seemed to have a calming influence on her. She swallowed and turned back to Bidwell. "Mr. Gilbert was out on Monday."

"What time did he go out?"

"A little after six o'clock."

"And got home at what time?"

"I don't know." Her face was grim.

Gilbert spoke again. "It was after you'd gone to bed, wasn't it, Katherine? I couldn't tell you the time myself, Inspector. It's a bit hazy. The early hours. That's about the best I can do."

Miss Trent said to Bidwell, "Will that be all?" There was an appreciable pause before she added "sir."

"Yes—thank you."

She cast a sidelong glance at Gilbert, who ignored her; then she walked slowly from the room. She pulled the door behind her, but Roger noticed that she did not fully close it.

There was silence for a moment. Gilbert looked from one of the two men to the other. Then he said to Bidwell, "You I know. Bidwell, isn't it?"

"That's right. This is—"

"Wait a minute—let me guess." He looked at Roger again, through narrowed eyes. "Matthews: am I right?"

Roger raised his eyebrows. "Correct."

"Linda's brother. Heard you were in town. Very sorry to hear about what happened. She was a nice girl."

A little taken aback, Roger just said, "Thanks." Not for the first time during the case, a conversation was taking not at all the course he had planned.

"I suppose it's about her death that you've called," Gilbert said. "I can't think why. There's nothing I can tell you."

"Where were you on Monday evening?" Bidwell said abruptly.

"I'm not obliged to answer that."

"You'd be advised to."

"Well, we'll see. I might oblige—if you ask me nicely. First, I want to know why you're asking. I thought you'd got the guy that did it. Grant, isn't it? Stephen Grant?"

In spite of years of training, Bidwell couldn't hold back a short intake of breath. "How did you know that?" he asked harshly.

Gilbert gave a chuckle—a deep, rich chuckle of genuine amusement and satisfaction. "There's very little goes on in Fermouth I don't know about, Bidwell. Very little."

Roger said quietly, "Then tell us who killed my sister."

"Didn't Grant?"

"He may have done. There's an element of doubt."

Gilbert gave a shrug. "Sorry, I've heard no whispers." He stared hard at Bidwell. "Surely you don't think it may have been me?"

"If I do, it might stop me thinking it if you told me where you were Monday evening."

Gilbert waved him down, with an arrogant, impatient gesture of the hand holding the cigarette. Bidwell was breathing heavily. Roger could understand his obvious hatred of the man.

Gilbert said, "You know I'd had nothing to do with Linda for seven—nearly eight—months."

"That's not our information."

Gilbert looked at him sharply. "You serious?"

"Perfectly serious. We have it on good authority that you were in regular touch with her and were on the phone to her as recently as last Wednesday."

Gilbert laughed. "That's a load of—" He broke off. "You know, Bidwell, when I moved here I decided I'd clean up my language. The way I spoke—it didn't go with this place, if you follow. There are some words I've never used since. You nearly made me break my rule. But I won't. I'll be polite. And say that is a load of garbage."

"We've got a witness, Mr. Gilbert."

"Witness? How can somebody witness both ends of a phone call?"

"We have somebody who was with Miss Matthews when she was speaking to you."

"And how does this somebody know it was me at the other end?"

"In the first place he or she heard Linda address you as Gil and—"

Gilbert cut in. "As what?"

"Gil."

"I've never been called 'Gil' in my life!"

"Maybe not by anybody else, but Linda—"

"No!" This came out in a sudden roar. Gilbert's face was starting to redden. Then he clearly made a great effort to get his temper under control, walked to the nearest table and ground his cigarette out into an ashtray.

Roger decided it was time he took some part in the proceedings. He said, "I really don't see why you should get so het up about a mere name, Mr. Gilbert. Linda always used diminutives and nicknames, even when nobody else did. She called Grant 'Steve,' when even his wife called him 'Stephen.' "

Gilbert turned slowly to face him. This time when he spoke his voice was ominously quiet. "And she called me 'Eddie.' All right?"

Roger shrugged. "If you say so."

Bidwell said, "Well, what she called you is a bit irrelevant. The fact is we also have a letter to Linda from a girl-friend—actually written the day after Linda died—following up a visit Linda must have made to her within the last week or so. In it she warns Linda against playing you fast and loose, and advises her to stop seeing Grant. She mentions your full name— Eddie Gilbert. And that was in response to what Linda had told her."

Gilbert stared at him without speaking. Then he let out his breath through his teeth while slowly shaking his head from side to side in a show of utter disbelief.

He said, "Well, I know I have enemies, who'd do anything to get at me —but I thought at least they'd do a better job of a frame than this! Phone calls! Letters! Unknown girl-friends! Sexless witnesses to one end of a phone call! It's pathetic! Listen, Bidwell, if you want to get me, you're going to have to do better than this."

He went right up to the chief inspector and spoke into his face. "Listen: you produce witnesses who have seen Linda and me together any time in the last seven months, giving times and places, and let me answer them. Because they'll be liars."

"All right," Roger said, "say we believe you. You don't deny you *did* know her."

"No, I've never tried to."

"It was you brought her to Fermouth?"

"Yeah, if you must know, it was."

"Mind telling me about it?"

"Why should I?"

"I was her brother. And I am trying to get at the truth about her death. I'm not convinced Grant killed her—though he may have done. You say you didn't. Then don't you want to know who did?"

"Sure I do, but—"

"Then why won't you cooperate?"

"I'll cooperate. But how can knowing what happened between her and me twelve months ago help you?"

"Let me be the judge of that."

Roger waited, almost seeing Gilbert's mind slowly ticking over. Of course, the other's question was perfectly legitimate, and the fact was that the information he was asking for would almost certainly *not* be of any help. However, up to now they'd got nothing out of Gilbert. If they could loosen him up a little, simply get him talking about Linda—then he just might give something away. By appealing to him in this manner, almost inviting him to cooperate in the investigation, simply as an interested party, Roger was making it very hard for him to refuse. And once you got a suspect talking it was often difficult for him to stop.

At last Gilbert gave a shrug. "Well, all right. I don't mind doing anything I can to help. As I said, she was a nice girl. What do you want to know?"

"When did you first meet her?"

"Would have been—oh, around March last year."

"Where?"

"Party up in Chelsea."

"And you started going out together?"

"Not regular, at first. I didn't get up to town all that often. But I'd usually ring her when I was planning a trip, and we'd get together."

"And eventually you invited her to come and live in Fermouth?"

"That's right. I told her I knew of this nice flat she could have. I gave her a grand towards her expenses. Beginning of July that was."

"And you paid her rent?"

"For a bit."

"Your wife was alive then, I believe."

"Yeah—but she was an invalid, wasn't she? I cared for her—ask anyone. But I needed to get away from the house now and then. I needed a bit of relaxation. I don't like just going out and picking up girls. I wanted one I could rely on always to be there. Linda suited me fine. She never had moods. She didn't want to be taken on the town. As long as she had her regular allowance, and the odd present thrown in as an extra, she was quite happy."

"And this went on how long?"

"Till my wife died in December. I didn't see Linda for a couple of weeks. Didn't feel I wanted to, somehow. But I went around eventually early in January. And she'd changed."

"How do you mean?"

"Well, she seemed to think now my wife was gone things were going to be different. She thought we were going to be a regular twosome—that I'd take her around, introduce her to people—have her out here to live eventually. Course, she didn't *say* all that straight out. But it came out gradual that's how her mind was working."

"And you weren't having any?"

"Look, I told you I liked her. But I made it clear from the start that living together wasn't on. Besides, now my wife was gone I had no intention of tying myself down again. I'd loved Sonia, but I wasn't going to let myself fall for any other bird. I was going to keep it casual—play the field."

"So you dropped Linda?" Roger's voice was hard.

"No, I did not. She dropped me. She made it clear she wasn't prepared to be just one of a crowd. So that was that."

"Must have been a new experience for you to be given the push by a girl," Roger said quietly. "Quite a blow to your ego that must have been."

Gilbert chuckled. He had recovered his temper and seemed genuinely amused. "If you think, sonny, that after the life I've led and the put-downs I've suffered I've got any ego left, you don't know much. I been given the push by plenty of birds in my time. This was no big deal. I told Linda that was OK by me, that I'd pay her rent for another month—which I was under no obligation to do, by the way—but that after that she was on her own. She said that was fair enough and we parted on quite good terms. I've never spoken to her since."

"Not even on the phone?"

"Not even on the phone. I caught a glimpse of her once in High Street about six or eight weeks ago. I was surprised she was still in town— thought she'd have gone back to London. That was the last time I saw her. Then on Tuesday I saw in the paper she'd been murdered and that a guy'd been detained. I made it my business to find out his name—just in case it was anybody I knew; but it wasn't. And that's it."

Roger was silent. He didn't believe Gilbert's story, but with no way of disproving it, he couldn't just call the man a liar. The only real evidence against him lay in Linda's inferred remarks to her friend "Toots"; but there was no proof of the truth of those remarks—nor indeed, in Toots' absence, any way of confirming they had ever been uttered. It made no sense either that Linda should lie about the affair to her friend; but on the other hand, no case that would stand up in court could be based on the letter alone. Roger foresaw long and laborious hours working through the names in the address book, trying to find somebody who knew Toots' true identity. A real live girl, willing to testify as to what Linda had told her, would be a very different kettle of fish from a mere letter signed by a nickname. Though even if they did succeed in identifying her, they still had to trace her and then get her back to England and into court, willing to give evidence against a notorious racketeer. It was a daunting prospect.

All these thoughts flashed through Roger's mind in a few seconds. There was now nothing more he could say to Gilbert about his story. However, there was still one faint chance of getting something out of the interview; and that was if Gilbert could produce no alibi for Monday evening. He was not, as he had said, obliged to do so; and even a refusal to give any information at all about how he'd spent the period would certainly not justify an arrest. All the same, such behaviour *would* look suspicious; and it would, if nothing else, be a psychological boost to the case against him.

As if he had read Roger's thoughts, Bidwell, who had been content to stand back and observe during the last five minutes, now returned to the attack.

"Right, Mr. Gilbert," he said, "that's all very interesting, and if it's true I can see no reason why you should refuse to tell us what you were doing at the time Linda was killed. I suppose, though, that you still decline?"

Gilbert shook his head. "No," he replied.

Both policemen looked at him sharply and Bidwell said, "No? You mean you won't tell us—you do decline?"

"No—I mean I will tell you—I don't decline."

"But you said earlier—"

"I know what I said earlier, Bidwell: that I wasn't obliged to tell you, but I might do so, if you asked me nicely. You haven't asked me nicely. But on the other hand I did tell Matthews I'd cooperate. I want to see this particular rat nailed, and it won't help giving you guys the run-around. So, here it is: I spent the whole of Monday evening with a girl."

"Oh yes? Name?"

"Carol Venning. She's got a flat at 17 Norwood Drive. I picked her up about half six and took her to an early dinner at the Carlton. We left there about seven forty-five and got back to her place just before eight. I stayed there until one in the morning, when I drove home. No, neither of us slipped out of the flat at all and there was nobody else present. We were alone there together the whole time. No one phoned. That's all I can tell you."

Bidwell and Roger exchanged glances. The story had the hallmarks of a prearranged alibi: simple, straightforward, dependent solely on the word of one person; but—providing she kept her head—virtually impossible to break down.

Bidwell took refuge in his favourite "I see." Then he asked, "And what did you do all the evening?"

Gilbert grinned. "Getting rather personal now, aren't we?"

"Murder is rather personal, Mr. Gilbert."

"All right, all right. Well, we watched TV part of the time."

"What—precisely?"

"A movie."

"Called?"

"Rambo II."

"That wasn't on television last Monday!"

"Didn't say it was—had it on the video."

"Surely it hasn't been released on video yet."

"No—not officially." Gilbert threw up his hands in mock horror. "Oh dear! Have I confessed to some sort of crime? Watching a pirated video tape? Lock me up, Inspector—I plead guilty."

Bidwell ignored the facetiousness. "I suppose you could describe the plot of this film?"

"What plot? You obviously haven't seen it. I could tell you what it's about—more or less."

"You still got the tape?"

"No—left it with her."

"So she'll have it?"

"Might do. Might have given it away. Or recorded over it. I told her I didn't want to see it again."

"You left there at 1 A.M. you say?"

"About that."

"Wouldn't it have been more convenient to stay the rest of the night there?"

"No, I like my own bed—and this house. Don't sleep away oftener than I have to these days."

"Then why not ask your friends back here?"

"I don't ask girls like Carol back here. Never have and never will. I got respect for my wife's memory."

He grinned suddenly. "Besides, what would Trent say? She thinks I'm playing cards with the boys when I'm out late."

Roger glanced at the door. It was still open about half an inch, but he could see no movement outside.

"She doesn't really approve even of that, of course," Gilbert was continuing, "but she can accept it. If I brought a bird home, she'd probably quit—and that'd be a pity, because she's good at her job. She fancies me, you know; so I keep her sweet by smiling at her a lot and letting her think it's only the memory of Sonia that stops me proposing. Not that that's any of your business, but now you know why I was at Carol's flat all Monday evening, OK?"

Gilbert was now very casual, very much in charge of the situation, enjoying showing off his skill at handling women, perfectly confident of his security. The king of the castle, Roger thought grimly. And there was nothing they could do about it.

He glanced at Bidwell who, although keeping a short rein on his temper, was plainly fuming, his lips drawn tight and his eyes dark.

The chief inspector met his gaze, gave the barest of shrugs, then looked at Gilbert.

"We will, of course, look into what—" he began, but Gilbert interrupted. "This Stephen Grant? He married?"

"Yes."

"Well, you give his wife a message from me. Tell her if there's anything I can do for her she's to get in touch with me. I know it can be pretty tough for a woman, when her man's inside. I'd like to help her, if I can."

Roger saw Bidwell open his mouth to utter what was no doubt going to be a curt retort, and he cut in quickly,

"Thank you. I'll pass the message on personally."

"Yes, you do that, son. Now, if that's everything . . ."

"For the moment," Bidwell said.

"Then I'll see you out."

He strolled with them to the front door and opened it. Primrose still standing outside suddenly sprang to life.

"Well, nice to have seen you, boys," Gilbert said airily. "Call again some time." He paused, then added, "Oh, and one more thing: give my love to Carol."

CHAPTER THIRTEEN

On the way back to town in the car Bidwell said shortly, "Well what do you make of him?"

"Formidable."

"He is, isn't he?" Bidwell sounded gratified at the reaction. Like the owner of an old fairground freak show it was clear he hadn't wanted his prize exhibit to be taken lightly.

"Charming at times, as you said, but quite cold underneath it. I wouldn't like to have him as an enemy, especially if I was a civilian."

"He expected us."

"Oh yes. He'd be bound to realise we'd get on to his connection with Linda sooner or later."

"How much of his story did you believe?"

"Quite a lot of it," Roger said. "All the first part. But, of course, I don't believe he hadn't been in touch with her since January."

"Well, the Toots letter makes it clear that that was a lie."

"I know. But on the other hand, I'm still not happy about *none* of his prints being found anywhere in the flat. If he was calling there regularly for all those months he'd put them in an awful lot of places."

Bidwell frowned. "What exactly are you saying?"

"Frankly, I don't know. But there is a contradiction. If he *was* telling the truth and hadn't been there since January—*then* there would have been time for his prints to have been wiped off every surface in the course of normal cleaning and handling. It did occur to me that perhaps he hadn't actually *been* there (until the night of the murder) but had only been speaking to Linda on the phone. But if he was still interested enough to keep ringing her—as we know from Mrs. H. that he was—the only reason he wouldn't go to the flat would be if Linda didn't want him there—that she had in fact chucked him. That would agree with her comments to Hopkins about people being unreasonable and thinking they own you. The trouble is it doesn't tie up with what she seems to have told Toots about pouring out her undying love to him, worrying in case he found out about Grant and so on."

Bidwell looked pensive. "We agreed she must have chucked Gilbert *after* she visited Toots, but we don't know just when that visit took place."

"Toots referred to it as being 'the other day.' That, surely, can't be more than two weeks ago. If Gilbert had been visiting there regularly as recently as that, could every one of his prints, from every object he might have touched in every room, have been completely obliterated?"

"Yes, I think they could," Bidwell replied. "Remember, Gilbert's been a professional criminal all his adult life. With a creep like that it's second nature to be careful about prints—to handle as few things as possible and remember those he does touch—even when he's not on a job. Add to that the fact that Mrs. Hopkins, if the state of the flat is anything to go by, is a very conscientious worker. Given both those things, I reckon he could have been calling there for months and still be able to get rid of all his dabs in ten minutes."

Roger nodded thoughtfully. "Yes, maybe you're right. No doubt I'm making too much of it."

"I'll tell you something else," Bidwell added. "The mere fact that we found *none* of his prints is suspicious in itself. After all, he's admitted he was a regular visitor there at one time. Therefore, it would be quite *natural* for his prints to be there. So, he must have dusted everything he touched. Why do that if he's innocent?"

He sighed. "Pity you can't arrest a man because his prints *weren't* found at the scene of a crime."

Roger smiled. "Do I take it you now definitely plump for Gilbert as the murderer?"

Bidwell was silent for a few seconds. Then he said, "I've got to guard against wishful thinking. Gilbert's the type of the killer. I can easily imagine him doing it—much easier than I can Grant. On the other hand, apart from that purely negative point of the absence of prints, there's not an iota of evidence against Gilbert. And *still* the case against Grant stands where it was at the beginning. It's not been weakened. Without something concrete against Gilbert I don't see how I can possibly let Grant go."

"Well, you haven't got very long to make up your mind."

"I know—don't remind me."

"Perhaps Gilbert's alibi won't hold up," Roger said hopefully.

"It will. We'll find the girl primed to perfection. Want to bet?"

"No thanks," said Roger.

Seventeen Norwood Drive was a small block of flats, less modern and less exclusive than Albany Court. A notice board in the entrance hall indicated that Carol Venning's apartment was on the second floor. There was no lift and Bidwell and Roger climbed the stairs.

Roger rang the bell and the door was answered almost immediately by a girl of about twenty, with long, flaming red hair. She was wearing shiny skin-tight scarlet trousers, with a shocking pink off-the-shoulder top and purple high-heeled shoes. Her fingernails were varnished deep crimson. She had a funny little snub nose and a too-large mouth, giving her a rather comical look and making it hard not to smile at her. However, she had very large, though rather vacant, hazel eyes; and these, helped by impeccable make-up and a good figure, enabled her to present an attractive appearance—though Roger wished she had been fitted with a knob that would enable him to turn the colour down.

Bidwell had his warrant card out again. "Miss Carol Venning? We're police officers. My name is Bidwell—"

Without waiting for him to finish she gave a flashing smile, revealing a perfect set of very white teeth. "Oh yes, do come in." She stood back, opening the door wide. "Please go into the lounge."

They passed through a tiny hallway into a sitting-room that presented an absolute contrast to the one in Linda's flat. It was crowded with furniture; ornaments, framed photos, china animals, knick-knacks of every kind covered all available surfaces. Travel posters dotted the walls. Yet there was a cheap shabbiness about the place. The carpet was wearing thin in several places, and so were the chair covers. The only expensive-looking objects in the room, both probably rented, were a television set with a 24-inch screen which was wired up to a video recorder. On the table next to the video was one cassette, its label clearly showing the title *Rambo II.*

Carol Venning followed them into the room, closing the door behind her. "Would you care for some coffee?" she asked.

Bidwell would have loved a cup, but he said formally, "Not just now, thank you, Miss. We wanted to ask you about—"

"Do please sit down."

"Oh thank you."

They both seated themselves on rather low chairs; Carol sat on an upright one opposite Bidwell and smiled encouragingly.

Bidwell cleared his throat. "We wanted to ask you about last Monday evening, Miss Venning—"

Again she interrupted before he could finish. "Oh yes. Well, I spent the entire evening in the company of a very dear friend of mine, Mr. Eddie Gilbert. We went to dinner at the Carlton restaurant, leaving here at six-thirty and arriving back at seven forty-five. We were here together the rest of the evening. We watched a film, I remember—that one, over there, *Rambo II.* And did various other things. Eddie eventually left at one o'clock the next morning. Was that everything you wished to know?" She gazed at him innocently.

Bidwell was breathing heavily. "You've been well primed, Miss Venning," he said.

Her eyes widened. "I beg your pardon? I don't understand."

"Are you aware of the maximum penalty for providing someone with a false alibi for the time of a major crime?"

She shook her head. "No. What is it?"

"Oh—er," Bidwell was a little taken aback. "Well, er, I'm not quite sure offhand exactly what it is. But I assure you, it's regarded as a very serious offence."

"Yes, I'm sure it must be."

"And you'd be willing to swear in court to what you've just told us?"

"Oh yes. Except for the odd two or three minutes—when I went to the powder room at the restaurant, and when I was in the kitchen here making coffee; things like that—we were together the whole time."

"I see." There was a depth of feeling in Bidwell's use of the phrase this time.

Roger said, "Known Gil a long time, have you?"

She gave a slight start, as if she'd forgotten his presence, and turned to face him; for a moment her expression seemed genuinely puzzled.

"Who?"

"Gil. Mr. Gilbert."

"Oh—Eddie." Her face cleared. "Well, not so as you'd say *very* long. But we hit it off from the start, you might say. We have such a lot in common."

"You mean art, music, literature—that sort of thing?"

"Er—yes. Sort of."

"You don't call him 'Gil,' though?"

"No. Is it a nickname?"

"Well, I thought it was. Isn't it?"

"I've never heard him called anything but Eddie."

"Ah, my mistake. Generous sort of chap, isn't he?"

"Eddie? Oh yes."

"Best of everything when you go out with him, I expect."

"Yes, that's right. He's a real gentleman."

"I'm sure. Did you know Linda Matthews?"

For a moment the sudden switch of direction took her aback, but she quickly recovered. "Not to speak to. I think I'd seen her around."

"Oh, where?"

"I think it was the hairdresser's. I remember seeing this really beautiful girl there once and asking one of the assistants who she was."

"She wasn't beautiful after she'd been strangled, Miss Venning. Have you ever seen a girl who's been strangled?"

A small shudder rippled through her slender body. "Certainly not."

"Well, I hope you never do. Trouble is a man who kills once can always kill again. It's easier the second time, easier still the third—and so on."

She looked a little startled. "But you've got him, haven't you?"

"We're holding somebody for questioning, but he hasn't been charged. There's certainly a degree of doubt. The killer might well be walking around free at this moment."

She gave a little laugh and a slight nervous shake of her shoulders. "Well, all I know is that he isn't Eddie. That's for sure."

"She was waiting for us," Bidwell said bitterly back in the car. "Every word rehearsed, down to the last comma."

Roger shrugged. "Well, it was only what we expected. No doubt Gilbert was on the phone to her before we were out of his drive."

"Yes, but she needn't have been so blatant about it. She could at least have pretended to have been surprised to see us—and to think for a few seconds about how she'd spent Monday evening. The way she behaved to us—it showed utter contempt."

Roger smiled. "That may not have been deliberate. She might be incapable of acting—and scared to death of making a mistake."

"Perhaps. And I suppose we should be glad in a way—if she'd really been with Gilbert, she wouldn't have to act—or be in any danger of making a mistake. All she'd have to do was tell the truth."

"Oh, her story's phoney, of course," Roger said, "but short of third degree I don't see any way of making her admit it. And even if we did prove she wasn't with Gilbert that evening, that's still no proof he killed Linda."

Bidwell stared at him. "Don't say *you* have doubts now?"

Roger shook his head. "Not really. Everything fits. I'm just thinking of nailing him. Frankly, as long as he keeps cool I don't see how we're going to do it."

While Roger and Bidwell were calling on Gilbert, Alison again visited Stephen in the police cells. She found him depressed—resigned now to being charged with the murder. Alison could find no way of cheering him up; conversation became more and more difficult and she didn't stay long.

Afterwards she went to see Innes Lloyd. He was kindly and tried to be reassuring, but was not very successful. They both knew that with every passing minute it was becoming increasingly likely Stephen would be charged. And once he were charged, irrespective of the eventual outcome, his connection with Linda would be public knowledge. And this Alison dreaded.

She drove home, filled with foreboding. In spite of all her brave words about getting Stephen off, it seemed she'd almost certainly failed. Was there anything else she could do, even at this eleventh hour? She racked her brains, but without result.

She hadn't been home ten minutes when she heard a ring at the front door. She hurried to open it. It was Roger.

Alison didn't waste time on greetings. "Any news?" she asked eagerly.

"Actually—yes," he said.

"Really? What?"

"May I come in?"

"Oh yes, of course."

She could hardly wait to get him settled in the same beautifully comfortable chair before saying urgently, "Well?"

"The address book's turned up."

"You've found it? That's marvellous! Where?"

"It arrived by post this morning at the flat."

She stared. "I don't understand."

"It had been sent on from London by some girl-friend of Linda's. Seems Linda had been visiting her a week or two ago and had accidentally dropped the book down inside a sofa. The girl just found it yesterday. She plainly didn't know Linda was dead."

Alison's eyes were wide. "I see. So the murderer didn't take it, after all?"

"No."

"Well, does it help? Does it identify Phil?"

"Not precisely. But the letter did."

Her face was bewildered. "What letter?"

"One from this girl—enclosed with the book. Linda had obviously been pouring out the story of her love life, and the letter warns her against two-timing this man friend—whom she'd apparently described as being dangerous and having a bad temper. Seems his name is Gil."

Alison gave a gasp. "Not Phil—or Bill?"

"No."

"Well, go on. Do you know anything more than that?"

"Oh yes. His full name is Eddie Gilbert."

"Eddie Gilbert?" Alison's hands rose to her mouth.

"Yes. Do you know him?"

"Not personally. But of course I know *of* him. I think everybody in Fermouth does. I remember the talk when he moved to the neighbourhood —shortly after we did. And Bertrand Innes Lloyd pointed him out to Stephen and me once, at the golf club dinner-dance. I think he acts for the people who own the house Gilbert lives in and has been trying to buy. Bertrand has to go out there quite often, and he hates doing so."

"Yes, I'm not surprised."

Alison sat down slowly. Her expression was dazed. "I can't take this in properly. This *will* mean Stephen's release, won't it?"

"Well, not right away."

"But why not—if Eddie Gilbert's been arrested?"

"He hasn't, Mrs. Grant."

"But he's going to be surely."

"Not immediately, I'm afraid."

She had gone pale. He hated doing this to her, but there was no choice. He said, "Bidwell and I called on him first thing this morning. He admits he was seeing Linda up to about January, but not since then."

"But that's a lie—if this letter . . ."

"I know. However, there's more. Unfortunately, he's got an alibi for the time of Linda's murder."

"Alibi? So what? He would have, wouldn't he? I mean, it's got to be bogus."

"No doubt. But it's a question of proving it."

She said angrily, "Oh, but this is absurd! You have a lead to a known criminal and you just leave him at large. Simply because somebody—another crook, I suppose—says that he was with him, you let him go on walking around scot free!"

He shrugged. "It's unavoidable. As I said, we've got no proof."

"But that doesn't stop you arresting someone! You didn't have any *real* proof against Stephen. There's nothing to stop you taking Gilbert in for questioning, is there?"

"Well in the first place, it's Bidwell's case, not mine, but I do go along with him fully on this. Technically we could pull Gilbert in—"

"Then you could grill him—break down his alibi."

"I doubt that very much. He's extremely tough. He's been grilled many times. He knows all the tricks. And we wouldn't be able to hold him. There's not an iota of evidence against him—no prints or any forensic evidence, no witnesses, nothing. Just the word of one girl, whom we can't even trace, because she didn't give her full name or even her address—and who's almost certainly gone abroad by now anyway. It's a useful lead against Gilbert—a start. And the good thing about it is that Bidwell now believes Gilbert did it."

"But he's going to hold on to Stephen, all the same?"

"I don't know. I don't think *he* knows yet."

"But how can he charge a man if he thinks somebody else is guilty?"

"It's not a question of what he *thinks.* It's a question of—"

"—of evidence, I know," she finished.

"Exactly. And the evidence against Stephen is precisely what it has been from the first."

She was silent, obviously wrapped in thought, staring down at the carpet.

Roger said, "Oh, by the way, Gilbert sent you a message."

She looked up, an expression of amazement on her face. "Sent *me* a message?"

"Yes: he said if there's anything he can do for you to get in touch with him. He knows it can be tough for a woman when her man's inside and he'd like to help if he can."

Alison's eyes blazed. "What utter arrogance! He's just laughing at us."

"He was laughing at the police certainly. He may have been sincere about you. There could be some vestigial conscience there somewhere."

"I don't believe it." She frowned. "Tell me: what sort of evidence would they need to arrest Gilbert?"

Roger pursed his lips. "Difficult to say offhand. Obviously fingerprints or an eyewitness are out of the question, but—"

She interrupted. "Suppose it could be proved his alibi was false?"

"Well, that would certainly be a step in the right direction. We couldn't get a *conviction* on that alone, but it would be grounds for pulling him in."

"Who's giving him the alibi?"

"A girl."

"A girl? That's good."

He looked puzzled. "Why?"

"Never mind. Tell me about her."

"Her name is Carol Venning. The story they both tell is that they went out to dinner at the Carlton, got back to her flat at seven forty-five, and then spent the entire evening there together, until Gilbert left at one the next morning."

"And what *makes* you sure she's lying?"

"Oh, she had it much too pat—all the times at her fingertips. And she came out with it parrot-fashion, as though she'd learnt it by heart."

"You think Gilbert paid her to lie for him?"

"Let's just say I wouldn't be a bit surprised."

Alison gave a satisfied nod. "Good, that's all I wanted to know."

"I wish you'd explain why you keep saying good."

"Because I can speak to another woman easier than a man; and if I know she was lying, then perhaps I can persuade her to tell the truth."

He said hastily, "Now Mrs. Grant, I don't think—"

"What harm can it do?"

"I don't know. But it could be dangerous. If Gilbert found out—"

"Oh, nonsense! What's he going to do? Put out a contract on me because I pay a visit to one of his girl-friends?"

"I don't think it's wise. I must ask you—"

"The answer's no. Now, you can't stop me. I'm a free citizen. If I want to pay a private call on another woman there's nothing you can do about it. And I'm going to. I've done virtually nothing to get Stephen out of this mess so far and this might just be my last chance. Now, are you going to tell me the girl's address, or do I have to look it up?"

CHAPTER FOURTEEN

Alison walked briskly along Norwood Drive, hesitated a moment outside number 17—then walked on. She felt decidedly nervous; even though she kept telling herself not to be a fool—that there was no cause to fear. If she followed the course she had led Roger Matthews to suppose she would follow, she would just stride boldly up to Carol Venning's door and ring the bell.

But it wasn't as easy as that. She had already been to the flat once—had gone right up to the door. But she had not rang the bell; in fact, she had positively scuttled away again, actually hoping the girl wouldn't come out and spot her. She was just thankful Roger hadn't been there to see her behaviour.

This time things had to be different. All the same, so much could go wrong. Yet everything depended on Carol's reaction. If it wasn't what Alison hoped it would be, the last chance of getting Stephen out of this jam would be gone. So, she told herself, she must wait, and get herself fully prepared for whatever the girl did.

Alison halted about thirty yards past the entrance to the building and took several deep breaths . . .

A girl came out of number 17 and looked up and down the road both ways. Alison stared at her. That had to be Carol Venning. She had been given a reluctant but good description of the girl by Roger, and there could not be two young women in one block with that shade of hair—and that taste in clothes. Carol was attired today in a tight, short-skirted dress in broad diagonal stripes of yellow and emerald green, with a blue and white polka-dot jacket over it. She had on very high-heeled orange shoes and a large white straw hat, adorned with multicoloured artificial flowers. To complete the ensemble she was carrying a big red plastic handbag.

Alison started to walk towards the girl. As she drew close, Carol looked in her direction—not at her but along the road, past her. The expression in her eyes was one of intense excitement and anticipation.

At that moment a taxi came along the road. Carol raised a hand, it pulled up by her, she opened the rear door and got in. She must have phoned for it, Alison decided, but been unable to contain her impatience long enough to wait in her apartment until it arrived.

The taxi drove off in the direction of the town centre. Alison stared after it for not more than a couple of seconds. Then she ran to her own car, which was parked just twenty yards down the road. She jumped in and roared off in pursuit of the taxi. She *had* to know where Carol went and what she did.

It was about two and a half hours later that Roger, sitting writing at the flat, was disturbed by the ringing of the telephone.

He lifted the receiver. "Matthews."

"It's Alison Grant."

"Oh, hallo."

"Listen—I went to see the Venning girl."

"Oh yes? Any luck?"

"I didn't actually speak to her. I was plucking up courage to go in, when she came out. And there was such an expression on her face—pleased as punch, almost gloating—that I followed her. She took a taxi to the shops. Mr. Matthews—for the last couple of hours she's been spending money like water."

"Is that so?" Roger said interestedly. "On what exactly?"

"Everything. Mostly clothes. She's bought dresses and coats and shoes and undies, and an evening gown—ghastly taste, most of it, but expensive. She's bought several pieces of very nice jewellery. And she's ordered a carpet and curtains for her flat. I should think altogether she must have spent twelve or thirteen hundred pounds. In about two hours."

Roger whistled. "You've been near her all the time, then?"

"Yes, I've been following her into the shops. I've had to buy all sorts of little things I don't want at all. She'd have noticed me for sure if she hadn't been so taken up with her purchases. But the really interesting point is this: she paid for everything in cash. She had a great bundle of ten pound notes in her bag. When she'd finished—or couldn't think of anything else to buy—she went into a Building Society and made quite a big deposit, again all in tenners. It looked at least five hundred pounds. And she still had some cash left. I think she must have had two thousand pounds with her when she started out."

Roger thought hard for a moment. He said, "This is really very intriguing, Mrs. Grant—and highly suggestive. You say the girl has ended her spree now?"

"Yes, eventually she got another taxi, and had the driver take her round the shops to collect her parcels—she'd left most of them for collection. Then he took her home. He helped her in with everything—they had to make three trips inside—and when she came back down the last time for the final few parcels she gave him a tip of ten pounds."

"It's obvious what you're thinking, Mrs. Grant—that this was the pay-off money from Gilbert."

"Well, it has to be that, doesn't it?"

"It certainly seems likely."

"What I was thinking was—if you could come and see her now you'd probably find the stuff spread all over the flat. She'd have a job to explain where she got the money. Perhaps you could make her say how she came by it."

"She'd be under no obligation to tell me."

"I know, but with your experience—I mean, couldn't you—what do you call it—lean on her a bit?"

He chuckled. "You're beginning to sound quite ruthless."

"I'm beginning to *feel* ruthless."

"You said I could *come* and see her now. Where are you?"

"In a phone box a few yards down the road from her flat. I thought, you see, that I could come in with you and tell her I'd been watching her all the afternoon. It might shake her up—get her nervous."

Roger hesitated. It was true that when interviewing a woman he liked always to have another woman present. Usually, he took a WPC along with him on such occasions. But here in Fermouth he had no authority to commandeer the services of one. The correct procedure now would be to contact Bidwell, pass on Alison Grant's message and leave the matter to him. But he knew Bidwell, together with Primrose, was out on another case. Roger was acquainted with nobody else on the local force. To locate another officer, senior enough to authorise an official call on Carol, and assign a WPC to accompany him would take time; especially as he would have to explain at length just what the situation was . . .

He came to a decision.

"Listen—as you know, I've got no authority in Fermouth. This is Bidwell's case. So I can only call on this girl unofficially—in my private capacity as Linda's brother."

"That's OK. If you like I'll do most of the talking—I feel up to it now. But I would like some moral support—and a witness."

"Very well," he said, "stay there and I'll be with you in a quarter of an hour."

For the second time that day Roger rang the doorbell of Carol Venning's flat. Alison, beside him, looked pale but determined.

Carol Venning opened the door. Rather disconcertingly, for three-thirty in the afternoon, she was wearing a full-length evening gown. It was mauve in some chiffony material, seemed mostly composed of frills and flounces and was covered in sequins. With it she was wearing maroon elbow-length gloves. She looked radiant, like a sixteen year old off to her first ball.

She beamed at them. "Yes?" Then she glanced down at herself and said in mock confusion, "Oh, do excuse me. I've only just bought this. What do you think?" She gave a gay little pirouette in the doorway.

"Charming," Roger said.

Alison said, "Miss Venning, could you spare us a few minutes?"

"What about?"

"It's in connection with the murder of Linda Matthews."

The smile partially faded from Carol's face, leaving it fixed in a kind of half smirk. She peered at them, and they realised for the first time that she was short-sighted. Probably too vain to wear glasses, Alison thought.

At that moment Carol recognised Roger. "You're the co—policeman who was here this morning."

"That's right, but I'm not here as a policeman now. I'm here unofficially."

"I—I don't understand."

"You see, I also happen to be Linda Matthews' brother."

The hazel eyes widened in alarm. "Oh," she said.

Alison said, "May we come in?"

Carol switched her gaze to her. "Who are you?"

"This lady is the wife of the man who's being held for Linda's murder," Roger told her.

Carol gave a little intake of breath, baring her white teeth. "You're— you're Stephen Grant's wife?"

Alison winced. Did everyone in this town know of Stephen's arrest?

She said coldly, "Yes."

"What do you want? I don't know noth—anything. I got nothing to say."

"But I have something to say to you," Alison answered firmly.

And without waiting for an invitation, she marched forward into the flat, virtually brushing the girl aside.

" 'Ere, what you doing? You can't come in like that—" Carol turned and trotted after her, leaving Roger to follow, closing the door behind him.

Alison gazed round the sitting-room, before saying to Roger. "See what I mean?"

He nodded. There were parcels and packages and carriers everywhere— on the floor, on the chairs, on the table. Only one had so far been opened— the box that had contained the evening gown—which was clearly Carol's especial pride. Sheets of tissue paper, plus the clothes she had been wearing, were strewn on the floor.

"You certainly didn't exaggerate, Mrs. Grant," he said.

"Look, what *is* this? 'Oo do you think you are, barging in 'ere, like you owned the place? Now get out, 'fore I call the cops. The real cops, that is." Carol stared angrily at Roger.

"Yes, you do that, Miss Venning," he said pleasantly. "I'm sure the local police would be very interested to see this little lot." He gestured round the room.

"What d'you mean?" Carol was highly indignant. "You suggestin' it's nicked? That's slander, that is. I paid for everythin' in this room—cash. Not even H.P."

"We know you did," Alison told her. "I saw you buy it all. I followed you all the time you were out."

Carol went pale. "You followed me? What for?"

"I wanted to see just how much you spent. It was well over a thousand pounds. Then you banked a lot more. And you came home with some left. You took about two thousand pounds out with you. I want to know where you got it."

"You got a cheek!" Carol's voice was rising to a squeak. "What's that to you. Mind your own bl—"

"I'll tell you what it is to me: my husband is in prison for a crime he didn't commit—"

"So you say!"

"Not only me. Even Chief Inspector Bidwell thinks he's innocent now. The enquiry's going to go on."

"So? What's that to me? Look, will you get out of here?"

"I think you know who really killed Linda. And I think you got that money for your part in covering it up."

There was an abrupt silence in the room. Carol didn't answer—didn't move. All the colour had now drained from her face. Roger suddenly felt sorry for her. Five minutes ago she had been so full of the joy of her new possessions. She probably hadn't had much enjoyment in her life. Pushed around. Exploited . . .

Then he hardened his heart. This girl was trying to save a man who had slowly choked the life out of his sister. That evening dress—and all her other purchases—were the proceeds of this. She deserved no sympathy at all.

At last Carol spoke. Her shrill indignation had gone. In its place was a cold anger. She said, very quietly, but with a voice full of passion, "That's a wicked lie."

Alison was plainly unimpressed. "Then where did you get it?"

"That's my business." Her lips were drawn into a tight line. There was not the slightest sign of her weakening.

Roger said, "Strictly speaking that's true, Miss Venning. You don't have to answer us. But if you don't there'll almost certainly come a time when you do have to answer somebody else."

"What do you mean?"

"In court, Miss Venning. You won't be able to say 'that's my business' then. If you refuse to answer you'll be sent to prison for contempt. And you *will* end up in court, I promise you. On the other hand, tell the truth now and I'll see to it that no charges are brought against you."

She said sullenly, "I 'aven't done nothing wrong." With every sentence her English was becoming more slovenly, the painstakingly acquired approximation to educated speech deserting her. To Alison it was a hopeful sign.

"Haven't you?" Roger said. "Well, if you can convince us of that you have nothing to worry about."

"I dunno what it is you want me to say."

"Tell us where you got that two thousand."

"I—I—" Her eyes flashed. "I drew it out the bank."

"And then put five hundred back again?"

"Yeah. Well, I didn' know 'ow much I was goin' to want, did I?"

"We can check on that, you know. Are you sure you don't want to change your story first? We won't hold it against you. I know you're nervous and a bit muddled. Anyone can make a mistake."

She moistened her lips. Then she said slowly, "Yeah, that's right. I was confused. I didn't get it from the bank. I won it on the 'orses."

"Oh, really?" Roger said.

"Yeah. I went to the races with a friend yesterday. Brighton. Had a bit of luck. A double I had a tenner on. The first won at ten to one and the second at twenty to one."

"My, my, you were lucky. What were the names of the horses?"

"I—I don't remember. I just liked the look of them. I pointed them out to my friend and asked him to put ten pounds on for me."

"And you don't recall their numbers either, I suppose?"

"That's right."

"Or the colours?"

"No."

"Well, what races were they in? First and second on the card? Second and third? You *must* remember that."

Again Carol was silent. Her eyes, while never alighting directly on Alison or Roger were flicking round, as if seeking to draw inspiration from some object in the room. At last she said—and there was now a note of desperation in her voice, "One was the second race."

Suddenly Roger gave a roar of anger. "Oh, come on, Miss Venning! I follow racing. I happen to know that the second race at Brighton yesterday was won by the favourite—which started at six to four on."

Carol Venning burst into tears. She flung herself down onto the sofa and let her head fall on her arms. In a muffled voice, between sobs, she gasped, "You're a beast. You're both beasts! Why can't you leave a girl alone? It's been so wonderful! I've never 'ad that much money in my life. Now you've spoilt everythink!"

Roger realised he'd gone too far. Feeling as powerless as most men faced by this particular phenomenon, he cast a helpless glance at Alison.

She stepped forward and spoke quietly in his ear. "Do you mind waiting outside, on the landing?"

"You sure?"

She nodded.

He whispered, "No rough stuff."

"No, of course not!" she hissed. "Don't be stupid!"

He grinned and slipped out of the flat. Alison sat down on the sofa, next to the still sobbing girl, and put a hand on her shoulder.

"Listen, Carol," she said gently. "We don't want to bully you. We're only trying to get at the truth. A girl's been murdered. A girl very much like you in lots of ways."

"Well, I didn' kill 'er," Carol sobbed.

In spite of everything, Alison couldn't suppress a smile. But her voice was still grave and low as she said, "I know that, dear; but we have to face the fact that with a man like that at large none of us is safe. Now I know my husband didn't do it. I've been married to him for twelve years and I know. He's quite incapable of strangling anybody. He just happened to be the one to discover the body. Don't you see, we've got to find out who really did it?"

Carol sat up and looked at her. Two big mascara-tinted tears were running down her face. She delicately brushed them away with her little fingers, leaving a grey smudge on each cheek-bone.

She said throatily, "Don't see what this 'as to do with my money."

Summoning up every ounce of her persuasive powers, Alison said, "Carol, there's nobody here but us two. Won't you tell me where you got that money? Please. I give you my solemn promise, I won't tell anybody unless you say I can. If I broke my word, you could always deny what you'd said, so why should I? I assure you I haven't got a microphone hidden on me. You can search me if you like. So please. Just between the two of us."

Carol sniffed. She seemed to have been impressed by Alison's speech.

"Well, it was a present, wasn't it?" she said.

"A present? From whom?"

"Dunno. It was anonymous."

"Oh, surely—"

"It's the truth, I tell you!" Carol sounded indignant.

"All right, I believe you," Alison assured her hastily. "But could you explain?"

"It came this morning. After those coppers left. Somebody pushed it through the letter-box in a big brown envelope. And I didn't see who it was. It might 'ave been there quarter of an hour before I saw it."

"But wasn't there a note with it, or anything?"

"Yeah, a short one. But it weren't signed."

"What did it say?"

Carol screwed up her eyes. "Not much. Just somethink like, *Thanks very much. Have fun.*"

"Have you still got it?"

"No, I burnt it."

"Blast," said Alison.

"I got the envelope. But it's just an ordinary one."

Carol was talking more freely now. One could even believe she was enjoying herself. She was obviously flattered by Alison's intense interest and by the weight that was being attached to her every word.

Alison said, "And you don't know who sent it?"

"No, I don't *know.*" There was the slightest emphasis on the last word.

"But you know it was a *man.* You said *he.*"

Carol looked at her pityingly. "Why would a woman ever give me a present?"

"But weren't you surprised to get a sum like that out of the blue?"

"Well, yes. I mean, I expected somethink. But nothin' like that much."

"Why did you expect to get something?"

"Well, it was just a sort of thank you—for not letting somebody down."

"He'd promised you a present?"

"No, not *promised.* He said I wouldn't regret it."

"I see. We *are* talking about Eddie Gilbert, aren't we?"

Carol gave a reluctant nod.

"He implied he'd give you a present for saying he was here the time Linda was murdered?"

"Well, more for *not* saying 'ee *wasn't.* He knew I could make things nasty for him, see, if I chose. I could tell the cops he wasn't 'ere that night. Or I could put the black on him. Course, I never would—I'd be much too scared. But 'ee didn't know that. So 'ee wanted to be sure and keep me sweet."

"And you're quite certain that two thousand pounds was from him?"

"Course it was."

"Even though it was anonymous?"

"Well." Carol fidgeted a little. "I—I didn' tell the *'xact* truth about that. The note wasn't signed properly, but he did put his initials—E.G."

Alison took a deep breath of satisfaction. She said, "Carol—would you tell this to the police?"

"No, I couldn't do that."

"Are you in love with Eddie?"

Carol's eyes dropped. "Well, not as you'd say reelly *in love.*" She paused. "I—I'm kind of scared of 'im, actually."

"So you'd really be glad not to see him again?"

"Well, I dunno." Carol looked doubtful. "He can be generous. As you can see." She gestured at her purchases. "And 'ee's quite nice to me. Sometimes." She sighed. "Suppose, on the 'ole, though, I'd be better off without 'im. I don't reckon he cares two 'oots for me, reelly. Only uses me, he does."

"Telling the police what you've told me would help to get rid of him."

"He'd half kill me."

"He couldn't if he was in jail."

"He's got friends, though. They'd get me. I ain't goin' to end up with me face slashed."

"The police would protect you. I know they would. Chief Inspector Bidwell is desperate to get Eddie put away."

Carol's brows narrowed. "I don't see how me telling the cops about Eddie's present is going to put 'im inside. Bribing a witness or somethink —that'd be it, would it?"

"That would be part of it—part of the whole case against him."

Carol thought deeply. At last she seemed to reach a decision. "I ain't going to frame him," she said decidedly.

"No, of course not. Just tell the truth."

"I ain't going back on our agreement, I ain't going to say 'ee wasn't here Monday night."

"Oh, but—"

"He was here. OK?" Carol spoke firmly.

Alison looked at her hard. She could tell the girl was going to be adamant on this point. She gave a slight shrug.

"OK," she said resignedly, "have it your way."

"But I don't mind telling about the money. If people want to draw their own conclusions, they can."

"Right," Alison said, "I'll go and get Mr. Matthews."

She went out to the landing. Roger, standing gazing ruminatively out of a window, spun round as he heard her.

"Any luck?" he asked.

"Well, we haven't broken his alibi. But I think we're getting somewhere."

Quickly she explained the gist of her conversation with Carol.

When she had finished he gave a nod of intense satisfaction.

"That's great," he said. "Better than I expected. Now let's go back in and get her statement down on paper quickly—before she changes her mind."

Ten minutes later Roger carefully folded up the paper on which Carol had, at his dictation, carefully written out and signed her statement, before he had added his signature as witness.

He said, "I'd like to get this transferred to an official typewritten statement as soon as possible, Miss Venning, so you will be asked to sign again when that's been done."

She gave a little shrug. "I suppose now I've signed it once it won't make any difference how many more times I do it."

"You've done the right thing, Miss Venning. You won't regret it."

"I 'ope not, that's all. I'm awful scared, though, honest. Eddie blacked me eye once—for much less than this."

"You should have brought charges."

"Against him? You're joking."

"Nobody should put up with that sort of thing," Roger said.

"Aw, it's all right. I'm used to it. People've been knocking me about all me life. Starting with me mum. Reckon there must be somethink about me what gets on people's nerves."

"Well, you don't have to be frightened now: Gilbert will have been arrested before anyone other than us and the local police know about this." He tapped his pocket.

"Got friends though, hasn't he?" Her English, Alison noticed, was slowly improving again.

"No," Roger said.

She looked at him sharply. "What?"

"This idea that every big racketeer has loyal friends who'll always take vengeance on anybody who shops their mate: it's a myth. Racketeers don't have friends—only associates, who are invariably delighted to see them go inside. Nonetheless, I'm certain the police will give you protection. In fact, I'm so confident of that, that if I'm wrong, *I'll* pay for the hire of a private detective to protect you. OK?"

She gave a watery smile. "OK."

"Now I must go and find Chief Inspector Bidwell," Roger said. "Coming, Mrs. Grant?"

Alison hesitated. "I don't think there's much more I can do at the moment; so I was wondering, if I'm welcome here, whether Miss Venning could find me a cup of tea?"

"Yes, course I could. Be a pleasure." Carol sounded surprised.

"You see, what I really want," Alison said, "is a chance to look at all these lovely new things you've bought. From what I've seen so far I'm green with envy."

Carol's eyes widened. "Oo, that'd be lovely. I've got some fancy cakes here, too. I'll just go and put the kettle on."

She disappeared into the kitchen. Alison was aware of Roger gazing at her quizzically.

She said defensively, "Well, we did spoil her big day. And she's scared. And she *did* make a statement. And there's nothing more miserable than having a lot of new things and no one to show them to."

He smiled. "And this from the 'ruthless' lady who wanted me to 'lean on' the girl."

CHAPTER FIFTEEN

Bidwell looked up from reading Carol Venning's statement. There was an expression of deep satisfaction on his face. "This is lovely," he said.

"Glad to have given you pleasure," Roger replied. "Sorry about going to see her off my own bat like that, without talking to you first, but—"

"Don't apologise," Bidwell interrupted. "This statement is worth a lot."

"Well, of course, it's not proof of his guilt," Roger said. "She still gives him an alibi."

"But no innocent person pays someone to back up a *genuine* alibi! Even the thickest jury could see that."

"I suppose there's no actual proof the money came from Gilbert—even though *we* know it did."

"Oh, there's proof enough. The girl says he promised she wouldn't regret backing him up, and that the note with the money was signed E.G. Gilbert will claim those are lies; or she might even go back on it, when it comes to testifying. The fact remains—she *did* receive the money. Her spending spree, which is something that *can* be established, proves that. Who else is going to send her two grand, in cash, out of the blue? The Chancellor of the Exchequer—just out of the goodness of his heart? Or the notorious ex-gangster who she's just alibied for the time of a murder? And, incidentally, any jury in this part of the world is bound to know he's an ex-gangster, even though we aren't allowed to mention previous convictions.

No, I grant you it's circumstantial evidence; but it's some of the strongest circumstantial evidence I've seen in a long time."

"And grounds enough for bringing Gilbert in?"

Bidwell absently picked up his pipe and tapped his teeth with the mouthpiece. Then he said, "I reckon that if Carol Venning will say all this in court, *and* if we can locate Toots, and she confirms what it seems your sister told her about Gilbert—then we'll get a conviction for murder."

"That's not quite what I asked," Roger said. "Without Toots—and without any other evidence, apart from Carol's statement—will you arrest Gilbert?"

Bidwell started slowly to pack his pipe. He said, "Once I confront Gilbert with this statement, I'm morally bound to arrest him—you promised the girl that."

Roger nodded. "Yes—sorry. Maybe I went too far there."

"No, I don't think so. We must retain her confidence. That way she may eventually come round all the way and admit the alibi was false, too. Trouble is, if I tell Gilbert about her statement, he might *admit* sending the money—say it was just a gift, a thank-you present for all the many happy hours spent in her company. OK—we know that's nonsense, but there's nothing in law that says it has to be false."

"You're saying we really do need something more?"

"Yes, I am. Oh, this statement is marvellous. It'll make devastating confirmatory evidence, once we get to court. But as I see it, its chief value lies in the fact that we are now morally certain of Eddie's guilt."

"And of Grant's innocence," Roger murmured.

Bidwell gave an unexpected smile. "All right, you win: and of Grant's innocence."

"His wife will be over the moon. May I ring her now and let her know?"

"Do you mind waiting just a bit longer?"

Then, as Roger looked surprised, he added, "You see, we still have a few hours before we need release Grant. Now Gilbert obviously hears about everything that goes on in this town. As long as he knows we're still holding Grant he'll feel fairly confident. But once he knows we've released him, he'll be on his guard. I want to avoid that as long as possible."

"Well, it's up to you, of course, Horace. But what can happen in so short a time to change the situation?"

"I don't know. But I'm a great believer in never throwing away even the slightest advantage. It's surprising the things that can turn up. Besides, I might even apply for permission to hold Grant for a final twenty-four hours. Ninety-six is the absolute maximum, remember, and that's not over till tomorrow night."

"I see. Bit hard on the Grants, though."

"Well, that would be a last resort. But at least let's hang on to the time we've got anyway."

"As you wish. However, I'd better let Mrs. Grant know about your reaction to Carol's statement—I'd never have got it without her."

Bidwell stood up. "Use this phone. I've got some things to do."

He left the room. Roger lifted the receiver and dialled the Grant's number. Alison's voice answered after about thirty seconds. She sounded a little breathless.

"Back from your tea party, then," he said.

"Oh, hallo. Yes, just this moment. I heard the phone in the porch."

"Did you succeed in cheering up Carol?"

"I think so. As a matter of fact, I'm rather afraid I've made a friend for life."

He chuckled. "Good for you."

"Well, it wasn't intended. But, you know, although she's what my grandmother would have called common as dirt, and isn't very intelligent, she's really very nice—good-natured and generous."

"That type often are."

"She actually insisted on giving me one of the jumpers she'd bought, which I happened to admire—about the only thing there I did *sincerely* admire. I was quite touched. And, by the way, she was very impressed by you—particularly when I told her you had a university degree in psychology. She seems to have taken quite a shine to you."

"Oh, help."

"But I just told you, she's very nice."

"Maybe. But, as *my* grandmother would have said, 'Don't touch her—you don't know where she's been.' "

Alison laughed. There was a constrained pause. They'd been making conversation, both avoiding the matter uppermost in their minds. Eventually she asked, "Did you—did you see Mr. Bidwell?"

"I did."

"What did he say?"

"He was very impressed. He agrees it certainly proves you-know-who faked his alibi."

"And—Stephen: he's going to be released—?"

Roger could sense her holding her breath for the answer. Hating himself, he said, "Not at the moment."

He heard her give a gasp of dismay. "But why not? Surely, he must know now Stephen didn't do it?"

Roger longed to say, Yes, of course he does. Stephen will be free very soon. But he was mindful of his position in the town. He had already pushed his nose into this case far more than was proper. The local man had taken it very well. But Roger was not going to push his luck now. So he hardened his heart and said deliberately,

"There's still no proof Carol's friend is the murderer. He might have faked an alibi for some other reason."

She was silent for such a long time that he was about to speak again when in a flat voice she said, "I understand."

"I'm sorry," Roger said.

"It's not your fault. So Gil—er, Carol's friend is not going to be investigated any further?"

"Oh, I wouldn't assume that. Things like this are always followed up."

"But Stephen *will* be charged?"

"I don't know," Roger lied.

There was another long pause before Alison said, "Well, thank you for letting me know."

"That was the least I could do. Now look, I know this is a stupid thing that everyone says but do try not to worry. I'll keep in touch, and if there are any developments I'll let you know immediately."

"Yes, do that, please. Goodbye."

"Goodbye, Mrs. Grant."

He put down the receiver. She had sounded absolutely shattered by his news. He told himself that by tomorrow at the latest her ordeal would be over. But it didn't make him feel much better. Twenty-four hours could be an awfully long time.

It was about half an hour later and Roger was back at the flat, his feet up, and a drink in his hand, when the phone rang. He gave a groan, heaved himself to his feet and answered.

"It's Alison Grant," said the familiar voice.

"Oh, hallo."

"Listen, could you come over here for a bit?"

"What—now?"

"If it's not inconvenient. I have an idea I want to put to you."

"Well, yes, I could make it. But I'm not sure it's very wise to—to . . ." He tailed off, not able to express himself.

"I'll cook you a meal, if you'd care for it," she said.

He smiled. "Bribing a police officer, Mrs. Grant? This could be serious."

"Look, forget it," she said, her voice suddenly cold. "I wasn't trying to corrupt you."

He said hastily, "No, please—I didn't mean that. It was just a weak joke. I'd like to come very much. Actually, I was just wondering what to do for the evening."

"Good," she said briskly. "As soon as you like, then."

"Right. See you." He rang off, suddenly feeling a lot more cheerful. Wise it might not be. But it was certainly going to be a lot pleasanter than sitting here for the next few hours.

CHAPTER SIXTEEN

"Well," Roger said lazily, "what's this great idea you want to talk about?"

He was sunk deep in what he was coming to think of as 'his' chair. He felt relaxed and contented. A pleasant aroma was wafting in from the direction of the kitchen. Somehow it was like coming home.

Alison was wandering round the room, making small unnecessary adjustments to ornaments. She seemed on edge. Not surprising, he told himself. Now suddenly she turned and sat down facing him. "I don't say it's a great idea. But you and Inspector Bidwell went to see Gilbert and got nothing out of him. Then you both went to see Carol and the same thing applied. Right?"

He nodded, puzzled.

"But when you and *I* went to see her, we *did* get somewhere."

"Certainly we did; or *you* did."

"I couldn't have done it on my own. Well—why shouldn't we try the same thing with Gilbert?"

Roger stared. "You mean go and see him together?"

"Yes."

He shook his head firmly. "Oh no."

"But why not?"

"For one thing, he's a different kettle of fish from Carol: he's a very dangerous man. Secondly, there was a good reason for visiting Carol—and quickly—after you'd seen her shopping spree; there's no such reason for calling on Gilbert. What excuse could you give?"

"You told me he offered to help me. I'll take him up on it."

"And ask him to do what?"

"Help me find the real killer."

"And what do you think he's going to say?"

"I don't know, but it'll put him in a very tricky position, won't it? Who knows what he might say? He might give himself away."

"Extremely unlikely. No, I'm sorry, Mrs. Grant, it's just not on. At least, not as far as I'm concerned. What you do is up to you, but I must say I think you'd be extremely foolish even to consider—"

From the hall came the sound of the telephone bell. Roger broke off and with a murmur of apology Alison got to her feet and went out.

Roger was thinking hard. Somehow he had to talk her out of this crazy scheme. He only hoped she wasn't going to be too stubborn about it.

Only half listening, he heard her lift the receiver and say, "Hallo?" Then she said, "Yes—speaking."

A moment later the note in her voice abruptly altered. "What do you know about that?" She sounded angry and Roger cocked an ear.

The next second he sat up, all attention, as he heard her give a gasp of amazement. With sudden urgency she asked, "Who is that?"

There was a short pause, then she said, "Yes, of course, but—"

She broke off. Then: "You have proof of that?" She spoke eagerly.

Roger was on his feet now, straining his ears for every word.

This time there was a slightly longer pause before Alison asked, "Yes, but what *is* this proof?"

A moment later, her voice rose as she said desperately, "No—wait—please—" She broke off, said, "Hallo?" and then there was silence. Roger heard her put the receiver down and a few seconds later, she reappeared in the doorway. Her face was ablaze with excitement. He felt her emotion communicated to him and asked urgently, "What was all that about?"

"It was a tip-off—an anonymous tip-off!" She sounded half incredulous, half triumphant.

"Saying what?"

"Saying where you could find proof of Eddie Gilbert's guilt."

"What? But where, for heaven's sake?"

"In the pot plant on the morning-room window ledge at his house."

They gazed at each other blankly. Then Roger said quietly, "There *was* one there."

"You mean that's the room where you saw Gilbert?"

He nodded, his mind awhirl.

"But—but what kind of proof could be there?"

"I don't know. Listen—tell me exactly what he said. Can you do that?" Roger took a notebook and pencil from his pocket.

"I don't know. Can you remember what *I* said?"

"I think so. You said *Hallo,* of course."

"And he said, *Is that Mrs. Stephen Grant?*"

"And you said, *Yes—speaking.*"

Alison screwed up her eyes. "Then he asked, *Is it your husband who's being held for the murder of Linda Matthews?*"

"And you said, *How did you know?* Or something like that." Roger was scribbling rapid shorthand.

"And he said, *I know who really did it.* I said, *Who is that?* And he said, *Never mind—do you want the real murderer caught?*"

"You said, *Yes* and started to ask him something."

"He told me to shut up and listen. Then he said, *Eddie Gilbert's your man.*"

"And you said, *You have proof of that?*"

Alison nodded. "That's right. Now let me get this exact." She closed her eyes. "He said, *I know where there is proof. Tell the police to look in the pot plant on the window ledge in his morning-room. That's where they'll find proof. Got that?*"

"Then you asked, *What is this proof?*"

"He said, *They'll soon find out. I have to go now.* And he rang off." Alison opened her eyes. "I think that was it."

Roger's pencil continued to fly across the paper for a few more seconds before he looked up. "Yes, that all fits in with my recollection of your end of it."

Alison sat down slowly. "Who on earth could it have been?"

"It *was* a man?"

"I don't know. I was going to come to that. One says 'he' automatically, but whoever it was spoke practically in a whisper the whole time. It's almost impossible to tell for sure then. It could well have been a woman."

"Then I think I know who it was."

Alison drew a deep breath. "Not *Carol?*"

"No, no. Miss Trent."

Her eyes widened. "Who's Miss Trent?"

"Gilbert's housekeeper. I'm pretty sure she was listening outside the door when we were talking to Gilbert this morning. If so, she heard Gilbert mention the name Stephen Grant, and could have got your number from the book. Gilbert was telling us about spending the evening with Carol. And he was making fun of Miss Trent."

"In what way?"

"Saying how she fancied him, and because she was good at her job he wanted to keep her, so he couldn't let her know about his girl-friends and kept her sweet by smiling at her a lot and letting her think it was only the memory of his wife stopped him proposing."

Alison's eyes were alight. She said, a catch in her voice, "And she knows he killed Linda—and this is her way of getting her own back."

"Seems like it." Roger was having difficulty in keeping his own excitement under control. He'd known too many anonymous tip-offs come to nothing to let himself build on this one yet.

"But why should she phone *me?*" Alison said wonderingly. "Why not the police?"

"It could be she was nervous of calling the police; she might think they could trace the call—as of course they could, given time. As to why *you*—well, you're the one person she could be absolutely certain would immediately tell the police."

"Well, I've done that," Alison said. "I've told you. What next?"

Roger looked at his watch. "I think a call to Bidwell. Somehow, for this, I don't believe he'll mind being disturbed at home. Excuse me."

He went out to the hall and picked up the phone book.

For the second time in twelve hours a police car containing Bidwell, Primrose and Roger swept through the narrow lane that led to The Cedars. This time a second car containing three constables followed.

In the first car there was an air of intense suppressed excitement. But also of nervousness. As if it was some sort of talisman, Bidwell constantly fingered the search warrant that nestled in his breast pocket.

"I hope to heaven that call wasn't a hoax," he said suddenly.

"It wasn't," Roger assured him quietly.

"OK, it wasn't. But suppose she—Miss Trent—if it *was* Miss Trent—has had second thoughts? Suppose she's confessed to Gilbert what she's done?"

"She'd never have the nerve."

"Perhaps not, but suppose she's just gone and removed this proof, or destroyed it?"

"Well, that'll be just too bad, won't it?" Roger snapped. "There's nothing we can do about it." Then he gave a sigh. "I'm sorry, Horace. I know you're on edge."

"It's just that I can foresee a lot of nastiness if this turns out to be a mare's nest. Gilbert'll have a field day complaining of police harrassment. Twice in one day, after all."

"Well, it's your decision," Roger said, "if you want to call the whole thing off . . ."

Bidwell shook his head. "Not likely. It's too good a chance to miss. I'd never forgive myself if I didn't follow it up. I'll risk the flack. Tell me again just what the woman said about the proof."

Roger did so.

"And there *was* a plant on the window ledge was there? I can't remember."

Primrose in the front seat, answered him. "Yes, sir: a poinsettia—big red leaves."

Bidwell gave a grunt. "Suppose—" he began, then broke off and fell silent.

A minute later the driver said, "Here we are, sir."

This time the big iron gates were closed. Primrose got out and went up to them. "Not locked," he called, and swung them back.

"Trusting cove," Roger murmured.

"Knows the local villains wouldn't touch him, that's all."

The car went through the gates, stopped for Primrose to get back in, then bowled up the drive to the house, the second car still following. They drew up—smoothly and quietly on this occasion—outside the front door. Bidwell took a deep breath. "Right, here we go."

The three of them got out. No lights were showing in the front of the house.

"Think he's scarpered?" Primrose asked.

"Soon find out."

Bidwell led the way to the front door and rang the bell. There was silence.

"He has, you know," Primrose began, but then a light came on in the hall. A moment later they heard Gilbert's voice shout, "Who's that?"

"Police," Bidwell called in his deepest tones.

Another few seconds passed and then the door was opened on a chain. "Ah, *not* all that trusting," Roger said.

They could see Gilbert's burly figure silhouetted against the light. He raised his hand to his eyes and peered at them. "What is it now?" He was plainly furious.

"We want to speak to you," Bidwell said curtly.

"Do you know what time it is?"

"Only too well, Mr. Gilbert."

"Then come back tomorrow."

"Mr. Gilbert, I have a search warrant for these premises and I intend to execute it—now."

Gilbert gave a roar. *"You have what?"*

"You heard. Now open up or I shall be compelled to make a forced entry."

For a moment Gilbert stood perfectly still and Roger thought he was going to defy them. Then he slowly closed the door, they heard the chain-bolt being withdrawn and the door was opened wide.

Bidwell marched into the hall, Roger and Primrose on his heels. Gilbert, who was in his shirt-sleeves, regarded them with hatred.

"You'll pay for this, Bidwell," he snarled, "forcing your way in here after ten o'clock at night. It's harrassment. I'll be putting in a formal complaint."

"Yes, you do that," Bidwell said calmly. He looked round. "Didn't think you answered your own doors, Gilbert. Where's Miss Trent?"

"If you must know, she's left, but—"

"Has she, indeed? Sudden, wasn't it?"

"Look, Bidwell, if you came all the way just to talk about—"

"I didn't. Read that." Bidwell took the search warrant from his pocket and put it in Gilbert's hands. Then he marched to the morning-room, threw open the door, felt for the switches and turned on the light. The curtains had not been drawn and the big scarlet leaves of the poinsettia on the window ledge stood out like glowing embers.

Bidwell briskly crossed the room. Gilbert hurried after him. Primrose followed closely on his heels and Roger closed the front door, then brought up the rear. The uniformed men, who had received their instructions earlier, remained temporarily in their car.

Gilbert was shouting. "Look, what you expect to find in here I don't know—"

He broke off as Bidwell picked up the plant pot and carried it back to the centre of the room, under the light. Roger and Primrose joined him and they all gazed at it. The soil in the pot showed no sign of being disturbed.

Gilbert gave a gasp of apparent disbelief. "What are you staring at that for? You all gone crazy?"

They ignored him. Bidwell said, "Paper, Freddie."

Primrose took a folded newspaper from his pocket, opened it out and laid it on the floor.

"We came prepared, you see," Bidwell said. He knelt down, and placed the pot in the middle of the paper. Then he took a firm grip on the stem of the plant and pulled sharply upwards. The plant came out of the pot, scattering loose soil all over the paper.

Roger was holding his breath. He momentarily tore his eyes away from Bidwell for a quick glance at Gilbert—who seemed to have been struck temporarily dumb by what was going on. He appeared to be bemused, and was staring down at the chief inspector, a dazed expression on his face.

Bidwell picked up the pot and tipped the remaining soil from it. Then he peered into the pot, making sure it was quite empty. Roger felt his heart sinking. Could the call have been a hoax, after all?

Only the plant itself now remained as a possible hiding place. Bidwell stared at it. Lumps of soil were still clinging to its roots. He shook it gently.

The next second there was a flash of gold in the air. Something had fallen from the plant. It landed on the newspaper, where it lay, gleaming brightly in the thin layer of soil. It was a diamond ring.

Roger let his breath out very slowly; Primrose muttered an inaudible exclamation; and Gilbert again found his voice.

"Look, I've never seen—"

Then, though he had not been cautioned, memories of other similar occasions over the years, and the advice of his solicitors to say nothing not absolutely necessary, must have come back to him and he stopped short.

Bidwell reached out a hand and daintily picked up the ring between the nails of his thumb and forefinger. He gently blew some specks of earth off it. Then he held it out to Primrose. "Well, Freddie? You were the one who got the description from the jeweller."

Primrose peered at the ring. "Fits it perfectly, sir."

"That's good enough for me." Bidwell got to his feet, took an envelope from his pocket, dropped the ring into it and returned it to his pocket.

"We'll have to get it properly identified, of course, but that's just a formality," he said.

He turned and looked at Gilbert. Somehow Bidwell seemed to Roger to be growing in stature. He took two steps forward. "Edward John Gilbert," he said, and Roger and Primrose, knowing what was coming braced themselves for fireworks. But Gilbert did not react at all, as Bidwell continued,

"I arrest you for the murder of Linda Mary Matthews, and I must warn you that anything you say will be taken down and may be given in evidence."

And then at last Gilbert responded. He smiled. "Been waiting for a chance like this for a long time, haven't you, Bidwell?" he said.

Bidwell ignored him. He looked at Roger.

"Didn't I say it's surprising the things that can turn up?" he asked.

CHAPTER SEVENTEEN

"Mr. Matthews!" Alison beamed delightedly. "Please do come in."

"Thank you."

As Roger entered the hall Stephen Grant came out of the sitting-room. Signs of strain still showed on his face, but he was smiling. He walked forward with outstretched hand. "Seems I have a great deal to thank you for," he said.

"Not really," Roger replied. "It's your wife you ought to be thanking."

"I know. And I assure you I have done so at length. Come into the sitting-room."

It was Friday morning. Immediately following Gilbert's arrest the previous night Stephen had been released. Not wanting to witness the formalities of Gilbert's charging, Roger had gone back to the flat and slept a sleep of emotional exhaustion for seven hours. When he awoke the very atmosphere of the apartment seemed somehow different. Imagination, he told himself. Though they did say the spirit of a murdered person could never rest until the killer had been brought to justice. Not that Eddie Gilbert had been brought to justice yet. A long road lay ahead. But he was behind bars. At the moment, this was all that really mattered.

Roger had gone to the police station for a chat with Bidwell, and had then made his way to the Grant's house. In the sitting-room all three sat down. Alison settled close to Stephen on the sofa holding on to his arm, as if afraid of losing him again. To Roger she was a new Alison, one positively glowing with happiness and contentment. As he looked at them Roger felt a pang of envy. It had been so much nicer before, with just the two of them. If only Stephen Grant *had* been the killer all along—fiercely Roger suppressed the thought.

"Well, what's the news?" Alison asked.

"What? Oh well, Gilbert's been charged, of course. Apparently he's not said anything—is just waiting for some high-priced shyster from London. The jeweller has identified the ring as Linda's without any doubt. Oh—you know about the ring?"

Stephen said, "Only what Bidwell told me briefly last night—that you'd found it in Gilbert's house."

"And was it in the pot plant?" Alison asked eagerly. "Where Miss Trent said?"

"It was."

Stephen shook his head in disbelief. "Incredible. Why on earth would he keep it?"

"Greed," Roger said simply. "Men like that—their whole life is built on avarice: the compulsion to accumulate more and more money and possessions. Oh, they can be generous on occasions—but they'll never ever throw anything valuable away, if they can possibly avoid it. Gilbert's an arrogant swine. He really thought he was completely in the clear. Given that, there was no way he was going to get rid of a diamond ring worth eighteen hundred pounds."

"But why keep it *there?*"

"Where would you have kept it?"

"Well, in the safe—I suppose he's got one."

"Which would normally be the very first place the police would look if he ever *was* suspected—of that crime or of any other."

"He could have buried it somewhere."

"Where? In his garden? He has a full-time gardener, who might have dug it up. He could have buried it somewhere out in the country. But if you're going to be quite sure you're not seen doing that, you have to do it at night. It's not easy to discover a good place, which you can be confident of finding again—which nobody else will find, and which won't be ploughed over, or something. What else could he do? Put it in the bank? The police can always get a court order to examine the contents of deposit boxes and if this was ever done in the course of trying to nail him on some lesser charge, and the ring found, he'd *really* be in the soup. He could ask a friend to mind it for him—and lay himself open to blackmail. No; it was dangerous to keep the ring at all; but if he was *determined* to keep it, I can't think of a better place than that pot plant. I mean, we would never have found it, if it hadn't been for the tip-off call."

Roger stopped and smiled. "Sorry for the lecture."

"Not at all. It's most interesting," Stephen said.

"Then I'll just add one more thing: there might have been another reason for keeping the ring there. Sheer bravado. I expect Gilbert's been finding life pretty boring in some ways for the last few years. He no doubt knew the police would be calling on him over this case. I imagine it gave him quite a kick to stand a few yards from that ring, talking to Bidwell and me yesterday morning."

Alison gave a little shiver. "That's horrible—sort of gloating over your trophies."

"Well, he's a pretty horrible man."

"How will he explain the ring, do you suppose?" Stephen asked.

Roger shrugged. "Say he's no idea how it got there. Claim the police must have planted it."

"Any chance of a jury believing that?"

"Not on top of the other evidence—his paying Carol Venning for a phony alibi; the letter from Linda's girl-friend, proving that he was seeing Linda shortly before her death; Mrs. Hopkins' testimony about the phone calls from 'Gil.' No, I'd say it's as watertight a case as you're ever likely to get."

Stephen was frowning. "There's no absolute proof it *was* Gilbert sent the girl that money, though, is there."

"I suppose, technically, the answer's no. But there's no doubt she *did* receive it. All the prosecution's got to do is ask who else would have sent her an anonymous gift of two thousand pounds."

In the hall the telephone bell rang. Stephen got to his feet. "Excuse me." He went out, leaving the door open.

Alison said, "It's lovely not to be scared every time the phone goes, wondering what you're going to be told next."

"I can imagine."

They heard Stephen say, "Hallo? Yes, that's right. Oh yes?"

Then, presumably covering the mouthpiece with his hand, he called, "It's only the bank, darling."

He obviously listened for a few seconds before saying in his normal tones, "Oh? No problem, I hope. The account's quite healthy, isn't it?"

There was another pause before Stephen's voice suddenly changed. *"What?* Oh, there must be some mistake!" He sounded shocked. He was silent for a moment, and when he next replied he was plainly angry.

"Look, I assure you we can't be overdrawn. I know there's quite a substantial balance—"

He broke off, then asked blankly, "What large withdrawal? Yesterday? No, my wife couldn't possibly—"

Alison got hastily to her feet. "Sounds as if he may be in for some sort of row," she said. "Better give him some privacy."

She moved quickly towards the door. But before she could get to it Stephen's voice came to them louder than ever—in words of utter incredulity:

"Two thousand pounds?"

Alison slammed the door. She said brightly, "Agency business, I think. Look, can I get you a cup of coffee?"

Before Roger could answer the door opened again and Stephen came back. He looked dazed. He said slowly,

"That was the assistant manager. Warning me that our joint account is overdrawn. Some cheques I sent off last week have come in this morning." He stared at Alison. "It would have been quite all right but for the cash withdrawal of two thousand pounds you made yesterday."

Roger had got slowly to his feet. He also was gazing at Alison. He whispered, *"You* sent Carol that money. It didn't come from Gilbert at all."

Stephen's face was a study in bafflement. He said hoarsely, "But, darling —why?"

Alison looked back and fore from one of them to the other. Then she raised her arms and let them fall to her sides in surrender. "Oh, all right," she said resignedly. "So I did. We knew Gilbert had murdered Linda. Somebody had to prove it, didn't they?"

"Yesterday morning," Alison said to Roger deliberately, "you came to see me and told me you'd identified Linda's man friend—the one Mrs. Hopkins had called Bill or Phil; that he was really Eddie Gilbert—a notorious criminal. You made it quite clear you believed he was the murderer. You said the trouble was that he had an alibi—which was no doubt bogus. You told me about Carol Venning. I asked myself how we could prove the alibi was bogus. Carol wasn't going to admit it. I wondered if he'd bribed her to give him the false alibi. I thought if we could prove *that,* it would make the alibi worthless: that no matter how much the girl swore he was with her at the time of the murder, if it was shown he'd paid her to say so, nobody would believe her. Then the whole idea came to me. I drew out the money, put it in a big envelope, with a note written in block capitals, and pushed it through Carol's letter-box. Then I just went away for a short while, came back and waited for her to come out. The rest you know. It all worked—except for the fact she burnt the note."

She looked at Stephen. "I thought it was worth two thousand to get you off—anyway, think what we'd save on legal fees. We had just enough in the current account. Of course, I didn't know those earlier cheques were going to come into the bank today—nor that they'd phone up about it when Mr. Matthews was here."

She fell silent. For a moment neither man said anything. Roger was too stunned to speak. He was trying to get his thoughts in some sort of order.

At last Stephen said, "Darling, you must have realised I'd find out eventually."

"Of course. I was going to tell you."

"But you couldn't have expected me to go along with it!"

She stared at him. "What do you mean?"

"I couldn't let Gilbert be convicted on false evidence!"

"Oh Stephen, don't be so pompous! What does it matter, so long as the right man's convicted? Why should he be allowed to get away with it, simply by cooking up a false alibi? I was only playing him at his own game."

Stephen gnawed at his lower lip. "I suppose there's something in that," he muttered.

"Of course there is!"

"Morally that may be right," Roger said, "but of course, *I* can't possibly go along with it. I'm going to have to tell Bidwell the truth."

Alison went pale. She said, "But that'll mean Gilbert getting off."

"It's possible. There's still the other evidence—the letter and the ring— but without proof of a bogus alibi an important link in the chain has been broken."

"But don't you care that he might get away with killing your sister?"

"Of course I care! But I am not going to connive at convicting a man on trumped-up evidence. We get him fairly and squarely or not at all."

Stephen said quietly, "Bidwell will be annoyed, won't he?"

"That's likely to be the understatement of the year."

"Is it possible Alison could be charged with an offence?"

Roger shrugged helplessly. "She's obviously guilty of something."

"What?" Alison cut in. "All I did was send someone two thousand pounds. Where's the crime?"

"For one thing you signed it with a false name—or false initials."

"As a matter of fact, I didn't. My middle name happens to be Edith. If I want to call myself Edith Grant and use the initials E.G. I'm perfectly entitled to do so."

"Oh, come on! You know you were trying to make it seem that Eddie Gilbert paid Carol Venning for a false alibi, when in fact he didn't. However, under the circumstances I think it's unlikely you'll be charged with any crime. That is, provided the matter's put right straight away."

"You mean you want me to go myself and tell Bidwell what I did?"

"I certainly think it would be best—from your own point of view."

"But I can't!" In sheer frustration, Alison took three or four little steps about the room. She faced Roger. "It's not that I'm afraid. But after all our work, it'll be like letting Gilbert go free—or the next best thing to it."

"No, it's not as bad as that," Roger said. "After all, we know his alibi *is* false. Perhaps we can prove that—" He broke off.

"What's the matter?" Stephen asked.

"I was thinking of Carol," Roger said slowly. "She gave Gilbert a false alibi. But she hasn't admitted that so far. If we could only get her to do so, the question of the money would be immaterial. If she would testify that he wasn't with her at the time of the murder, yet promised her she wouldn't regret it if she said he was—then the chain would be complete again: the bogus alibi proved."

"But she refused point-blank to admit that before," Alison protested. "Why should she do so now?"

"Well, it just occurred to me that if she knew the real source of that two grand and that Gilbert hadn't been quite so generous to her as she'd imagined then she might have second thoughts."

Alison stood quite still, letting the idea sink in. "I wonder," she breathed. She looked at Stephen. "What do you think, darling?"

"Well, I haven't met the girl. But I should think it's worth trying. Would you see her, Mr. Matthews—tell her the whole story?"

Roger hesitated.

"It would come best from you," Alison urged. "She likes you."

"She likes you, too."

"Not quite the same though, is it? Besides, it would be embarrassing for both of us for me to tell her that money was from me."

"Yes, I can see that." Roger came to a decision. "All right, I'll do it."

"And you won't see Bidwell until after you've spoken to Carol?"

"On one condition: that if I fail you'll come with me yourself to see him —straight away."

"Very well. I promise."

"Good." Roger looked at his watch. "Wonder if she's in now?"

"Do you want to phone her and find out?"

"No, I don't think so. She might make some excuse not to see me. I'd rather just turn up and hope for the best."

Roger made towards the hall. "Now stay here, both of you. Do nothing till I get back. And start praying I can make the girl see sense."

"Oo, it's you," said Carol Venning. She stared at Roger, big-eyed.

"Hallo, Miss Venning. Can you spare me a few minutes?"

"Er, what for?" She was looking decidedly nervous.

"Just a talk." Then as she hesitated he added, "It's all right. I promise not to bully you today, or try to catch you out. But it *is* rather important."

"All right, then."

She stood aside and he went in. The parcels had all been cleared away, and she'd been making an effort to clean up the sitting-room.

She said apologetically, "I'm in an awful state—I been doing a bit of work." She was dressed today in jeans and a plain white shirt; she was wearing very little make-up, and in fact looked considerably better than she had the previous day.

"You look fine to me," he said truthfully.

"Would you care to sit down?" she asked formally.

"Thank you." He did so.

"Would you care for some coffee?"

About to refuse, it occurred to him that it might help to break the ice.

"Thank you. That would be very nice."

He sat there until she came in with a tray containing what was obviously her best china. It seemed a long time before he was finally sipping some steaming liquid.

She poured one for herself, then said, "Er, what can I do for you?"

"It's about that money."

She stiffened. "Now, don't you go saying it was stolen or somethink."

"No, no—nothing like that. But, I've got a surprise for you: it didn't come from whom you thought."

"What do you mean?"

"Eddie Gilbert didn't send it to you."

She stared. "What?"

He repeated the words. "Course he did," she said scornfully.

"No, I assure you he didn't. I can tell you who did. I only found out myself this morning. It was Alison Grant."

Carol's mouth fell open. "What the 'eck she want to send me two thousand nicker for?"

"She wanted you to think it came from Eddie, so you'd sign the statement saying as much. Then we—the police—would believe he'd bribed you to give him a false alibi; he'd be arrested and it would let her husband off the hook."

Carol blinked. "I don't understand."

"Well, Alison Grant wanted to make it seem—"

She interrupted. "No, don't bother. I won't understand at the end. But you are levelling with me?"

"Yes, I promise you: it's absolutely true."

She suddenly looked alarmed. "Hey—you're not saying she wants it back, are you?"

"No, no." He hastened to reassure her. "Nothing like that."

She relaxed a little. "That's all right, then." The next moment she suddenly sat up as something seemed to click. "That means Eddie didn't send me a penny, then?"

"No, he didn't."

"Aw, would you believe it! He promised he'd see me all right."

"I know."

She put down her cup and leaned back sadly. "I really thought he meant it, too. Still, I suppose he had other things to think about. All the same, it would serve him right if I rung him up and gave 'im a real piece of my mind."

"He's not at home," Roger said. "He's in police custody."

Carol gave a squeak of amazement. "Eh? What's that?"

"He was arrested last night. I was there."

"Cor . . ." Carol's expression was blank. "I never thought they'd get 'im again. Was it because of me statement?"

"Not really. Though that will help to keep him there."

"What's it for, then?"

"Well, the murder."

"Murder!" Carol gave a start. "Of your sister?"

"That's right."

"But that's daft! He was with me all the evening."

Roger put down his cup. "That's what I wanted to talk to you about. Now, I know that naturally you have a certain loyalty to him, and—"

"Not now, I don't."

"Then that's all to the good. Because there's a real chance he might get away with this murder—unless you tell the truth. If I give you my solemn word that you won't get into any sort of trouble—"

"But I 'ave told the truth."

"Please, Miss Venning—Carol—it's desperately important. I respect loyalty, but it can be carried too far. Please don't continue to cover for him in this way—"

Suddenly Carol jumped to her feet and stood staring down at him. She folded her arms in an unconsciously flamboyant gesture. Her face was indignant.

"Look—what is this? I told Alison yesterday I wasn't going to frame Eddie."

"Nobody wants you to. Just tell the truth."

"But I keep telling you! I've told you the truth!" She was shouting now. "I'm sick of saying it. Eddie and me was together from half past six onwards. There's no way he could have killed your sister."

There was an air of such utter sincerity in her voice and in her face that Roger suddenly felt himself going cold. He said slowly, "But if that's the case, why did you expect him to pay you for saying so—for telling the truth?"

"Listen: when he heard about the murder he was scared. He *used* to see Linda and he thought how the cops'd try to pin the killing on him. He said, 'Thank the Lord we were together the whole evening, or I might really find myself in lumber.' So I said, joking like, 'Oh, so you're relying on me to keep you out of the nick, are you? Good job you can trust me, innit? I'd only have to say you went off for an hour, wouldn't I?' Well, he went real white. He said, 'You wouldn't do that, would you, love—you wouldn't let me down? And I said, 'Don't be daft, you know I wouldn't. And I won't blackmail you, either.' And he said, 'You're a good kid, Carol, I'll see you don't regret it.' So nach'ly when that money come, signed E.G., I thought it was from him."

Roger said dazedly, "But when Chief Inspector Bidwell and I spoke to you, you sounded as if you'd rehearsed what you were going to say."

"Well, course we had. I mean, you can forget times and things, can't you? We didn't want to contradict each other, without meaning to—me say we set out at quarter past six, him at half past, just 'cos we didn't go over it together and get it all straight. When you're talking to the cops you gotta be very careful about things like that. Ask yourself now—suppose we had said things like that what didn't tie up: wouldn't you have jumped on it?"

Slowly Roger nodded. "Yes, I'm afraid we would."

"Well, there you are, then."

"And you're willing to swear in court—you're swearing to me now—that Eddie Gilbert couldn't have killed my sister?"

"That's the gospel truth—honest. Look, I may not be much. I'm not proud of my life. I'm not very bright, and to a lot of people I'm a bit of a joke. If I croaked tomorrow nobody'd reelly care. But I got me standards. I wouldn't stand here and tell lies to shield a man who'd strangled a girl— no matter who he was. That wouldn't be right."

Suddenly and very surprisingly there was an air of immense natural dignity about her. Roger gazed at the girl, abruptly seeing her in quite a new light. He took a deep breath.

"Carol," he said, "I believe you. I'm very sorry I ever doubted you."

"Aw, that's all right," she said.

"It was just that money. It did make things look queer. But it was simply a misunderstanding. My fault, I'm sure."

"No, 'spect it was me. Usually is."

"Well, whose fault it was doesn't really matter. Anyway, thank you very much for putting me right."

He stood up. She looked disappointed. "You going already?"

"I'm afraid I must. This has changed everything. I've got to go and undo a lot of damage."

"So there we are," Roger said. "It's unbelievable—but I believe her. We've got the wrong man." He ran his fingers through his hair. "Lord, what do we do now?"

"But that letter," Alison protested, "you said it mentioned Stephen— and Eddie Gilbert."

"Well, probably the truth is that Gilbert was still seeing Linda. He was no doubt lying when he said they hadn't met for seven months. But he *didn't* see her the night she was killed. I'm convinced of that now."

Stephen said weakly, "But the ring . . ."

"I know," Roger cut in. "Don't ask me to explain. Obviously whoever took it is the murderer. I suppose it must have been planted in Gilbert's place. But don't ask me by whom."

He gave a sigh. "What a fine, logical explanation I had for Gilbert himself having put it there! How you can fool yourself into believing something when you really want to."

"Look," Stephen said, "are you absolutely sure the girl's telling the truth now? Couldn't she be fooling you?"

Roger shook his head. "No. There aren't many occasions when you can tell for certain whether a person is telling you the truth or lying. But occasionally in my business you *can* tell—without any doubt at all. This was one of those times. Believe me."

"It's infuriating!" Alison said bitterly. "Carol insisted to *me* Gilbert was with her the whole evening. But I assumed she was not only lying, but actually meant me to realise she was. It was the way in which she said it—a heavy, significant sort of way: *'He was with me. OK?'* It was almost as though she was winking, or giving me a nudge in the ribs, as she said it. And really, I suppose, it was just her way of emphasising she was telling the truth. Anyway"—Alison stood up—"I suppose I must keep my promise and go and make my confession. Are you ready, Stephen?"

He hesitated and turned his head away. "I—I don't think I can come with you, darling."

She looked at him in surprise. "You can't?"

He seemed embarrassed. "No, I'm sorry. I spent three days in that place and it gives me the heebie-jeebies to think of going back. I've got this crazy feeling they'd keep me there again, especially now as they're going to have to let Gilbert out." He gave an awkward sort of laugh. "Stupid, isn't it?"

"Oh, darling, of course I understand. I'm sorry. I shouldn't have asked you."

"Look, why don't you get Innes Lloyd to go with you?" Stephen said. "I think, anyway, you ought to see him before you go to the police—find out your exact legal position."

"Yes, I suppose that's not a bad idea," she said slowly. She looked at Roger. "Will you come with me to him—help me to explain all about our visit to Carol and everything?"

"Yes, if you'd really like me to. But I'll have to leave you then—before you start discussing your legal position. I *am* a police officer, after all."

"That's fair enough. I'll go and phone him and see if he can see us right away."

She went out to the phone and dialled the number of the solicitor's private line. There was no reply, so she next looked up the main office number and tried that. Innes Lloyd's secretary answered. Alison explained who she was and what she wanted, listened for a few seconds, said, "I see. Thank you, I'll be there," rang off and went back to the sitting-room.

"He's out to lunch at the moment, with an old army friend," she said. "He'll be back at two-thirty. She's sure he'll see me then—he hasn't got any other appointments till three-thirty."

"I hadn't even realised it was lunchtime," Roger said ruefully.

"I don't think any of us had. Will you stay and have some with us? Just a snack."

"I ought to find Bidwell right away and report my latest interview with Carol. But anything to put off the evil hour. And a snack would be fine. I'm not really hungry."

"This was going to be a real day of celebration for us," she said bitterly as she went out to the kitchen.

"I want you to answer me something truthfully," Alison said.

"What's that?" Roger asked.

"When Mr. Bidwell hears my confession, and all about your latest talk with Carol, and that you now believe her—is he likely to arrest Stephen again?"

The two of them were on their way to Innes Lloyd's office in the MG Metro. Roger took advantage of a right-hand turn in heavy traffic to delay his reply for a few seconds, but when they were moving freely again, Alison said,

"Well?"

"I think it's most unlikely."

"Why?"

"Because he agreed with me Stephen was innocent."

"Only because he was convinced by then Gilbert had done it. Now you're going to tell him Gilbert is innocent. The position will be exactly as it was before. Why shouldn't he rearrest Stephen?"

"I'm not able to promise you anything, but I just can't see it happening. In the first place, I think that he'd feel a fool to do such a thing."

"But he's got to charge somebody soon."

"Not necessarily. Frankly, I'm getting the feeling that this may be one of those cases in which nobody is ever charged."

A minute or so later he found a parking space about fifty yards from Innes Lloyd's office. They got out and walked along the pavement. It was twenty-five past two and as they approached the office building they spotted Innes Lloyd standing outside the entrance in jovial conversation with a military-looking man of about his own age.

"Oh, he's back," said Alison. "Good."

Roger said, "What do we do—go straight past into the office or wait until he's free and let him take us in?"

"Let's just wait for a few seconds."

They drew near the two men. Innes Lloyd had his back to them and his companion suddenly stuck out his hand.

"Well, jolly nice to see you again, old boy," he said. "Many thanks for lunch. My regards to your wife."

Innes Lloyd took the man's hand as Roger and Alison stopped a few feet behind him.

"Nice to see you, too, Charles," he said. "My best to Helen. Let's keep in touch."

"Yes, let's."

"Goodbye, Charles."

"So long, Bill," said the other man.

CHAPTER EIGHTEEN

It was Saturday morning and Bertrand Innes Lloyd was alone in his private office, catching up with some important paperwork. The outer office was unoccupied and the main door locked; so he was not expecting to be disturbed. It was therefore with a twinge of irritation that he heard a knock on his personal door leading to the corridor. He sighed, rose, crossed the room and opened it.

His eyebrows went up. "Chief Inspector Bidwell—Mr. Matthews. This is a surprise. What can I do for you?"

"We need to speak to you, sir," Bidwell replied formally.

"What, now? Oh, can't it wait? I've got a considerable amount of work to finish before lunch and I'm playing golf this afternoon."

"No, sir, it can't wait; it's quite important."

"I see. Then you'd better come in."

He stood aside and they entered. He closed the door, saying rather impatiently, "Well, what is it?"

Neither Bidwell nor Roger answered directly. It was Roger who spoke. "Bertrand Innes Lloyd," he said softly. "The initials make up the name Bill. It's obvious once you've realised it."

Innes Lloyd licked his lips. "So? I—what of it?"

"It's your nickname, isn't it, sir?" Bidwell said.

"No! Of course not!" The retort came sharply.

"Oh, come on!" Roger protested. "Mrs. Grant and I were within a few feet of you outside this building yesterday at two-thirty. You were saying goodbye to a friend."

The solicitor frowned. "I didn't see you."

"No, we turned on our heels and walked quickly away. But not before we'd clearly heard him say 'So long, Bill.' "

Innes Lloyd had gone a little pale. "Well, er, it's true that as a young man I wasn't fond of the name Bertrand. In the army and at university I was called Bill. The man you saw me with yesterday was an old army friend. Nobody else has called me Bill for years."

"I think they have, sir," Bidwell said quietly. "I think your mistress called you Bill."

"Mistress? How dare you! I have no mistress—"

"No, you don't—now. Because she died five days ago."

"You're mad! This is sheer nonsense—"

"Linda always used nicknames or abbreviations," Roger said reflectively. "She'd never have called you by a name like Bertrand. And I can't imagine you letting her call you Bert. So you resurrected Bill—just for her. I expect it gave you a kick—made you feel a real young blade again. Such a good name, isn't it? Dashing, easy-going, all-round sporting, decent and honest. Good old Bill!"

Innes Lloyd backed away towards his desk. "I—I don't know what you mean. If you're suggesting Linda Matthews and I were—"

"Oh, don't try and deny it, sir," Bidwell cut in. "We found several sets of unidentifiable prints in Linda Matthews' flat. But yesterday we lifted your prints from the doorhandle of your car—immediately after you were seen to get out of the vehicle, lock it and try the handle. They match those at the flat."

Innes Lloyd's face had changed from white to green. He tried to speak, but all that came out was a strangled, "I—I—I . . ."

Bidwell continued remorselessly, "You met Linda Matthews about six or seven months ago—after she'd broken up with Eddie Gilbert. You fell for her in a big way. You paid her rent. And you made her an allowance—not such a big one as Gilbert, but adequate. The affair continued for about three months. Then, however, something happened: Linda met—and fell in love with—Stephen Grant. She told you it was over between you. But you couldn't accept that. You continued to pester her, mostly on the phone. You couldn't risk visiting the apartment, because you never knew when her new lover might be there. You didn't know at that stage who he was, because Linda was discreet—she never talked of her old beaux to the new ones—or vice-versa. But you made it your business to find out—just as you'd earlier found out about her previous relationship with Gilbert. Perhaps you just hung about the block one day, saw Grant going in or leaving and put two and two together."

Innes Lloyd groped blindly for the back of a chair and dropped down into it. He looked absolutely ghastly and Roger began to feel slightly alarmed about him.

But Bidwell plainly had no such worries. After pausing for a few seconds to give the solicitor a chance to reply he carried on inexorably,

"Last Saturday you played golf with Stephen Grant and he mentioned he was going to Dublin early on Monday. You knew that would be your chance to see Linda again and try to persuade her to come back to you. You went out Monday evening. You visited an old dying client, who wanted to change his will, and later you had some drinks in the bar of the yacht club. But not all of your time between seven-thirty and nine-thirty is accounted for. You had plenty of time to go to Linda's apartment."

Still Innes Lloyd didn't answer. His mouth was open and he seemed to have difficulty in breathing. He wasn't even looking at Bidwell.

Again the chief inspector stopped for just a few seconds. Then he said harshly, "Oh, come on—why not admit it? You begged her to come back to you. She refused. Did Grant actually ring up while you were there? Did she tell you to get out because he was on his way? Whatever happened, you had a flaming row. You saw red, snatched up that scarf and strangled her."

Bidwell paused once more. Then: "Didn't you?" he shouted.

Innes Lloyd took hold of the corner of his desk and somehow pulled himself to his feet. He stood swaying. He made a great effort and started to speak.

Then suddenly his face contorted. One hand went to his heart. He gave a gasp of agony—and fell forward onto the floor.

CHAPTER NINETEEN

"Well," Roger said, "the doctors seem to think that he will survive, though it's obviously been impossible to question him further. And heaven knows when, if ever, he'll be fit enough to come to trial."

He was back with Stephen and Alison. He looked—and felt—tired and pale. He'd had many more physically wearing cases than this one—which strictly hadn't even been his case—but rarely had one taken more out of him. Presumably, he thought, it was the emotional involvement; he'd been answerable to nobody but himself, could have quit any time, and had no responsibility to lift even a finger to help towards its solution. There was nothing but his own self-imposed moral obligation. And that had been a stricter taskmaster than a dozen police commissioners.

"Poor Marjorie," Alison said softly. "She's at the hospital now, I suppose?"

"She was half an hour ago."

"I must get in touch with her as soon as possible and ask if there's anything I can do. I don't suppose there will be, but one likes to show willing. Does she know about—well, about what he did?"

Roger shook his head. "Neither Bidwell nor I told her. After the ambulance came and took him away we simply went to his house, broke it to her that he'd been taken ill and drove her to the hospital."

"So, she's got that shock still to come."

Stephen shook his head in incredulity. "Innes Lloyd and Linda . . . I still can't take it in."

"I was slow," Roger said. "I should have realised a long time ago that he knew her."

"But how could you have?" Alison asked.

"You remember that night you introduced me to him? Almost his first words were, 'I never even knew she had a brother.' That's not the sort of thing you say about a stranger—someone you'd never even heard of until after she were dead."

Alison nodded. "Of course—you're quite right. I should have noticed that, too."

"Not necessarily." Roger smiled. "After all, you're not a detective."

"It's the hypocrisy of the man that gets me," Stephen said. "Acting as my solicitor—urging *me* to tell the truth—letting me go through all that! I suppose he'd have actually let me go to jail for life, rather than own up."

"Of course, it must be admitted he never intended you to be involved," Roger said, "even though you had, as he saw it, stolen Linda from him and he must have hated you. It was no doubt a tremendous shock to him to hear *you* were under arrest. He'd had quite a different fall guy in mind."

"You mean Eddie Gilbert?"

"Precisely."

"It was Innes Lloyd who hid that ring in the plant pot?"

Roger nodded. "Of course, a lot of this has to be conjecture at the moment. But he must have found out about Linda and Gilbert. He'd been to The Cedars a number of times in connection with Gilbert's projected purchase of the property, and he could always find a legitimate excuse to call again. He'd also know the routine: that if Gilbert wasn't immediately available—as he wouldn't be if Innes Lloyd called early enough—Miss Trent would put him in the morning-room. He must have gone out early on Tuesday."

"And it was he who phoned here with the tip-off about where to look for the evidence?"

"Obviously." Roger looked at Alison. "You did say it could have been a man or a woman's voice, didn't you?"

Alison, who had been rather silent, nodded briefly. Her earlier elation at having Stephen home seemed to have subsided. Reaction to the strain of the last few days had set in and she was largely content to listen.

"So," Roger said to Stephen, "Innes Lloyd did get off the hook eventually, even if he had to frame somebody else to do it."

Stephen did not reply. He still did not look particularly forgiving, and made an obvious attempt to change the subject.

"How's Bidwell taking all this?" he asked. "He must be bucked to have got his man—at last."

"More frustrated than bucked, I think," Roger said. "True he has got his man—third time lucky, as you might say—but he *still* can't charge anyone; and he may never be able to. However, he has had some very worthwhile compensation. This is strictly confidential, but Bidwell thought it a pity not to get all the mileage he could out of that warrant to search The Cedars, so he had his men go over every inch of it. They found a kilo of heroin in a locked drawer in Gilbert's bedroom. So it seems friend Eddie will *not* be purchasing The Cedars, after all, and in fact will be leaving the neighbourhood for a considerable period. Which fact has brought a certain cheerfulness to Bidwell's countenance, in spite of everything else."

"That's very good news," Stephen said.

"Especially for Carol, I imagine," Alison added.

"Well, once we knew the true source of that two thousand quid it was obvious she wouldn't be in any danger from Gilbert; he never even knew about it or about that E.G. note or her statement. But I agree she'll certainly be better off with him out of the way."

Alison made a face. "As things turned out, that was really money down the drain, wasn't it?"

"I'm not so sure: if you *hadn't* done it and I hadn't found out about it, you and I would never have gone to see Innes Lloyd yesterday and wouldn't have heard that chap call him 'Bill.' "

She smiled. "You cheer me."

"The strange thing was both you and Innes Lloyd trying independently to pin the murder on Gilbert."

Stephen said quickly, "The difference being that Alison genuinely believed Gilbert had done it. Innes Lloyd knew he hadn't."

"Oh, agreed," Roger said. "I'm not comparing the two actions."

"*You* thought Gilbert had done it," Alison said to Roger. "As soon as you'd read that letter from Toots."

"I did. So did Bidwell. He seemed the obvious suspect." He paused. "You know, the one thing I don't understand about that letter was that although the girl mentioned both you"—he nodded to Stephen—"and Gilbert she didn't make any reference to Innes Lloyd—not even simply to the name Bill."

Alison shrugged. "Presumably she didn't know about him."

"No, but *Linda* knew about him! If she'd been pouring out the story of her convoluted love life, why not mention the man who was making himself such a pest? And if she *did* mention him, why didn't the other girl say anything about him in her letter?"

"I don't see that as a problem," Stephen said. "The girl was advising Linda not to play fast and loose with two men. Well apparently Linda wasn't seeing Innes Lloyd then. True, he was ringing her up all the time, but there was nothing she could do about that."

Roger nodded thoughtfully. "Yes, I suppose that's the answer. In spite of Gilbert's denials he and Linda must have been continuing to see each other all along—probably because she was frightened of him—and even though he'd apparently stopped making her a regular allowance."

"I can understand that," Stephen said. "What I can't understand is why she should agree to see Innes Lloyd as well. She can't have been frightened of *him.*"

"Until we can question him we can't know—probably not even then. Maybe it was only after Linda started to fear she'd lost you that she gave in to his pestering and agreed to see him again. Incidentally, the fact that she made a will last Thursday makes me think she may have spent some time with him on Wednesday; Innes Lloyd seems just the sort who'd go to spend a romantic evening with a girl and pass much of the time lecturing her on the dangers of intestacy."

"And then she invited him back again on Monday?"

"Possibly. Again we're in the realm of guesswork. Maybe she only agreed to see him on Wednesday in order to try and persuade him things were over between them. In which case it could be that on Monday he turned up there unannounced, having learnt you were going to be out of town that night. However, either before he arrived, or perhaps while he was actually there, you phoned Linda from the airport and informed her you were on your way."

"Whereupon she told Innes Lloyd he had to leave?"

"I imagine that's what happened. And it has to be said that if she *had* arranged a date with him, it was appallingly bad behaviour on her part. Which is why I like to think Innes Lloyd in fact came unannounced. Either way, though, she gave him marching orders. They had a blazing row, he lost his head and . . ."

Roger tailed off. There was silence for a few seconds. To break it, he continued, "As I say, we can't know all the details. We may fill in some of them later on: if Innes Lloyd recovers, if Toots ever turns up—"

He broke off and frowned. Then he looked at Alison, a slightly puzzled expression on his face. "By the way, how did you know just now that that letter was signed 'Toots'?"

It was two seconds that did it—the two seconds that elapsed before Alison replied.

"You told me," she said. Her voice was casual.

If she'd answered instantaneously he would probably have believed her, have accepted that his memory was at fault. But that barely noticeable hesitation told him that she had been caught off balance and had had to grope hastily round for an answer.

"I didn't," he said, and he stared at her. She licked her lips and suddenly he felt his jaw literally drop.

He whispered, "Don't say—don't say *that* was you as well!"

She didn't answer. Stephen gave an incredulous gasp. "Alison? *You* wrote that letter?"

"That was part of your plan, too," Roger was almost speaking to himself. "Part of your plan to prove Gilbert was the killer. Like the bribe to Carol."

At last Alison spoke. "Of course not!" she said. "I did nothing of the sort. Don't be ridiculous!"

"But you *must* have!" Roger said. "I *know* I didn't mention the name Toots to you. Oh, come on! Don't hold out on us. I mean, you shouldn't have done it, but it's over now and all's well that—"

Roger stopped as a sudden realisation struck him like a heavy punch in the solar plexus. Hardly conscious of what he was doing he found himself standing up. The room seemed to be going round. He said hoarsely, having difficulty in getting the words out,

"The address book. It came with the letter. You had Linda's address book. You must have been at the flat . . . You—you killed her. You murdered my sister . . ."

"Matthews, what are you saying?"

Stephen was shouting. He too jumped to his feet. "Are you out of your mind?"

"Look at her!" Roger yelled. He pointed at Alison, who was sitting quite still. She had gone deathly pale. "She's not denying it!"

"Well, of course not! You've frightened her out of her wits! Darling—tell him he's a fool."

Then, as he looked more closely at her face, Stephen's confidence seemed to waver. "Alison," he said urgently. "Please. Tell him that . . ." He didn't finish. A growing horror came into his expression. Once more he said, "Alison . . ." Then, as she still said nothing, he gave a groan. It was a sound of utter despair. He dropped back into his chair and buried his head in his hands.

At last Alison spoke. She looked up pleadingly at Roger. "Please," she said, "don't hate me. I didn't mean to do it. It just happened. She was going to take Stephen from me, you see. I pleaded with her to give him up. But she wouldn't listen. She laughed at me. She was triumphant—jubilant. She'd just had a call from Stephen. She flaunted her ring. She said he was going to leave me and marry her. I had to do something to stop her. I really didn't have any choice. You must see that. You must."

"I found out about the affair months ago," Alison said. I knew there was *somebody* long before I knew who it was. Just from Stephen's manner. So one day I followed him to the apartment block. It wasn't too hard after that to find out who the girl was. I watched Linda several times—followed her in the street, studied her in cafés. She was very beautiful. I thought at first it was just an infatuation and would quickly pass. But as the weeks went by it seemed it wasn't going to and I knew I had to do something. I decided to go and see her.

"It had to be a time when Stephen was away, and the trip to Dublin seemed a good opportunity. I went there in the evening. She was there, alone. I introduced myself. She was quite shaken at first, I think, to find out I knew about her. But she soon recovered herself. I've told you the sort of things that happened then. I don't want to talk about that anymore. But eventually I saw I wasn't going to get anywhere. At one stage she turned her back on me. The silk scarf was lying on a chair and on an impulse I just snatched it up, and—well, I needn't go into that. Afterwards I was appalled at what I'd done, but it was too late, then. I searched the flat to see if I could find any traces of Stephen having been there. But there was nothing—apart from the address book. His name was in that—under 'S.' I was going to tear the page out—but that would only make the police look for somebody with a name beginning with S. That might lead them to Stephen, and though he—or so I thought—had a perfect alibi they might put two and two together and think of me. So there was no choice but to take the book with me. I'd worn gloves, so I knew I wouldn't have left my fingerprints anywhere. I left the flat quite openly. No one saw me, which was just luck. Nobody would have recognised me if they had seen me, as I was still wearing my disguise, but if a woman *had* been spotted leaving, then obviously later, when Stephen's connection with her came out, again I might have been suspected."

Alison paused. Roger said quietly, "The ring."

"Oh yes. Well, I must admit I tore that off her finger after—after it happened. I just couldn't bear to see it there. As I explained, she sort of flaunted it in my face. I took it away with me. I thought it might make the motive look like robbery. But I knew it was too risky to keep, so I just dropped it down by the base of a tree in the street and ground it down into the earth with my heel.

"I couldn't do that with the address book, though. I just didn't know what to do with it. My first idea was to tear it up and throw the pieces out of the car window. But there were so many pages and I knew I'd have to rip them up very small, which would take an age, and I kept imagining somebody seeing me scattering paper out of the window and later reporting it; or one of the pages slipping down inside the seat or something and Stephen finding it. All highly unlikely but I wasn't thinking very calmly. Next I thought I might throw the book in the sea and I went down to the front. But it was a lovely evening and there were still lots of people about. I couldn't risk being seen throwing the book away; besides it might be washed up again. I drove out to the country, meaning to bury it. But every time I came to what seemed a suitable spot a car came along. It was really frustrating. Eventually my nerves wouldn't take the strain anymore and I decided that after all the least risky thing I could do would be take it home and burn it."

Alison paused again. Neither of the men said anything. Stephen's head had dropped forward. One hand was to his forehead and it could just be seen that his eyes were closed.

Alison continued. "I got home and then I more or less collapsed. I couldn't do anything except just sit. Eventually I had a drink and recovered a bit. I got the book out to burn it. But I couldn't resist having a quick look through it first. I'd just started when I heard someone in the hall. I nearly jumped out of my skin. It was Stephen, of course. I was absolutely horrified. I'd chosen that day especially because I thought he'd have an alibi—and here he was! It was clear something awful had happened to him. It occurred to me at once that he might have been to Linda's. I just hoped desperately that he hadn't. Anyway, at last the police arrived. All the time they were here the address book was tucked in the side of this very chair."

She cast a glance at Stephen. "Thank heavens you let them search you and didn't demand they get a warrant. They'd have certainly found the book and then the fat would have been in the fire."

Stephen didn't look up. Alison hesitated, then got to her feet. Roger stiffened.

"It's all right," she said. "I just want a drink of water."

She went out to the kitchen, he heard the tap running, then she returned carrying a tumbler and sat down again. She took a sip, then said,

"The one thing that concerned me then was getting Stephen out of jail. I knew the only way would be to put the blame on somebody else. But who? There were scores of names in the address book, but it would be no use just to pick out one at random—I might select one who'd turn out to be abroad, or ill, or even dead. Then we went to see Mrs. Hopkins and she told us about the man called Phil or Bill. I rushed home after you left me and went through every name in that book. But there wasn't a single Phil or Bill among them. It was infuriating. And all because Innes Lloyd's private office number is so easy to remember—one she didn't need to write down. However, I did eventually come across the name Eddie Gilbert. I knew about him, of course—and it suddenly occurred to me that the name Mrs. Hopkins heard could have been Gil. The more I thought about it the more it seemed he *had* to be the man. He was wealthy and unscrupulous, and it was so feasible that Linda would call him Gil and Mrs. Hopkins mishear it. But how could I draw your attention to him?

"I puzzled about it a long time and then thought of this idea of a letter from an imaginary girl-friend of Linda's, implicating Gilbert and referring to him as Gil. I planned it that night—though I wasn't going to write it until I was sure there weren't any snags. It took an awful lot of working out. For one thing I had to make the girl seem real, yet ensure that the police couldn't even try to trace her. I thought of all sorts of little things—like writing 'Steven' with a 'v'—so it would look as though the writer was a stranger to him. Unfortunately, nobody seemed to notice that."

Roger thought, she's really proud of herself—even now. She'd like to be complimented on her cleverness.

But she was continuing. "Of course, what I didn't know was that Linda and Eddie Gilbert had split up so long ago. I really thought it had been 'Gil' who'd been pestering Linda with phone calls all the time—not Innes Lloyd. And that obviously answers your question about why there was no reference to 'Bill' in the letter.

"The next thing I did that night was go out and retrieve the ring. It was a risk, but I thought if I could plant it on Gilbert it could be the additional evidence that would clinch the case."

"You did something else while you were out, didn't you?" Roger asked quietly.

"Oh, you mean attack that barmaid? Yes. That was a mistake—a spur-of-the-moment thing. Of course, I never intended to kill her. But it came to me that if I could put around the belief there was a mad strangler on the prowl, attacking girls at random, and that the second attack took place while Stephen was locked up, the police might be convinced he was innocent of the first crime. When you came to see me on Wednesday evening I was waiting all the time for you to mention it; I couldn't understand why you didn't. In the end it was Marjorie who brought it up. It was only then I learned about the copy-cat thing and why you didn't link the two attacks."

She paused. Roger didn't speak. He knew he didn't have to ask too many questions. As long as he just went on listening it would all come out.

Sure enough, she went on after just a few seconds. "Even when I did that I knew it was only a second line of attack and I was still going to have to carry on with my other plan. Wednesday morning, quite early, I went out to The Cedars. Innes Lloyd had told us all about Eddie Gilbert having a housekeeper. I had my old identity card from my early market research days, with my maiden name on it, together with some old questionnaires that I'd kept as souvenirs; and, of course, I knew all the correct procedure, the phrases to use and so on. Miss Trent came to the door and I told her I was doing research into spending patterns in upper-class households, and could she spare me ten minutes. That 'upper class' bit won her over straight away, and she asked me into the morning-room. I started with irrelevant questions, very formal, and gradually got more friendly and casual—did her employer do much entertaining, did he patronise restaurants, night-clubs, et cetera? Eventually I managed to extract the information that he'd been out playing cards with some male friends on the Monday evening. After I'd been there twenty minutes, Miss Trent had mellowed enough to offer me some coffee. I accepted and when she went out to get it, it was easy to slip the ring into the plant pot. It wasn't the ideal place; I'd been hoping to put it in a drawer but the only ones in the room were locked. You must realize that from the beginning I was improvising the whole time. I could never plan my exact course of action completely in advance. I just had to take things as they came—and hope.

"All the same, when I left The Cedars I'd achieved two things. I'd planted the ring. And secondly I'd discovered Gilbert was *not* abroad, or out of town, or sick, but had been out and about in Fermouth on the Monday evening. True, it was likely he had an alibi, but on the other hand, his card-playing friends would probably be criminal types, so equally probably the police wouldn't believe the alibi. They might not be able to *break* it but from my point of view that wasn't important. I didn't particularly want Gilbert *convicted;* I just wanted the police convinced of his guilt, so they'd let Stephen go. Anyway, as soon as I left The Cedars I went home and wrote the letter, just as I'd planned it the previous night. I put the address book in the envelope with it because I thought that would prove the letter's authenticity—and that Eddie Gilbert had been a friend of Linda's. At that stage it didn't matter the police seeing Stephen's name in it. I didn't want to post it locally, though, because I thought you'd see the postmark and never believe that somebody living in Fermouth wouldn't know about Linda's murder. So I took the train to London, with that manuscript for Stephen's secretary, and posted the letter and address book to Linda's flat while I was there. I was a bit worried in case when you got it the next morning and saw the London postmark you'd remember I'd been up to town that day and put two and two together; but it couldn't be helped and apparently you didn't, anyway."

"The postmark wasn't readable," Roger said quietly.

"Then that was about my only stroke of luck."

Alison took another sip of water and put the glass down carefully. "That's about all, I think," she said. "You know what happened. Gilbert *hadn't* been playing cards: he'd been with Carol. In spite of the fact that you doubted the alibi she gave him, he still wasn't arrested and Stephen wasn't released. You pointed out there was no real evidence against Gilbert at all.

"Well"—Alison shrugged—"the rest of it was a matter of having to keep on providing additional evidence. First the money to Carol, to make out

Gilbert paid for his alibi. But that didn't succeed: Stephen *still* wasn't released. Yet I was sure that if only the police could find that ring, everything would be all right. Hence my final ploy—the anonymous phone call. Do you know how I managed that?"

"Presumably you arranged for a friend to phone you at a specific time. I obviously don't know what reason you gave."

She shook her head; there was a self-satisfied expression on her face. "Nobody phoned me. I was talking to myself the whole time."

"But the phone rang."

"No, it didn't. You heard a *recording* of the telephone bell. It was simple. I loaded our recorder with a new blank tape, placed it by the phone and pressed 'Record.' Then I went to the end of the road and dialled our own number from the phone box there. I let it ring six times, came home, turned off the recorder and rewound the tape. I now had a recording of our telephone bell about five minutes into an otherwise blank tape. I put the recorder—it's the low, flat type—in the drawer of the hall table under the phone, leaving it open a few inches. Just before I let you in I pressed the 'Play' button. I then simply had to make conversation for five minutes—all that nonsense about going to see Gilbert—until the tape reached the point of the bell's recording, and in here it sounded as though our phone started to ring. I just had to stop the recorder at the same moment I lifted the receiver."

Roger nodded slowly. "Very ingenious. Ingenuity worthy of a better cause."

"A better cause than securing the release of my husband—in jail for a murder he didn't commit?"

"There was another way to get him out."

"What do you mean?"

"Confess."

"But then *I'd* be in and *he'd* be out. We'd still be apart. What would be the point of that?"

Roger got to his feet. "Well, you are going to be apart for a very long time, I'm afraid."

"Don't be so sure of that," she said.

"What do you mean?" He spoke sharply.

"Simply that you have no witnesses to any of this. Nor is there any evidence. And naturally I shall deny it all."

"Miss Trent—" he began.

"Oh, if you can find her she'll no doubt testify that somebody—whom she may or not recognise as me—was out at The Cedars, asking about

Eddie Gilbert's movements. I shall admit that. I suspected he might be the murderer and was making enquiries. But when she told me he had an alibi for Monday evening, that was the end of it and I left. I certainly never planted that ring in the pot. So you've got nothing against me at all. And I don't think you'd get much cooperation from Inspector Bidwell, either, if you tried it. First he accused Stephen of the murder, and had to let him go —largely because of you. Then he arrested Eddie Gilbert and had to let him go—largely because of you. If you go to him now and tell him Innes Lloyd is innocent, and *I'm* the guilty party he'll laugh in your face. He'll think you're obsessed. Particularly when Stephen and I flatly deny I confessed to anything even remotely criminal." She smiled sweetly.

"Are you out of your mind?"

They both gave a start and swung round. It was Stephen who had positively roared the words. He was on his feet and his eyes were blazing.

"Do you think I'd lie to save you?" he shouted. "I'll confirm every word he says!"

Alison seemed to wilt—like a flower caught in a blast of heat from a forest fire.

"But Stephen—darling—I did it for you." Her voice was a whisper of unmitigated horror. "I love you. I couldn't lose you. You love me—you've said so—over and over again."

"That was before—before you admitted this appalling thing. Do you think I could ever love a woman who could strangle another woman in cold blood—and then try to pin the blame on somebody else?"

"It wasn't in cold blood!" Alison wailed. "I lost my head—"

"Lies! You went disguised. You were wearing gloves—in August. You chose a time when you thought I had an alibi. Maybe you hoped to persuade her to give me up. But you went fully prepared to kill her if she refused."

"Stephen, she was worthless—a gold-digging, promiscuous little slut—"

"So am I worthless—a lying, promiscuous weakling. Perhaps that's what drew Linda and me together. But at least I know what I am. I think Linda knew what she was, too. But you—you see nothing wrong with what you've done at all. You disgust me!" He spun on his heels and strode towards the door.

She cried desperately, "Stephen! Where are you going?"

He stopped, turned and stared at her. "I don't know. Away. Out. Anywhere. Our marriage is over—as though it had never been. As far as I'm concerned it's been annulled. Understand?"

He looked at Roger. "Tell Bidwell I'll be in touch with him soon—to give a full statement."

He disappeared into the hall and the next moment they heard the front door slam.

Roger waited a few seconds before also moving towards the hall—and towards the telephone.

It was then that Alison started to scream.

CHAPTER TWENTY

"She loved not wisely but too well," said Detective Sergeant Primrose sagely.

Bidwell groaned. "Oh, Freddie, spare us the platitudes!"

"Sorry, sir." Primrose sounded hurt.

"I'm afraid he's right, all the same," Roger said. "It was murder for love. Always rather horrible."

Bidwell nodded. "Yes, indeed. Still, all's well that—" He caught Primrose's eye and broke off. "Anyway, thanks for your help," he said hastily to Roger.

"I fear I was more hindrance than help. And, you know, I should have suspected her from the start. Actually, I very nearly did."

"How do you mean?"

"It was something she said. You know how occasionally a person makes a remark that puzzles you slightly? You mean to ask them about it. Then the conversation changes tack or you get distracted—and it's gone. You're just left with a vague feeling of something you don't understand. Well, Alison made a remark like that. It momentarily struck me as strange—but afterwards I couldn't for the life of me remember what it was. And of course it went out of my mind. It's only just come back. It was a tiny point, really, but the first time we met she referred to me as Linda's next of kin. How did she know that? There was no way she could have been told that both our parents are dead. Besides, it's almost exclusively a legal term —a strange one for a nonlawyer to employ. Normally a person would use an expression like 'a close relative.' The answer, of course, is that she'd read the term in Linda's will, where she uses the phrase 'my brother and next of kin, Roger Matthews.' When Alison heard my name and used the word 'brother,' 'next of kin' slipped out automatically. I might have nailed her there and then."

"Oh, I don't think you could have been expected to spot that," Bidwell said.

"Perhaps not. And anyway we got there in the end."

"Yes—at the fourth attempt."

"Better late—" Primrose began.

Roger said hurriedly, "How's Innes Lloyd?"

"Oh, improving. They say now he will definitely pull through."

"That's a relief. If he'd pegged out I'd have really felt we'd killed him. Any need for his wife to know he was Linda's 'Bill'?"

"I don't see why."

"I'm glad—for her. Though it's more than he deserves."

He paused, then said, "Tell me, Horace: did you ever suspect anybody else of the murder?"

"Er." Bidwell hesitated. He seemed embarrassed.

"Come on—out with it. You did, didn't you?"

Bidwell nodded.

"Who?"

"Well—you, as a matter of fact."

"Yes, I'm not surprised." Roger was quite unperturbed. "I should have in your shoes. I certainly had a motive. And you only had my word for it that I hadn't been in touch with Linda for five years. Suppose we'd been in regular contact? Suppose she'd phoned me last Thursday, saying she'd just made a will, leaving everything to me? She'd have certainly let *me* into her flat when she was there alone. When did you clear me in your mind?"

"When I phoned the Yard and discovered you were on duty all Monday evening—and that unless an inspector, a sergeant and two constables were in cahoots with you, you had an unbreakable alibi."

Roger smiled. "Evening duty sometimes has its compensations." He got to his feet.

"You off now?" Bidwell asked.

"Shortly. I've got a few things to do. For one thing, start making arrangements for the funeral."

"Will you have it in Fermouth?"

"No, this wasn't a good town for her. It'll be in Norfolk. There is a family plot. Most of her early friends—the people she grew up with—live there. Some of them might turn up—for our parents' sake, if not for hers or mine."

He looked at his watch. "Anyway, I must dash. I have one other very important visit to pay before I leave town."

When Roger had made his farewells and left, Bidwell sat back and started to fill his pipe. "Well, thank heavens that one's over. Not one of my greatest successes."

"Never mind, *patron,* there'll be plenty more."

"Heaven forb—" Bidwell broke off. *"What* did you call me?"

"Patron. It's what Sergeant Lucas calls Maigret."

Bidwell paused in his pipe filling. *"Patron,* eh?" He looked thoughtful and Primrose held his breath. Then regretfully the chief inspector shook his head. "No, won't do. Not in Fermouth. I think you'd better go back to 'sir,' Freddie."

"Thank you, sir," said Primrose, with great relief.

Roger rang the bell of the little flat at 17 Norwood Drive and after a few seconds the door was opened and Carol Venning was staring at him in amazement.

"It's you," she said.

Roger smiled. "I believe you're right." He brought his hand from behind his back and presented her with a large bunch of yellow roses.

Her eyes bulged. "For me?"

"That's the general idea."

"Cor . . . they're lovely." She took them gingerly, still gazing at them in disbelief.

"May I come in for a minute?"

"What?" She blinked. "Oh, sorry. Yes—please do."

She stood aside and he went in.

She said dazedly, "I can't remember the last time anyone gave me flowers."

"Didn't Eddie ever give you any?"

"Not 'im. Oh, he'd give me things sometimes—bits of jewellery and stuff. Nothing *very* good, and it was always things I had to wear to go out with him. And I always felt he might ask for 'em back. You know. He never gave me nothing useless, like flowers. Nobody does. Oh, won't you sit down?"

"Thanks."

He did so, and she stood facing him, holding the roses in front of her, like a bride.

She said, "Wasn't it awful about Mrs. Grant?"

"Yes. Awful."

"She really took me in. Did she take you in, too?"

"Yes."

"Bit stuck on 'er, weren't you?"

He hesitated, before nodding slowly.

"Thought so. I can always tell. I'm awful sorry. I liked her, too. We 'ad a lovely time Thursday, after you'd gone. I reelly enjoyed it. I'll never forget it. And she was reelly nice about my new clothes and jewellery. Though I knew she didn't reelly think much of the clothes—not deep down."

"What made you think that?"

"Oh, I dunno. Nothing she said. I could just tell. I didn't mind. I know I got no taste, reelly. I just like bright things. They cheer me up. Alison did that, too. So, in spite of what she did, I suppose I'll always have a bit of a soft spot for her. I'm sorry. I shouldn't say that to *you,* I know. And I thought Linda was reelly beautiful—just like I'd like to look. It's just awful she's dead."

"Thank you, Carol. And don't apologise for feeling like that about Alison. She liked you, too."

"Honest?"

"Honest. I don't think she expected to, when we first came here. Neither did I, as a matter of fact—knowing you were Eddie Gilbert's girl. But she said you were really very nice—good-natured and generous."

"Well, that's a relief."

"Relief?"

"Yeah. I mean, she might get off, and anyway she'll get out one day. And, well, when she doesn't like a girl, she reelly shows it, if you see what I mean."

He smiled. "I certainly do."

"Look, it's awful nice to see you, but why d'you come?"

"Well, I'm going back to London very soon and I wanted to see you once more before I left."

Her face fell. "Oh. So the flowers are a sort of goodbye present?"

"Partly. And an apology."

"What for?"

"Bullying you like I did the other day. And for lying to you."

"Lying to me? How?"

"Well, you see, I don't know a thing about racing."

"You mean all that stuff 'bout what 'orse had won that race: you made it up?"

" 'Fraid so."

"Cor, you are a beast! I ought to belt you one. But I will accept your apology." She made a clumsy attempt at a mock curtsy.

He said, "Carol, sit down, will you? I want to talk to you."

She eyed him shrewdly for a moment. Then she said, "You're going to give me a sermon, aren't you?"

"I don't intend to. It'll only take a few seconds. Please."

She hesitated; then, still holding the flowers sat down slowly. "I suppose you're going to say you want to talk to me like a brother."

"I wasn't going to *say* it—but yes, I do. I did it once before—to a girl just about your age. It didn't do much good. I put things badly. I want to try and do better now."

" 'Ave a go, then," she said.

"Well, in the first place, Gilbert will certainly be going down for a very long time. And there's no way he can find out about that statement you signed. So you've nothing to be frightened of. Carol—it's a chance for you to make a new start. The other day you said that you weren't much—you were a bit of a joke—if you croaked nobody would really care. None of that's true. You've got a lot going for you. You're pretty. You're kind-hearted and generous—Mrs. Grant was right about that. You're straight as a die. And you haven't got an ounce of malice or rancour in your make-up. There's nothing about you that should get on any decent person's nerves— quite the opposite. Because, in fact, Carol Venning, you're something rather special. I'm just ashamed it took me too long to realise it—but I did have other things on my mind. So: don't sell yourself short. Don't waste your life. Keep away from men like Eddie Gilbert. Get a proper job—*you* won't have any problem. Be able to say you *are* proud of your life. If you go on as you are you might just end up like my sister. And if that happened—well I, for one, would *really* care. OK?"

She said, "You're not kidding me, are you? You reely mean it, don't you?"

She wasn't actually asking questions. She was thinking aloud.

But he answered nonetheless. "Most certainly I do."

"Cor—an' you a psychologist. You can think all that of *me.*"

She spoke wonderingly. He took a card from his pocket and handed it to her. "There's my home address and number, and that's my extension at Scotland Yard. If there's ever anything I can do for you, you get in touch with me. And any time you just feel like a chat, phone me—any time. But especially if anybody even threatens to lay a finger on you. Because I can make them very, very sorry indeed. Will you do that?"

"OK."

"Promise?"

"Oh, I promise, all right, don't worry. I'll probably be ringing you up all the time, I'm warning you."

"That'll be fine by me. Because you and I are going to keep in touch. And for starters I'll be coming to see you in a month or two—if that's all right with you."

Her face brightened. "Oo, yes, smashing."

"Mind you, I'll want three things then."

"What's that?"

"Tea. Fancy cakes. And to see a real change in your life-style."

He held out his hand. "Is it a deal?"

She looked at him silently for several seconds. Then she blinked rapidly three or four times and took his hand. "It's a deal, brother," she said.

ABOUT THE AUTHOR

JAMES ANDERSON is the author of seven other crime novels which have been published in hardcover and paperback editions in both England and the United States—and have been translated into German, Italian, Portuguese, Dutch, Swedish, and Norwegian. *Additional Evidence* is Mr. Anderson's second novel for the Crime Club. His first, *Assault and Matrimony*, was a recent made-for-TV movie starring Jill Eikenberry and Michael Tucker.